PENGUIN (P) CLASSICS

MAGGIE: A GIRL OF THE STREETS
AND OTHER TALES OF NEW YORK

Stephen Crane (1871–1900) was born in Newark, New Jersey, the youngest in a family of fourteen children. His father was a prominent Methodist minister and his mother, niece of a Methodist bishop, was a leading churchwoman. After brief attendances at Lafayette College and then Syracuse University Crane joined his brother's news agency in New Jersey and, while continuing to pursue freelance journalism, drifted into the bohemia of lower Manhattan. His first novel, *Maggie: A Girl of the Streets* (1893) failed to find a reading public but was enthusiastically received by Hamlin Garland and William Dean Howells, who encouraged his literary career. With his next novel, *The Red Badge of Courage* (1895), he became an instant, international celebrity. As a journalist Crane reported from the American West, Mexico, Greece, and Cuba, as well as New York, and also converted a number of his experiences into fiction. The stories and sketches he wrote following the composition of *The Red Badge of Courage* are among the finest short works in all of American literature. In 1899 Crane and his wife, Cora, settled in England where his tubercular condition was aggravated by the relentless work schedule he undertook in order to meet his debts. He died in a sanitarium in Germany in June 1900.

Larzer Ziff is the author of a number of books on American literary culture, among them *The American 1890s*, winner of the Christian Gauss Award. A member of the American Academy of Arts and Sciences, he is Research Professor of English at The Johns Hopkins University.

MAGGIE: A GIRL OF THE STREETS

AND OTHER TALES OF NEW YORK

STEPHEN CRANE

EDITED WITH AN INTRODUCTION BY LARZER ZIFF
WITH THE ASSISTANCE OF THEO DAVIS

PENGUIN BOOKS

PENGUIN BOOKS

Published by the Penguin Group

Penguin Group (USA) Inc., 375 Hudson Street, New York, New York 10014, U.S.A.

Penguin Books Ltd, 80 Strand, London WC2R 0RL, England

Penguin Books Australia Ltd, 250 Camberwell Road, Camberwell, Victoria 3124, Australia

Penguin Books Canada Ltd, 10 Alcorn Avenue, Toronto, Ontario, Canada M4V 3B2

Penguin Books India (P) Ltd, 11 Community Centre, Panchsheel Park, New Delhi – 110 017, India

Penguin Books (N.Z.) Ltd, Cnr Rosedale and Airborne Roads, Albany, Auckland, New Zealand

Penguin Books (South Africa) (Pty) Ltd, 24 Sturdee Avenue,
Rosebank, Johannesburg 2196, South Africa

Penguin Books Ltd, Registered Offices: 80 Strand, London WC2R 0RL, England

This volume first published in Penguin Books 2000

7   9   10   8   6

Introduction and notes copyright © Larzer Ziff, 2000
All rights reserved

LIBRARY OF CONGRESS CATALOGING-IN-PUBLICATION DATA
Crane, Stephen, 1871–1900.
Maggie, a girl of the streets, and other tales of New York / Stephen Crane;
edited with an introduction by Larzer Ziff; with the assistance of Theo Davis.
p.   cm. — (Penguin classics)
Includes bibliographical references.
Contents: Maggie—George's mother—The broken-down van—An ominous
baby—A great mistake—A dark-brown dog—An experiment in misery—An
experiment in luxury—Mr. Binks' day off—The men in the storm—When
man falls, a crowd gathers—An eloquence of grief—Adventures of a novelist.
ISBN 0 14 04.3797 5
1. City and town life—New York (State)—New York—Fiction.   2. New York
(N.Y.)—fiction.   I. Ziff, Larzer, 1927–   II. Davis, Theo.   III. Title.   IV. Series.
PS1449.C85A6   2000
813'.4—dc21   99–462421

Printed in the United States of America
Set in Sabon

CONTENTS

INTRODUCTION:
STEPHEN CRANE'S NEW YORK

Stephen Crane's characteristic literary form was the brief, vivid, self-contained unit. Even his novels, short as they are, are made up of a series of sharply realized episodes, each of which is almost a complete story in itself. Unlike his contemporary Frank Norris, he did not seek to spread his characters and actions across a broad panorama in pursuit of the effects of epic, nor, like another contemporary, Theodore Dreiser, did he seek to build his fictive worlds through the inexorable massing of the sticks and stones of life. We find Norris's California or Dreiser's Chicago in their large novels, but Stephen Crane's New York comes to us in two short novels, *Maggie* and *George's Mother*, and in a wealth of short pieces—stories, sketches, reports—that he wrote before he and that city came to an unamiable parting of the ways in 1896.

This edition offers Crane's New York through a reprinting of the two so-called Bowery novels and a selection from the range of brilliant, sharply incised sketches and stories he wrote for newspapers and magazines in 1892–94, the artistically fertile years of his hectic residence in a hectic city. It concludes with his 1896 newspaper report of the conflict that led to his departure from the city in that year.

As if in anticipation of the early death that claimed him in 1900 before his twenty-ninth birthday, Stephen Crane was always in a hurry. Yet his sense of urgency rarely led to careless writing. Rather it propelled a style in which selected images and swiftly drawn episodes are made to yield effects that had more conventionally been elicited through extended plotting. Before Crane, novels set in New York presented that city as quantitatively different from the villages, towns, and other cities of nineteenth-century America. More people lived there than anywhere else, but those people were portrayed as maintaining pretty much the same patterns of behavior that informed American life prior to the rise of large cities.

Crane's New York pieces, however, are like the colored fragments of a kaleidoscope that when placed in juxtaposition reveal a completely new picture. Quantitative difference has resulted in qualitative difference. To live in New York, acutely alone yet always a member of a crowd, is to develop a sense of self and acquire a standard of conduct distinctly different from any previous models. Collectively, Crane's New York works usher into the national literature the twentieth-century American metropolis as a unique environment that shapes a new kind of person.

Nineteen-year-old Stephen Crane entered Lafayette College in September 1890 and within three months accumulated a sufficient number of "academic deficiencies" to necessitate his withdrawal. Shortly thereafter, however, he managed to gain entrance to Syracuse University as a special student—perhaps because his mother's uncle, Bishop Jesse Truesdell Peck, had been one of its founders—but his stay there was also short-lived. Crane expended a good deal of energy playing for the university's baseball team (as catcher and shortstop) and received an A in English literature. But he failed all other subjects and when the summer recess arrived he departed for Asbury Park, New Jersey, where his widowed mother lived, never to return.

While at Syracuse, Crane had written stories and sketches and served as a stringer for the New York *Tribune*. He continued to

experiment with stories and sketches when in Asbury Park in the
summer of 1891 he began a full-time career as a freelance writer,
supplying reports about summer-season activities on the Jersey
Shore to the *Tribune* and other newspapers. Among these summer projects was further work on *Maggie*, a version of which had
been begun at Syracuse in the spring. College friends later re-
called that while there Crane had frequented the night police
courts, talked with street people, and spent social hours in music
halls where, in their words, "daringly clad girls" danced and
sang. It is clear that before he had ever visited the streets of New
York he had already envisaged *Maggie* and begun accumulating
material for it, a procedure that would be characteristic of his
later literary practice as well. Typically, he made his forays into
life—conducted his research, as it were—in order to find details
that would support what he already had envisioned rather than
to gather experiences upon which he could then exercise his
imagination. His great Civil War novel, for example, which rendered with precision what it was like to be under fire, was written before he had ever witnessed a military engagement; it was
the novel itself that led him to seek out a war he could observe.
Crane's imagination was always in advance of his experience,
and in the sometimes exaggerated luridness of its details *Maggie*
bears this mark of being a fiction projected upon the screen of life
by an incandescent imagination rather than a narrative of experienced life passed through its lens.

In 1892 Crane began making visits to New York's Bowery
from his residence in New Jersey, and then in October of that
year he moved to New York, worked on a revision of his novel,
and began life in the series of apartments and studios in lower
Manhattan that he shared with fellow bohemians from 1892 to
1894. Early in 1893, *Maggie* was published at Crane's own ex-
pense by a small print shop on New York's Sixth Avenue. Below
the title on the book's mustard-yellow cover were two subtitles,
"A Girl of the Streets," and "(A Story of New York)." The cover
also proclaimed that the price was fifty cents and the author was

Johnston Smith. "Commonest name I could think of," Crane told a friend. "I had an editor named Johnson and put in the 't,' and no one could find me in the mob of Smiths."

Apparently almost no one found the small book either. Of the 1,100 copies printed Crane kept one for himself and gave away about 100 others. The rest served for kindling in whatever New York apartment or studio he was at the moment sharing with fellow artists in the impecunious days following the book's publication. Today a surviving copy of *Maggie* is among the rarest and costliest of first editions of modern American literature.

It has been conjectured that Crane used a pseudonym—sought to get lost among the Smiths—because as a young author who was yet to find a public he was cautious about immediately identifying himself with a work that he himself regarded as shocking in its implication that its heroine was driven to prostitution by her circumstances rather than drawn to it because of an inherently sinful nature. In the closing decades of the nineteenth century New York's wealthier citizens, taking alarm at the size and condition of the city's "other half," as reformer Jacob Riis labeled the distressed classes, had launched a number of moral reform agencies, the most prominent of which adhered to the belief that poverty was caused by laziness and a life of prostitution was willingly chosen by depraved women too shiftless to seek more honest means of earning money. A strong distinction was drawn between the deserving poor and those who were inherently degraded, and assistance was firmly withheld from all whom the reformers in their wisdom chose to assign to the latter category. In *Maggie* Crane scorned the distinction, not by polemically attacking it but by ignoring it, representing a reality that bore no relation whatsoever to the platitudes advanced by the legions of moral righteousness.

Another significant branch of reform, however, centered on the need to improve the social conditions that led to degradation rather than to punish the victims of poverty and vice. In 1886, running for the office of mayor of New York, the reformer Henry

George had asked in a campaign speech what it was that "forces girls upon the streets and our boys into grog shops and penitentiaries." *Maggie* is very much about what it is that forces girls upon the streets, and Crane's later work, *George's Mother*, is concerned with what it is that forces boys into the grog shop.

In outline, Maggie's story is one that was told often by concerned observers. A month before the publication of *Maggie*, an article in the *Arena*, a magazine to which Crane later contributed pieces such as "An Ominous Baby," ran an article entitled "The Woes of the New York Working Girl" that spoke of young women "dragging themselves from dirty, vermin-thronged beds at five in the morning, being blackguarded and beaten by drunken parents, being tempted by rakes whose very lust seems a haven of refuge to them." And of course the seduction and abandonment that terminate in the death of the heroine is a novelistic theme almost as old as the novel itself.

The manner in which Crane tells the familiar tale, however, is entirely original and so electrically revivifies the well-known structure of oppressive circumstances, seductive charms, heartless abandonment, prostitution, and death that it becomes a story never told before. Although the plot of *Maggie* advances chronologically from chapter to chapter, it unfolds in distinct scenes, none of which necessarily follows from the preceding. Each unit stands by itself, its integrity further emphasized by Crane's at times beginning a chapter away from his central characters before bringing them into focus—as if, at the outset, we might be dealing with another cast of characters than those whom we already know.

Consider the following sets of consecutive sentences. "Maggie's red mother, stretched on the floor, blasphemed and gave her daughter a bad name. An orchestra of yellow silk women and bald-headed men on an elevated stage near the centre of a great green-hued hall, played a popular waltz." And: "She wondered if the culture and refinement she had seen imitated, perhaps grotesquely, by the heroine on the stage, could be acquired by a girl who lived in a tenement house and worked in a shirt factory. A group of urchins were intent upon the side door of a saloon." The first set ends Chapter VI and begins VII; the second ends Chapter VIII and begins IX.

The consecutive sentences of each set contrast sharply in that the location of the action is abruptly changed but also because in the change of scene we lose sight of the characters we have thus far been following and must wait to relocate them in the new setting. So, for example, the scene in the entertainment saloon is set before Maggie and Pete are placed in it rather than after we follow them into it. In cinematic terms, Crane pans the hall before focusing on his actors, and this opening contrasts in focus as well as content with the sharply realized figure of the "red mother" stretched on the floor with which the previous scene closed. In the second set, the first sentence is concerned with interiority, with the wistful movement of Maggie's thought, while the second sentence is decidedly exterior, a street scene outside a door. Objectivity contrasts with subjectivity, and as the new scene unfolds we must again wait a moment before an unnamed character emerges from the saloon. We must hesitate yet a second or two more before we recognize her as Maggie's mother.

Such interrupted continuities evoke a world that is larger than and overshadows the lives of the characters. They are, to be sure, at the center of our attention, but their brief appearances occur between briefer disappearances. They are constantly framed by shifting scenery that leads us time and again to reapproach them after temporarily losing sight of them in the city. Although Maggie is certainly the heroine of this little drama, she does not take the stage more frequently than the others, which further contributes to the sense that this is indeed, as the subtitle insists, a story of New York.

But, after observing the apparent contrasts within the sets of sentences, we note also underlying coherence. In the first set of sentences, most obviously it is the color register of red, yellow, and green that binds the scenes together. The red of Maggie's mother is the emblem of her violently destructive dissolution. The yellow silk of the women in the orchestra is less menacing, even perhaps wanly cheerful, and yet in conjunction with the bald-headed men the yellow also suggests that the waltz in the green-hued hall is but a temporary stay against inevitable decay. And although Maggie's shy wondering as to whether a girl in her circumstances could ever attain the culture and refinement she saw grotesquely imitated in the melodrama she attended contrasts strongly with the urchins outside the door, the two are continuous as well. The urchins also have gathered to attend a drama, one of real life that answers the question Maggie has just asked herself with a decisive negative.

Throughout *Maggie*, Crane works against the conventions of realism—the representation of precisely realized details that accumulate into a persuasive model of the actual world—even while in good part abiding by them. His gift was for incisive brevity rather than for the irresistible solidity of detail that constitutes the represented world of an author such as Dreiser. In consequence he had to achieve his effects swiftly, by taking even common details and pushing them over the edge of realism into that of expression: a "careening building," a "hilarious hall," "squat and ignorant stables." We recognize that there is not enough furniture in the Johnson household for the family members to keep up the demolition Crane assigns to them but we also recognize the truth of their lives that the destruction is meant to express, although the excess may somewhat detract from the intended effect.

In Chapter XVII, however, Crane's technique of moving actualizing details from the particulars of a realistic scene onto the level of expressive truth is frictionless: the effect is extraordinary. As Maggie walks from the well-lit theater district through the darkening streets of the factory district to the oily, lapping waters of the river, each particular of the scene emerges with a striking clarity. Yet for all the convincing substantiality of the details, we recognize that her stroll is not a single evening's walk but the progress of her entire career as a prostitute. At the outset she has a "handsome cloak" and "well-shod" feet, indications of a woman successful at her profession, but as she moves from one encounter to the next, she progresses downward in the attractiveness of her partners—would-be partners on the particular night but actual partners in a downward career. This descent in effect speaks of her own deteriorating condition, until the torn and greasy garments of the abhorrent figure she encounters at the end suggest not only what her own fine clothing will eventually come to, but indeed the condition she has finally reached in her career of prostitution.

The features of this final apparition suggest venereal disease, and it is significant that he does not, on one hand, pass her by, as did the men of her earlier encounters, nor, on the other, engage her as would a client. Rather, "chuckling and leering" he follows her—a specter of drink, filth, and disease, less "realistic" yet more expressive than the men earlier depicted—and tracks her to her end at an "impossible distance" from the glittering avenues of her beginning. The city that constrained individuality as it framed the preceding scenes here finally annihilates it. In her last appearance, Maggie has become nameless: a "girl of the crimson legions."

In the spring of 1893, a half year after the publication of *Maggie*, Crane began writing *The Red Badge of Courage*. It was first published in abbreviated serial form in 1894 and then in its entirety in book form in 1895. Its success was sensational, and in the following year, capitalizing upon the novel's great popularity and its author's widespread fame, the publishing house of Appleton eagerly published a slightly revised version of *Maggie*, now identified as by Stephen Crane, the author of *The Red Badge of Courage*.

But back in 1893 the seven hundred dollars Crane spent to have *Maggie* published (he was later to say that the publishers, a firm of religious and medical printers, "did me dirt") was the entirety of the inheritance left him by his mother, who had died in the previous year. Daughter of a well-known Methodist minister,

Mary Helen Peck had married another eminent Methodist minister, the Reverend Jonathan Townley Crane, with whom she had fourteen children. Stephen, born in 1871, was the youngest. His father died when Stephen was nine. A devout Christian throughout her life, Mary Helen Crane was busy in church activities, headed the Asbury Park chapter of the Women's Christian Temperance Union (an organization in which Crane was to enroll George's mother) and contributed paid work to Methodist journals. In addition to the investments he sold in order to pay for *Maggie*, Crane's literary talent also may well have been an inheritance from his mother.

But beginning with *Maggie* and continuing throughout his brief and spectacular career, Crane satirized what he saw as conventional Christianity's disconnection from the world he and his characters inhabited: Jimmie attends service in a mission church only to have the preacher distance himself from his auditors while assuring them they are damned; in her distress, Maggie, who "had heard of the Grace of God," timidly accosts a minister on the street who "gave a convulsive movement and saved his respectability by a vigorous side-step"; and in the novel's final scene, Maggie's mother's behavior parodies the rhetoric of Christian forgiveness. Banal as it is, stage melodrama with its assurance that the rich are scoundrels who will fall before the uprightness of the virtuous poor parallels the teachings of religion in Crane's world, both hypocritically denying the reality of exploited lives by assuring the distressed classes that they are essentially better off than their exploiters.

George's Mother is more conventional in its narrative form than is *Maggie*. The principal characters are kept in focus and followed from chapter to chapter rather than approached through a series of city scenes, and the plot seems generated by their willed acts rather than by the force of circumstances. Whereas *Maggie* can justifiably be called "A Story of New York" and Maggie's individuality finally dissolves into "a girl of the streets," *George's Mother* is pretty much the story of what happened to these particular characters, or, as William Dean Howells phrased it, "It is the study of a situation merely: a poor inadequate woman, of a commonplace religiosity, whose son goes to the bad."

Maggie's fall occurs at the novel's midpoint, *between* chapters IX and X rather than within any chapter, emphasizing Crane's view that what is at issue is not the alleged sinfulness of her act but its cause and its consequence: Chapter IX ends, " 'Go teh hell an' good riddance.' / She went."; and X begins, "Jimmie had an idea it wasn't common courtesy for a friend to come to one's home and ruin one's sister." Kelcey's corresponding fall into alcohol also occurs at the midpoint of *George's Mother*, but it is fully rendered in three chapters—VIII, IX, and X—that follow the continuous events of Bleecker's party from beginning to end. The difference between Crane's treatment of these two falls, each centrally located, epitomizes his changed narrative technique.

If *George's Mother* appears to be the more conventional work, it is, nonetheless, a work well worth reading. To quote Howells again, "The wonder of it is the courage which deals with persons so absolutely average, and the art that graces them with the beauty of the author's compassion for everything that errs and suffers." Crane's irony beats back the sentimental and the maudlin readings that the situation of Mrs. Kelcey and her errant son would seem to invite, but it is not deployed to wither them. Rather, Crane fixes them in a clear-eyed gaze that invites sympathetic comprehension of their bewilderments. They are country people, *in* the city but not *of* it, each viewing it as a great theater of sin.

For George's mother, this leads to a fearful retreat behind the banal beliefs she brought with her from the country. For George, the sinful city is a mystery he longs somehow to enter into, but his desire to lose country habits and learn city ways is, finally, more pathetic than his mother's narrow-minded fearfulness: "The saloons contained the mystery of a street for him. When he knew its saloons he comprehended the street." His aspiration goes no higher and he therefore sinks.

With an understated irony that amounts to a joke to be shared only with the reader who has also read *Maggie*, Crane wryly makes Maggie the immediate, albeit unconscious, cause of George's downfall, even as Pete was the conscious cause of hers. Maggie Johnson, whom George sees on the stairs of the tenement house in which they both live, becomes the object of his desire and the subject of his fantasies, yet in his awkward self-consciousness he finds no way of approaching her. ("Say, Mag, I'm stuck on yer shape," is the way that city-smart Pete initiated his approach.) Terrified by the possibility of rejection and the consequent collapse of his fantasy world, George hesitates, awaiting some dreamed-of moment when a disaster will require him to rescue Maggie and win her adoring love, until one day he sees the dapper Pete call upon Maggie, and with this glimpse of the well-dressed, fast-talking Pete his sense of his own inadequacies overwhelms him. "There came over him all the self-pity that comes when the soul is turned back from a road," and his career as a drinking companion commences.

Although not published until 1896, *George's Mother* was written shortly after *Maggie* was published. In that same period of his New York residence (1892–94) Crane wrote most of his striking stories and sketches of the city. Maggie's little brother Tommie, dead before the end of the novel, is resurrected in three of them, "An Ominous Baby," "A Great Mistake," and "A Dark-Brown Dog," and almost all the other short works of the period are also concerned with life in the Bowery, a district that in Crane's day was becoming synonymous with poverty and the attendant vices of filth, drink, crime, and degradation.

A financial panic in 1893 had initiated five years of severe depression and massive unemployment with some twenty thousand homeless as well as jobless. "People piled up in parks and squares, in the Salvation Army Hall, on Blackwell's Island, and in Bowery lodging houses."* This was Crane's turf, and he strode across it with a will.

The three Tommie stories were written immediately after the publication of *Maggie*, although they were not then published. James B. Colvert observes that the "young child as pure ego, as candid and unabashed aggressor" appealed to Crane because it represented "primitive forces in nature powerfully resistant to constraints of human laws and conventions." In his inexperience, Tommie, the "baby," knows no reason why his will should not be served—save his awareness that those with superior physical force will attempt to thwart him in the service of their own desires. No higher principles govern in Tommie's world. Although his struggles are clothed in the diction of revolt against property and against religion, both institutions are as predatory as he.

In "An Ominous Baby," Tommie makes off with the toy he has wrested from the wealthy child and then weeps "with the air of a wronged one who has at last succeeded in achieving his rights." In "A Great Mistake" the boy's eyes are raised to the vendor's face "with deep respect, worship, as if he saw omnipotence," and a biblical phrase introduces the godlike vendor's detection of the theft of the forbidden fruit: "And it was written that the Italian should at this moment open his eyes."

To note this, however, is not to contend that Crane is explicitly parodying the Bible in that story nor that he is mounting an explicit social criticism in the previous story. He was not, in the usual sense of the phrase, an author of "social protest" but rather was concerned with conveying the elemental forces that for him were truly at work behind the facade of social and religious regulations. The child too young to receive the world as other than a

---

*Edwin G. Burrows and Mike Wallace, *Gotham, A History of New York City to 1898* (New York: Oxford University Press, 1999), p. 1186.

series of desires was his vehicle. As Keith Gandal has suggested, Crane was an ethnographer of slum life, not a moralist.

A newly emerging popular art was soon to reveal how remarkably prescient was Crane's use of the child, a conventional symbol of innocent virtue, as the epitome of anarchic force. On February 6, 1896, Joseph Pulitzer's New York *World* published a picture that historians of the genre today recognize as the first newspaper comic strip. Its hero, the "Yellow Kid," was a boy who always dressed in a long nightgown, thereby emphasizing his infancy even as the jug-handled ears protruding from his bald head and the worldly-wise leer on his lips hinted at a cunning beyond his years.

His speech was conveyed by words printed on his nightgown and it was in the same register of slang as that of Crane's Bowery inhabitants. Yellow-haired Tommie asks the affluent child "Is dat yours?" The Yellow Kid says things such as "Dis gang tinks dey kin queer me but wait an see." The Yellow Kid is depicted time and again in one or another violent act against either authority or convention, upending well-dressed citizens, dismaying policemen, and scattering bystanders. He became so sensational a popular favorite that William Randolph Hearst hired its creator, Richard Felton Outcault, away from the *World* to his New York *Journal*, which led Pulitzer in turn to employ another artist to continue the cartoon in the *World*. There were thus two Yellow Kids running against each other in the competing newspapers—a phenomenon that gave rise to the term "yellow journalism."

In a period of severe economic depression, the Kid converted mass resentment of authority into laughter by running off with a horseless carriage, the vehicle of the rich, or, with ludicrous inappropriateness, appearing on the golf links. ("I am playin dis game and I dont want no fresh mug te gimme tips SEE.") The similarities he shares with Tommie illustrate how perceptive were Crane's journalistic instincts. But the dissimilarities illustrate the difference between mass entertainment and literary artistry. In a time of severe economic depression, the Kid finally acts as a safety valve, draining the dispossessed's outrage at the conspicuous luxuries of the privileged into laughter at the amusing spectacle of one of their own discomfiting the stuffed shirts. But the Tommie stories convey a terrible truth made all the more appalling by the fact that it is not a truth conventionally said to emerge from the mouth of babes.

Although Crane's New York pieces were printed in newspapers—many of the best as feature articles in the Sunday editions of the New York *Press* during the spring and summer of 1894—they were not a reporter's stenographic accounts of witnessed events but sketches of street life that moved halfway toward fiction in their concern with atmosphere and their attention to impressions; the reactions of the narrators or other spectators to depicted incidents are characteristically of an importance equal to that of the incident itself. "The Broken-Down Van," written for the *Tribune* in 1892, is an experiment in description in which the drama of the breakdown is made to organize the larger street scene, with the residents of the East Side—sweatshop employees, policemen, beer-toting children, an ogling barber— passing to and fro across the stage in a manner to suggest the way in which the pace and clamor of their streets shape the quality of their lives.

The American literary tradition of local color that emerged in the second half of the nineteenth century was primarily concerned with the unique, folkloric relationship existing between inhabitants and landscape in one or another provincial region of the United States—Bret Harte's California or Sarah Orne Jewett's Maine, for example. Crane, in sketches such as "The Broken-Down Van," carried this subgenre into the city, where it had rarely been situated before, depicting the distinctive folkways that had arisen to meet the demands of the urban environment together with the slang that was the city's very own lexicon.

"When Man Falls, a Crowd Gathers" is perhaps the most telling of the local-color pieces in the breathtaking economy with which Crane captures the sense of the city as the site of crowds and thus of anonymity, of callousness and yet of succor. It is in such pieces that he apprehends the way in which the city's sheer quantitative difference from other human sites, a place where thousands upon thousands move past one another with streams converging into crowds, results in a qualitative difference, a place where life is conducted differently. Here Crane begins to move past New York itself into a study of the nature of urbanism and the patterns of behavior destined to replace those that had been nurtured for centuries in the countries and the countrysides from which those who now were massed in the city were drawn.

With New York as the stage of his drama, Crane organized other sketches along a narrative line, moving them closer to the boundaries of fiction than pieces such as "The Broken-Down Van" without ever quite crossing that line. The two "Experiment" pieces are concerned with social investigations into the contrasting worlds of the destitute and the wealthy. They are also experimental in a literary sense as Crane explores the way in which the meaning that eludes objective description may be rendered through making the witnessing author's imaginings part of the depicted reality.

For example, the youth spending the night in a Bowery flophouse listens to the moans and shrieks of a man lying in a corner of the cot-crowded room:

To the youth these were not merely the shrieks of a vision pierced man. They were an utterance of the meaning of the room and its occupants. It was to him the protest of the wretch who feels the touch of the imperturbable granite wheels and who then cries with an impersonal eloquence, with a strength not from him, giving voice to the wail of a whole section, a class, a people. This, weaving into the young man's brain and mingling with his views of these vast and somber shadows that like mighty black fingers curled around the naked bodies, made the young man so that he did not sleep, but lay carving biographies for these men from his meager experience. At times the fellow in the corner howled in a writhing agony of his imaginations.

The "mighty black fingers" glide away from literal reality—yet this subjectivity operates strongly to reinforce the objective picture placed before the reader's eyes even as it moves the realistically observed details onto the plane of expression.

In "An Experiment in Luxury," as in the previous sketch, accompanying and underlying the depiction of the actual scene is the author's uncomfortable awareness of his own inadequate reaction to what he is witnessing. Spending an evening in the opulent mansion of a wealthy friend, he is disturbed at his failure truly to feel the outrage to which his knowledge of the sufferings of tens of thousands should lead him. The "mystery" of the social condition, as he phrases it, is that some sit amidst luxury and chat idly while others are being "blackened and mashed" by life in the lower places.

And yet even as he recognizes this, his involuntary awe at the luxury that surrounds him exasperatingly illustrates how the "mystery" is sustained: "For what reason did his nature so deeply respect all this? . . . There was one side of him that said there were finer things in life, but the other side did homage." He recognizes, that is, that by "nature" he is complicitous in the maintenance of what his intellect tells him is a system of massive social injustice.

"The Men in the Storm" is a powerful forerunner of the naturalism of Dreiser and Steinbeck and their telling narratives of the price paid in human dignity for the economic depressions that were the dark side of the American dream. The circumstances under which Crane wrote it were pictured verbally by the artist Corwin K. Linson, a friend of Crane's who also sketched and painted notable portraits of him. One day after a bitter night of driving snows, Linson went to the League of Art Students Building, where Crane was rooming, to find his haggard friend lying in bed. "Pulling a manuscript from under his pillow," Linson said, "he tossed it to me." After standing for hours with the inadequately clothed men, Crane had rushed back to write the sketch before going to sleep. Looking at Crane's worn condition Linson asked why he had not dressed more warmly and was answered with a question, "How would I know how those poor devils felt if I was warm myself?"

The story "Mr. Binks' Day Off" is to some extent uncharacteristic of Crane's New York period in dealing with middle-class—at least lower-middle-class—characters as well as in moving them out of the city for a day. "The sense of a city is battle," says Crane and, far from deploring this, the Binkses find something unbearable about the calm placidity of the rural town they visit. Finally, they do lapse into an afternoon of bucolic content, but the view of the city they acquire from the vantage point of the country does not support the customary idea that man made the turbulent city while God made the tranquil country. Rather, with a Crane-like touch of irony, in the country they put aside the expressions about gold as a curse and the sneers at the rush for spoils that they indulged in the city and "In the light of their contempt for this stillness, the conflicts of the city were exalted." The story echoes "When Man Falls" in its quiet insistence that urban values do not just contrast with rural values but are irresistibly replacing them.

In January 1895 Stephen Crane left New York for a tour of the West and Mexico, returning in April 1896 to resume his career in freelance journalism. He sold sketches of city life, such as an incident on a streetcar or a description of bicyclists speeding down Broadway, to newspaper syndicates, and, appreciating his eye for the underside of big-city life, the New York *Journal* commissioned him to do a series of articles on the Tenderloin. For one of these, in September 1896, he attended the Jefferson Market Court and there witnessed the hearing he described in the brilliant sketch "An Eloquence of Grief." "People pity those who need none," Crane wrote, "and the guilty sob alone." The great wonder of this piece is that without explicit comment and without any emotive language, his dispassionate description of the incident—culminating in the sentence "Then it was that a great cry rang through the court-room, the cry of this girl who believed that she was lost"—extends the withheld pity.

In further pursuit of Tenderloin scenes, one night in the same month Crane met with two chorus girls and interviewed them at the Broadway Garden, a known resort of prostitutes. There they were joined by Dora Clark, a friend of the chorus girls, and the four left together at about two in the morning. What followed— the arrest of Dora Clark for solicitation and Crane's appearance on her behalf in court—was described by him in the New York *Journal* of September 20 under the headline "ADVENTURES OF A NOVELIST."

Another sometime visitor to Tenderloin scenes in that year was Teddy Roosevelt, one of the four members of the Police Board appointed in 1895 to reform a corrupt police force and clear the city of the vicious activities that force had protected. Accompanied by Jacob Riis, the noted authority on slum life, Commissioner Roosevelt would walk the nighttime streets in disguise to check on how policemen were performing their duties. Roosevelt had welcomed Crane's earlier studies of the Bowery such as *Maggie*, but when Crane bore witness against a policeman, as he did in the Dora Clark case, Roosevelt was quick to discredit him as a man who frequented prostitutes, drank heavily, and took drugs—based, apparently, on the absence of moralizing when Crane depicted such matters in his sketches. Many another agreed with Roosevelt, while every New York police officer recognized Crane on sight and was determined to harass the man who had testified against a fellow officer. In the city of his greatest creative period Stephen Crane had become persona non grata. His departure for Florida in November 1896, en route to Cuba and coverage of the Cuban revolution, ended his remarkable New York career.

Crane returned to New York three more times, but always in transit from one site of death to another. When the Greco-Turkish War broke out he passed through New York in March of 1897 on his way from Florida to cover that conflict, and at its close in June chose to return to London rather than America. When the Spanish-American War broke out, however, he rushed back to New York in order to enlist in the navy, but the tuberculosis that was to end his life was already evident and, failing the physical examination, he went to Havana as a war correspondent. Then at war's end, for a third and final time, he passed through the city en route back to England and the society of admiring literary friends such as Henry James, H. G. Wells, Ford Madox Ford, and especially Joseph Conrad.

Settled in Sussex, Crane undertook a killing schedule, racing to meet the deadlines of journals to which he had promised work even as he attempted also to write stories and novels. He left himself no time to rest, and rest he critically needed as the tuberculosis he had for too long attempted to deny relentlessly advanced upon him. Finally, in May 1900, unable even to rise to his feet, he was carried to a sanitarium in Germany's Black Forest, and there in the following month, age twenty-eight years seven months, Stephen Crane died. His final journey was to burial in Hillside, New Jersey.

SUGGESTIONS FOR FURTHER READING

BIOGRAPHY

Benfey, Christopher. *The Double Life of Stephen Crane* (New York, 1992). The best single discussion of Crane's life and work.

Berryman, John. *Stephen Crane* (New York, 1960) offers brilliant critical interpretation but is unreliable with regard to the facts of Crane's life.

Davis, Linda H. *Badge of Courage: The Life of Stephen Crane* (Boston, 1998).

Linson, Corwin K. *My Stephen Crane* (Syracuse, 1958), a memoir by Crane's friend, is always fascinating although not always trustworthy.

Wertheim, Stanley, and Paul Sorrentino. *The Crane Log* (New York, 1994) is a rich "documentary life," informative on every page.

LETTERS

The Correspondence of Stephen Crane, ed. Stanley Wertheim and Paul Sorrentino (New York, 1988), 2 vols.

Stephen Crane: Letters, ed. R. W. Stallman and Lillian Gilkes (New York, 1960).

CRITICISM: BOOKS

Colvert, James B. *Stephen Crane* (San Diego, 1984).

Gandal, Keith. *The Virtues of the Vicious* (New York, 1997).

Haliburton, David. *The Color of the Sky: A Study of Stephen Crane* (Cambridge, U.K., 1989).

Robertson, Michael. *Stephen Crane, Journalism, and the Making of Modern America* (New York, 1997).

Solomon, Eric. *Stephen Crane: From Parody to Realism* (Cambridge, Mass., 1966).

CRITICISM: ARTICLES

Bloom, Harold, ed. *Stephen Crane* (New York, 1987) contains articles on some of Crane's New York works.

Colvert, James. "Stephen Crane and Postmodern Theory," *American Literary Realism* 28:1 (Fall 1995).

Pizer, Donald. "*Maggie* and the Naturalistic Aesthetic of Length," *American Literary Realism* 28:1 (Fall 1995).

A NOTE ON THE TEXTS

The text of *Maggie* follows that of the first edition, 1893, rather than the 1896 edition in which revisions appear to be the work of an editor rather than of Crane. For a discussion of the superiority of the 1893 text, see Hershel Parker and Brian Higgins, "Maggie's 'Last Night,' " *Studies in the Novel* 10:1 (Spring 1978), 64–75.

All other works printed here follow the texts approved by the Center for Editions of American Authors as published in *The Works of Stephen Crane*, ed. Fredson Bowers (Charlottesville: University Press of Virginia), 10 vols. *George's Mother* is in Volume I (1969); the remaining pieces are in Volume VIII (1973).

When two dates follow a work in the table of contents, the first refers to the presumed year in which composition was completed and the second to the year of the work's initial appearance in print.

MAGGIE

A

GIRL OF THE STREETS

(A Story of New York)

BY

JOHNSTON SMITH

MAGGIE:
A GIRL OF THE STREETS
(A Story of New York)

Chapter I

A very little boy stood upon a heap of gravel for the honor of Rum Alley. He was throwing stones at howling urchins from Devil's Row who were circling madly about the heap and pelting at him.

His infantile countenance was livid with fury. His small body was writhing in the delivery of great, crimson oaths.

"Run, Jimmie, run! Dey'll get yehs," screamed a retreating Rum Alley child.

"Naw," responded Jimmie with a valiant roar, "dese micks can't make me run."

Howls of renewed wrath went up from Devil's Row throats. Tattered gamins on the right made a furious assault on the gravel heap. On their small, convulsed faces there shone the grins of true assassins. As they charged, they threw stones and cursed in shrill chorus.

The little champion of Rum Alley stumbled precipitately down the other side. His coat had been torn to shreds in a scuffle, and his hat was gone. He had bruises on twenty parts of his body, and blood was dripping from a cut in his head. His wan features wore a look of a tiny, insane demon.

On the ground, children from Devil's Row closed in on their antagonist. He crooked his left arm defensively about his head and fought with cursing fury. The little boys ran to and fro, dodging, hurling stones and swearing in barbaric trebles.

From a window of an apartment house that upreared its form from amid squat, ignorant stables, there leaned a curious woman. Some laborers, unloading a scow at a dock at the river, paused for a moment and regarded the fight. The engineer of a passive tugboat hung lazily to a railing and watched. Over on the Island, a worm of yellow convicts came from the shadow of a grey ominous building and crawled slowly along the river's bank. ✒

A stone had smashed into Jimmie's mouth. Blood was bubbling over his chin and down upon his ragged shirt. Tears made furrows on his dirt-stained cheeks. His thin legs had begun to tremble and turn weak, causing his small body to reel. His roaring curses of the first part of the fight had changed to a blasphemous chatter.

In the yells of the whirling mob of Devil's Row children there were notes of joy like songs of triumphant savagery. The little boys seemed to leer gloatingly at the blood upon the other child's face.

Down the avenue came boastfully sauntering a lad of sixteen years, although the chronic sneer of an ideal manhood already sat upon his lips. His hat was tipped with an air of challenge over his eye. Between his teeth, a cigar stump was tilted at the angle of defiance. He walked with a certain swing of the shoulders which appalled the timid. He glanced over into the vacant lot in which the little raving boys from Devil's Row seethed about the shrieking and tearful child from Rum Alley.

"Gee!" he murmured with interest, "A scrap. Gee!"

He strode over to the cursing circle, swinging his shoulders in a manner which denoted that he held victory in his fists. He approached at the back of one of the most deeply engaged of the Devil's Row children.

"Ah, what deh hell," he said, and smote the deeply-engaged one on the back of the head. The little boy fell to the ground and gave a hoarse, tremendous howl. He scrambled to his feet, and perceiving, evidently, the size of his assailant, ran quickly off, shouting alarms. The entire Devil's Row party followed him.

They came to a stand a short distance away and yelled taunting oaths at the boy with the chronic sneer. The latter, momentarily, paid no attention to them.

"What deh hell, Jimmie?" he asked of the small champion.

Jimmie wiped his blood-wet features with his sleeve.

"Well, it was dis way, Pete, see! I was goin' teh lick dat Riley kid and dey all pitched on me."

Some Rum Alley children now came forward. The party stood for a moment exchanging vainglorious remarks with Devil's Row. A few stones were thrown at long distances, and words of challenge passed between small warriors. Then the Rum Alley contingent turned slowly in the direction of their home street. They began to give, each to each, distorted versions of the fight. Causes of retreat in particular cases were magnified. Blows dealt in the fight were enlarged to catapultian power, and stones thrown were alleged to have hurtled with infinite accuracy. Valor grew strong again, and the little boys began to swear with great spirit.

"Ah, we blokies kin lick deh hull damn Row," said a child, swaggering.

Little Jimmie was striving to stanch the flow of blood from his cut lips. Scowling, he turned upon the speaker.

"Ah, where deh hell was yeh when I was doin' all deh fightin'?" he demanded. "Youse kids makes me tired."

"Ah, go ahn," replied the other argumentatively.

Jimmie replied with heavy contempt. "Ah, youse can't fight, Blue Billie! I kin lick yeh wid one han'."

"Ah, go ahn," replied Billie again.

"Ah," said Jimmie threateningly.

"Ah," said the other in the same tone.

They struck at each other, clinched, and rolled over on the cobble stones.

"Smash 'im, Jimmie, kick deh damn guts out of 'im," yelled Pete, the lad with the chronic sneer, in tones of delight.

The small combatants pounded and kicked, scratched and

tore. They began to weep and their curses struggled in their throats with sobs. The other little boys clasped their hands and wriggled their legs in excitement. They formed a bobbing circle about the pair.

A tiny spectator was suddenly agitated.

"Cheese it, Jimmie, cheese it! Here comes yer fader," he yelled.

The circle of little boys instantly parted. They drew away and waited in ecstatic awe for that which was about to happen. The two little boys fighting in the modes of four thousand years ago, did not hear the warning.

Up the avenue there plodded slowly a man with sullen eyes. He was carrying a dinner pail and smoking an apple-wood pipe.

As he neared the spot where the little boys strove, he regarded them listlessly. But suddenly he roared an oath and advanced upon the rolling fighters.

"Here, you Jim, git up, now, while I belt yer life out, you damned disorderly brat."

He began to kick into the chaotic mass on the ground. The boy Billie felt a heavy boot strike his head. He made a furious effort and disentangled himself from Jimmie. He tottered away, damning.

Jimmie arose painfully from the ground and confronting his father, began to curse him. His parent kicked him. "Come home, now," he cried, "an' stop yer jawin', er I'll lam the everlasting head off yehs."

They departed. The man paced placidly along with the apple-wood emblem of serenity between his teeth. The boy followed a dozen feet in the rear. He swore luridly, for he felt that it was degradation for one who aimed to be some vague soldier, or a man of blood with a sort of sublime license, to be taken home by a father.

Chapter II

Eventually they entered into a dark region where, from a careening building, a dozen gruesome doorways gave up loads of babies to the street and the gutter. A wind of early autumn raised yellow dust from cobbles and swirled it against an hundred windows. Long streamers of garments fluttered from fire-escapes. In all unhandy places there were buckets, brooms, rags and bottles. In the street infants played or fought with other infants or sat stupidly in the way of vehicles. Formidable women, with uncombed hair and disordered dress, gossiped while leaning on railings, or screamed in frantic quarrels. Withered persons, in curious postures of submission to something, sat smoking pipes in obscure corners. A thousand odors of cooking food came forth to the street. The building quivered and creaked from the weight of humanity stamping about in its bowels.

A small ragged girl dragged a red, bawling infant along the crowded ways. He was hanging back, baby-like, bracing his wrinkled, bare legs.

The little girl cried out: "Ah, Tommie, come ahn. Dere's Jimmie and fader. Don't be a-pullin' me back."

She jerked the baby's arm impatiently. He fell on his face, roaring. With a second jerk she pulled him to his feet, and they went on. With the obstinacy of his order, he protested against being dragged in a chosen direction. He made heroic endeavors to keep

7

on his legs, denounce his sister and consume a bit of orange peeling which he chewed between the times of his infantile orations.

As the sullen-eyed man, followed by the blood-covered boy, drew near, the little girl burst into reproachful cries. "Ah, Jimmie, youse bin fightin' agin."

The urchin swelled disdainfully.

"Ah, what deh hell, Mag. See?"

The little girl upbraided him. "Youse allus fightin', Jimmie, an' yeh knows it puts mudder out when yehs come home half dead, an' it's like we'll all get a poundin'."

She began to weep. The babe threw back his head and roared at his prospects.

"Ah, what deh hell!" cried Jimmie. "Shut up er I'll smack yer mout'. See?"

As his sister continued her lamentations, he suddenly swore and struck her. The little girl reeled and, recovering herself, burst into tears and quaveringly cursed him. As she slowly retreated her brother advanced dealing her cuffs. The father heard and turned about.

"Stop that, Jim, d'yeh hear? Leave yer sister alone on the street. It's like I can never beat any sense into yer damned wooden head."

The urchin raised his voice in defiance to his parent and continued his attacks. The babe bawled tremendously, protesting with great violence. During his sister's hasty manoeuvres, he was dragged by the arm.

Finally the procession plunged into one of the gruesome doorways. They crawled up dark stairways and along cold, gloomy halls. At last the father pushed open a door and they entered a lighted room in which a large woman was rampant.

She stopped in a career from a seething stove to a pan-covered table. As the father and children filed in she peered at them.

"Eh, what? Been fightin' agin, by Gawd!" She threw herself upon Jimmie. The urchin tried to dart behind the others and in the scuffle the babe, Tommie, was knocked down. He protested with his usual vehemence, because they had bruised his tender shins against a table leg.

The mother's massive shoulders heaved with anger. Grasping the urchin by the neck and shoulder she shook him until he rattled. She dragged him to an unholy sink, and, soaking a rag in water, began to scrub his lacerated face with it. Jimmie screamed in pain and tried to twist his shoulders out of the clasp of the huge arms.

The babe sat on the floor watching the scene, his face in contortions like that of a woman at a tragedy. The father, with a newly-ladened pipe in his mouth, crouched on a backless chair near the stove. Jimmie's cries annoyed him. He turned about and bellowed at his wife:

"Let the damned kid alone for a minute, will yeh, Mary? Yer allus poundin' 'im. When I come nights I can't git no rest 'cause yer allus poundin' a kid. Let up, d'yeh hear? Don't be allus poundin' a kid."

The woman's operations on the urchin instantly increased in violence. At last she tossed him to a corner where he limply lay cursing and weeping.

The wife put her immense hands on her hips and with a chieftain-like stride approached her husband.

"Ho," she said, with a great grunt of contempt. "An' what in the devil are you stickin' your nose for?"

The babe crawled under the table and, turning, peered out cautiously. The ragged girl retreated and the urchin in the corner drew his legs carefully beneath him.

The man puffed his pipe calmly and put his great mudded boots on the back part of the stove.

"Go teh hell," he murmured, tranquilly.

The woman screamed and shook her fists before her husband's eyes. The rough yellow of her face and neck flared suddenly crimson. She began to howl.

He puffed imperturbably at his pipe for a time, but finally

arose and began to look out at the window into the darkening chaos of back yards.

"You've been drinkin', Mary," he said. "You'd better let up on the bot', ol' woman, or you'll git done."

"You're a liar. I ain't had a drop," she roared in reply.

They had a lurid altercation, in which they damned each other's souls with frequence.

The babe was staring out from under the table, his small face working in his excitement.

The ragged girl went stealthily over to the corner where the urchin lay.

"Are yehs hurted much, Jimmie?" she whispered timidly.

"Not a damn bit! See?" growled the little boy.

"Will I wash deh blood?"

"Naw!"

"Will I"—

"When I catch dat Riley kid I'll break 'is face! Dat's right! See?"

He turned his face to the wall as if resolved to grimly bide his time.

In the quarrel between husband and wife, the woman was victor. The man grabbed his hat and rushed from the room, apparently determined upon a vengeful drunk. She followed to the door and thundered at him as he made his way down stairs.

She returned and stirred up the room until her children were bobbing about like bubbles.

"Git outa deh way," she persistently bawled, waving feet with their dishevelled shoes near the heads of her children. She shrouded herself, puffing and snorting, in a cloud of steam at the stove, and eventually extracted a frying-pan full of potatoes that hissed.

She flourished it. "Come teh yer suppers, now," she cried with sudden exasperation. "Hurry up, now, er I'll help yeh!"

The children scrambled hastily. With prodigious clatter they arranged themselves at table. The babe sat with his feet dangling

high from a precarious infant chair and gorged his small stomach. Jimmie forced, with feverish rapidity, the grease-enveloped
pieces between his wounded lips. Maggie, with side glances of
fear of interruption, ate like a small pursued tigress.

The mother sat blinking at them. She delivered reproaches,
swallowed potatoes and drank from a yellow-brown bottle. After
a time her mood changed and she wept as she carried little Tommie into another room and laid him to sleep with his fists dou-
bled in an old quilt of faded red and green grandeur. Then she
came and moaned by the stove. She rocked to and fro upon a
chair, shedding tears and crooning miserably to the two children
about their "poor mother" and "yer fader, damn 'is soul."

The little girl plodded between the table and the chair with a
dish-pan on it. She tottered on her small legs beneath burdens of
dishes.

Jimmie sat nursing his various wounds. He cast furtive glances
at his mother. His practised eye perceived her gradually emerge
from a muddled mist of sentiment until her brain burned in
drunken heat. He sat breathless.

Maggie broke a plate.

The mother started to her feet as if propelled.

"Good Gawd," she howled. Her eyes glittered on her child
with sudden hatred. The fervent red of her face turned almost to
purple. The little boy ran to the halls, shrieking like a monk in an
earthquake.

He floundered about in darkness until he found the stairs. He
stumbled, panic-stricken, to the next floor. An old woman
opened a door. A light behind her threw a flare on the urchin's
quivering face.

"Eh, Gawd, child, what is it dis time? Is yer fader beatin' yer
mudder, or yer mudder beatin' yer fader?"

Chapter III

Jimmie and the old woman listened long in the hall. Above the muffled roar of conversation, the dismal wailings of babies at night, the thumping of feet in unseen corridors and rooms, mingled with the sound of varied hoarse shoutings in the street and the rattling of wheels over cobbles, they heard the screams of the child and the roars of the mother die away to a feeble moaning and a subdued bass muttering.

The old woman was a gnarled and leathery personage who could don, at will, an expression of great virtue. She possessed a small music-box capable of one tune, and a collection of "God bless yehs" pitched in assorted keys of fervency. Each day she took a position upon the stones of Fifth Avenue, where she crooked her legs under her and crouched immovable and hideous, like an idol. She received daily a small sum in pennies. It was contributed, for the most part, by persons who did not make their homes in that vicinity.

Once, when a lady had dropped her purse on the sidewalk, the gnarled woman had grabbed it and smuggled it with great dexterity beneath her cloak. When she was arrested she had cursed the lady into a partial swoon, and with her aged limbs, twisted from rheumatism, had almost kicked the stomach out of a huge policeman whose conduct upon that occasion she referred to when she said: "The police, damn 'em."

"Eh, Jimmie, it's cursed shame," she said. "Go, now, like a dear an' buy me a can, an' if yer mudder raises 'ell all night yehs can sleep here."

Jimmie took a tendered tin-pail and seven pennies and departed. He passed into the side door of a saloon and went to the bar. Straining up on his toes he raised the pail and pennies as high as his arms would let him. He saw two hands thrust down and take them. Directly the same hands let down the filled pail and he left.

In front of the gruesome doorway he met a lurching figure. It was his father, swaying about on uncertain legs.

"Give me deh can. See?" said the man, threateningly.

"Ah, come off! I got dis can fer dat ol' woman an' it 'ud be dirt teh swipe it. See?" cried Jimmie.

The father wrenched the pail from the urchin. He grasped it in both hands and lifted it to his mouth. He glued his lips to the under edge and tilted his head. His hairy throat swelled until it seemed to grow near his chin. There was a tremendous gulping movement and the beer was gone.

The man caught his breath and laughed. He hit his son on the head with the empty pail. As it rolled clanging into the street, Jimmie began to scream and kicked repeatedly at his father's shins.

"Look at deh dirt what yeh done me," he yelled. "Deh ol' woman 'ill be raisin' hell."

He retreated to the middle of the street, but the man did not pursue. He staggered toward the door.

"I'll club hell outa yeh when I ketch yeh," he shouted, and disappeared.

During the evening he had been standing against a bar drinking whiskies and declaring to all comers, confidentially: "My home reg'lar livin' hell! Damndes' place! Reg'lar hell! Why do I come an' drin' whisk' here thish way? 'Cause home reg'lar livin' hell!"

Jimmie waited a long time in the street and then crept warily up through the building. He passed with great caution the door of the gnarled woman, and finally stopped outside his home and listened.

He could hear his mother moving heavily about among the furniture of the room. She was chanting in a mournful voice, occasionally interjecting bursts of volcanic wrath at the father, who, Jimmie judged, had sunk down on the floor or in a corner.

"Why deh blazes don' chere try teh keep Jim from fightin'? I'll break yer jaw," she suddenly bellowed.

The man mumbled with drunken indifference. "Ah, wha' deh hell. W'a's odds? Wha' makes kick?"

"Because he tears 'is clothes, yeh damn fool," cried the woman in supreme wrath.

The husband seemed to become aroused. "Go teh hell," he thundered fiercely in reply. There was a crash against the door and something broke into clattering fragments. Jimmie partially suppressed a howl and darted down the stairway. Below he paused and listened. He heard howls and curses, groans and shrieks, confusingly in chorus as if a battle were raging. With all was the crash of splintering furniture. The eyes of the urchin glared in fear that one of them would discover him.

Curious faces appeared in door-ways, and whispered comments passed to and fro. "Ol' Johnson's raisin' hell agin."

Jimmie stood until the noises ceased and the other inhabitants of the tenement had all yawned and shut their doors. Then he crawled upstairs with the caution of an invader of a panther den. Sounds of labored breathing came through the broken door-panels. He pushed the door open and entered, quaking.

A glow from the fire threw red hues over the bare floor, the cracked and soiled plastering, and the overturned and broken furniture.

→ In the middle of the floor lay his mother asleep. In one corner of the room his father's limp body hung across the seat of a chair.

The urchin stole forward. He began to shiver in dread of

awakening his parents. His mother's great chest was heaving painfully. Jimmie paused and looked down at her. Her face was inflamed and swollen from drinking. Her yellow brows shaded eye-lids that had grown blue. Her tangled hair tossed in waves over her forehead. Her mouth was set in the same lines of vindictive hatred that it had, perhaps, borne during the fight. Her bare, red arms were thrown out above her head in positions of exhaustion, something, mayhap, like those of a sated villain.

The urchin bended over his mother. He was fearful lest she should open her eyes, and the dread within him was so strong, that he could not forbear to stare, but hung as if fascinated over the woman's grim face.

Suddenly her eyes opened. The urchin found himself looking straight into that expression, which, it would seem, had the power to change his blood to salt. He howled piercingly and fell backward.

The woman floundered for a moment, tossed her arms about her head as if in combat, and again began to snore.

Jimmie crawled back in the shadows and waited. A noise in the next room had followed his cry at the discovery that his mother was awake. He grovelled in the gloom, the eyes from out his drawn face riveted upon the intervening door.

He heard it creak, and then the sound of a small voice came to him. "Jimmie! Jimmie! Are yehs dere?" it whispered. The urchin started. The thin, white face of his sister looked at him from the door-way of the other room. She crept to him across the floor.

The father had not moved, but lay in the same death-like sleep. The mother writhed in uneasy slumber, her chest wheezing as if she were in the agonies of strangulation. Out at the window a florid moon was peering over dark roofs, and in the distance the waters of a river glimmered pallidly.

The small frame of the ragged girl was quivering. Her features were haggard from weeping, and her eyes gleamed from fear. She grasped the urchin's arm in her little trembling hands and they huddled in a corner. The eyes of both were drawn, by some force, to stare at the woman's face, for they thought she need only to awake and all fiends would come from below.

They crouched until the ghost-mists of dawn appeared at the window, drawing close to the panes, and looking in at the prostrate, heaving body of the mother.

Chapter IV

The babe, Tommie, died. He went away in a white, insignificant coffin, his small waxen hand clutching a flower that the girl, Maggie, had stolen from an Italian.

She and Jimmie lived.

The inexperienced fibres of the boy's eyes were hardened at an early age. He became a young man of leather. He lived some red years without laboring. During that time his sneer became chronic. He studied human nature in the gutter, and found it no worse than he thought he had reason to believe it. He never conceived a respect for the world, because he had begun with no idols that it had smashed.

He clad his soul in armor by means of happening hilariously in at a mission church where a man composed his sermons of "yous." While they got warm at the stove, he told his hearers just where he calculated they stood with the Lord. Many of the sinners were impatient over the pictured depths of their degradation. They were waiting for soup-tickets.

A reader of words of wind-demons might have been able to see the portions of a dialogue pass to and fro between the exhorter and his hearers.

"You are damned," said the preacher. And the reader of sounds might have seen the reply go forth from the ragged people: "Where's our soup?"

Jimmie and a companion sat in a rear seat and commented upon the things that didn't concern them, with all the freedom of English gentlemen. When they grew thirsty and went out their minds confused the speaker with Christ.

Momentarily, Jimmie was sullen with thoughts of a hopeless altitude where grew fruit. His companion said that if he should ever meet God he would ask for a million dollars and a bottle of beer.

Jimmie's occupation for a long time was to stand on street-corners and watch the world go by, dreaming blood-red dreams at the passing of pretty women. He menaced mankind at the intersections of streets.

On the corners he was in life and of life. The world was going on and he was there to perceive it.

He maintained a belligerent attitude toward all well-dressed men. To him fine raiment was allied to weakness, and all good coats covered faint hearts. He and his order were kings, to a certain extent, over the men of untarnished clothes, because these latter dreaded, perhaps, to be either killed or laughed at.

Above all things he despised obvious Christians and ciphers with the chrysanthemums of aristocracy in their button-holes. He considered himself above both of these classes. He was afraid of neither the devil nor the leader of society.

When he had a dollar in his pocket his satisfaction with existence was the greatest thing in the world. So, eventually, he felt obliged to work. His father died and his mother's years were divided up into periods of thirty days.

He became a truck driver. He was given the charge of a painstaking pair of horses and a large rattling truck. He invaded the turmoil and tumble of the down-town streets and learned to breathe maledictory defiance at the police who occasionally used to climb up, drag him from his perch and beat him.

In the lower part of the city he daily involved himself in hideous tangles. If he and his team chanced to be in the rear he preserved a demeanor of serenity, crossing his legs and bursting forth into yells when foot passengers took dangerous dives beneath the noses of his champing horses. He smoked his pipe calmly for he knew that his pay was marching on.

If in the front and the key-truck of chaos, he entered terrifically into the quarrel that was raging to and fro among the drivers on their high seats, and sometimes roared oaths and violently got himself arrested.

After a time his sneer grew so that it turned its glare upon all things. He became so sharp that he believed in nothing. To him the police were always actuated by malignant impulses and the rest of the world was composed, for the most part, of despicable creatures who were all trying to take advantage of him and with whom, in defense, he was obliged to quarrel on all possible occasions. He himself occupied a downtrodden position that had a private but distinct element of grandeur in its isolation.

The most complete cases of aggravated idiocy were, to his mind, rampant upon the front platforms of all of the street cars. At first his tongue strove with these beings, but he eventually was superior. He became immured like an African cow. In him grew a majestic contempt for those strings of street cars that followed him like intent bugs.

He fell into the habit, when starting on a long journey, of fixing his eye on a high and distant object, commanding his horses to begin, and then going into a sort of a trance of observation. Multitudes of drivers might howl in his rear, and passengers might load him with opprobrium, he would not awaken until some blue policeman turned red and began to frenziedly tear bridles and beat the soft noses of the responsible horses.

When he paused to contemplate the attitude of the police toward himself and his fellows, he believed that they were the only men in the city who had no rights. When driving about, he felt that he was held liable by the police for anything that might occur in the streets, and was the common prey of all energetic officials. In revenge, he resolved never to move out of the way of anything, until formidable circumstances, or a much larger man than himself forced him to it.

Foot-passengers were mere pestering flies with an insane disregard for their legs and his convenience. He could not conceive their maniacal desires to cross the streets. Their madness smote him with eternal amazement. He was continually storming at them from his throne. He sat aloft and denounced their frantic leaps, plunges, dives and straddles.

When they would thrust at, or parry, the noses of his champing horses, making them swing their heads and move their feet, disturbing a solid dreamy repose, he swore at the men as fools, for he himself could perceive that Providence had caused it clearly to be written, that he and his team had the unalienable right to stand in the proper path of the sun chariot, and if they so minded, obstruct its mission or take a wheel off.

And, perhaps, if the god-driver had an ungovernable desire to step down, put up his flame colored fists and manfully dispute the right of way, he would have probably been immediately opposed by a scowling mortal with two sets of very hard knuckles.

It is possible, perhaps, that this young man would have derided, in an axle-wide alley, the approach of a flying ferry boat. Yet he achieved a respect for a fire engine. As one charged toward his truck, he would drive fearfully upon a side-walk, threatening untold people with annihilation. When an engine would strike a mass of blocked trucks, splitting it into fragments, as a blow annihilates a cake of ice, Jimmie's team could usually be observed high and safe, with whole wheels, on the side-walk. The fearful coming of the engine could break up the most intricate muddle of heavy vehicles at which the police had been swearing for the half of an hour.

A fire-engine was enshrined in his heart as an appalling thing that he loved with a distant dog-like devotion. They had been known to overturn street-cars. Those leaping horses, striking sparks from the cobbles in their forward lunge, were creatures to be ineffably admired. The clang of the gong pierced his breast like a noise of remembered war.

When Jimmie was a little boy, he began to be arrested. Before he reached a great age, he had a fair record.

He developed too great a tendency to climb down from his truck and fight with other drivers. He had been in quite a number of miscellaneous fights, and in some general barroom rows that had become known to the police. Once he had been arrested for assaulting a Chinaman. Two women in different parts of the city, and entirely unknown to each other, caused him considerable annoyance by breaking forth, simultaneously, at fateful intervals, into wailings about marriage and support and infants.

Nevertheless, he had, on a certain star-lit evening, said wonderingly and quite reverently: "Deh moon looks like hell, don't it?"

Chapter V

The girl, Maggie, blossomed in a mud puddle. She grew to be a most rare and wonderful production of a tenement district, a pretty girl.

None of the dirt of Rum Alley seemed to be in her veins. The philosophers up-stairs, down-stairs and on the same floor, puzzled over it.

When a child, playing and fighting with gamins in the street, dirt disguised her. Attired in tatters and grime, she went unseen.

There came a time, however, when the young men of the vicinity, said: "Dat Johnson goil is a puty good looker." About this period her brother remarked to her: "Mag, I'll tell yeh dis! See? Yeh've edder got teh go teh hell or go teh work!" Whereupon she went to work, having the feminine aversion of going to hell.

By a chance, she got a position in an establishment where they made collars and cuffs. She received a stool and a machine in a room where sat twenty girls of various shades of yellow discontent. She perched on the stool and treadled at her machine all day, turning out collars, the name of whose brand could be noted for its irrelevancy to anything in connection with collars. At night she returned home to her mother.

Jimmie grew large enough to take the vague position of head of the family. As incumbent of that office, he stumbled up-stairs late at night, as his father had done before him. He reeled about the room, swearing at his relations, or went to sleep on the floor.

The mother had gradually arisen to that degree of fame that she could bandy words with her acquaintances among the police-justices. Court-officials called her by her first name. When she appeared they pursued a course which had been theirs for months. They invariably grinned and cried out: "Hello, Mary, you here again?" Her grey head wagged in many a court. She always besieged the bench with voluble excuses, explanations, apologies and prayers. Her flaming face and rolling eyes were a sort of familiar sight on the island. She measured time by means of sprees, and was eternally swollen and dishevelled.

One day the young man, Pete, who as a lad had smitten the Devil's Row urchin in the back of the head and put to flight the antagonists of his friend, Jimmie, strutted upon the scene. He met Jimmie one day on the street, promised to take him to a boxing match in Williamsburg, and called for him in the evening.

Maggie observed Pete.

He sat on a table in the Johnson home and dangled his checked legs with an enticing nonchalance. His hair was curled down over his forehead in an oiled bang. His rather pugged nose seemed to revolt from contact with a bristling moustache of short, wire-like hairs. His blue double-breasted coat, edged with black braid, buttoned close to a red puff tie, and his patent-leather shoes, looked like murder-fitted weapons.

His mannerisms stamped him as a man who had a correct sense of his personal superiority. There was valor and contempt for circumstances in the glance of his eye. He waved his hands like a man of the world, who dismisses religion and philosophy, and says "Fudge." He had certainly seen everything and with each curl of his lip, he declared that it amounted to nothing. Maggie thought he must be a very elegant and graceful bartender.

He was telling tales to Jimmie.

Maggie watched him furtively, with half-closed eyes, lit with a vague interest.

"Hully gee! Dey makes me tired," he said. "Mos' e'ry day some farmer comes in an' tries teh run deh shop. See? But deh gits t'rowed right out! I jolt dem right out in deh street before dey knows where dey is! See?"

"Sure," said Jimmie.

"Dere was a mug come in deh place deh odder day wid an idear he wus goin' teh own deh place! Hully gee, he wus goin' teh own deh place! I see he had a still on an' I didn' wanna giv 'im no stuff, so I says: 'Git deh hell outa here an' don' make no trouble,' I says like dat! See? 'Git deh hell outa here an' don' make no trouble;' like dat. 'Git deh hell outa here,' I says. See?"

Jimmie nodded understandingly. Over his features played an eager desire to state the amount of his valor in a similar crisis, but the narrator proceeded.

"Well, deh blokie he says: 'T'hell wid it! I ain' lookin' for no scrap,' he says (See?) 'but' he says, 'I'm spectable cit'zen an' I wanna drink an' purtydamnsoon, too.' See? 'Deh hell,' I says. Like dat! 'Deh hell,' I says. See? 'Don' make no trouble,' I says. Like dat. 'Don' make no trouble.' See? Den deh mug he squared off an' said he was fine as silk wid his dukes (See?) an' he wanned a drink damnquick. Dat's what he said. See?"

"Sure," repeated Jimmie.

Pete continued. "Say, I jes' jumped deh bar an' deh way I plunked dat blokie was great. See? Dat's right! In deh jaw! See? Hully gee, he t'rowed a spittoon true deh front windee. Say, I taut I'd drop dead. But deh boss, he comes in after an' he says, 'Pete, yehs done jes' right! Yeh've gota keep order an' it's all right.' See? 'It's all right,' he says. Dat's what he said."

The two held a technical discussion.

"Dat bloke was a dandy," said Pete, in conclusion, "but he had'n' oughta made no trouble. Dat's what I says teh dem: 'Don' come in here an' make no trouble,' I says, like dat. 'Don' make no trouble.' See?"

As Jimmie and his friend exchanged tales descriptive of their prowess, Maggie leaned back in the shadow. Her eyes dwelt wonderingly and rather wistfully upon Pete's face. The broken furniture, grimey walls, and general disorder and dirt of her home of a sudden appeared before her and began to take a potential aspect. Pete's aristocratic person looked as if it might soil. She looked keenly at him, occasionally, wondering if he was feeling contempt. But Pete seemed to be enveloped in reminiscence.

"Hully gee," said he, "dose mugs can't phase me. Dey knows I kin wipe up deh street wid any tree of dem."

When he said, "Ah, what deh hell," his voice was burdened with disdain for the inevitable and contempt for anything that fate might compel him to endure.

Maggie perceived that here was the beau ideal of a man. Her dim thoughts were often searching for far away lands where, as God says, the little hills sing together in the morning. Under the trees of her dream-gardens there had always walked a lover.

Chapter VI

Pete took note of Maggie.

"Say, Mag, I'm stuck on yer shape. It's outa sight," he said, parenthetically, with an affable grin.

As he became aware that she was listening closely, he grew still more eloquent in his descriptions of various happenings in his career. It appeared that he was invincible in fights.

"Why," he said, referring to a man with whom he had had a misunderstanding, "dat mug scrapped like a damn dago. Dat's right. He was dead easy. See? He tau't he was a scrapper! But he foun' out diff'ent! Hully gee."

He walked to and fro in the small room, which seemed then to grow even smaller and unfit to hold his dignity, the attribute of a supreme warrior. That swing of the shoulders that had frozen the timid when he was but a lad had increased with his growth and education at the ratio of ten to one. It, combined with the sneer upon his mouth, told mankind that there was nothing in space which could appall him. Maggie marvelled at him and surrounded him with greatness. She vaguely tried to calculate the altitude of the pinnacle from which he must have looked down upon her.

"I met a chump deh odder day way up in deh city," he said. "I was goin' teh see a frien' of mine. When I was a-crossin' deh street deh chump runned plump inteh me, an' den he turns

aroun' an' says, 'Yer insolen' ruffin,' he says, like dat. 'Oh, gee,' I
says, 'oh, gee, go teh hell and git off deh eart',' I says, like dat.
See? 'Go teh hell an' git off deh eart',' like dat. Den deh blokie he
got wild. He says I was a contempt'ble scoun'el, er someting like
dat, an' he says I was doom' teh everlastin' pe'dition an' all
like dat. 'Gee,' I says, 'gee! Deh hell I am,' I says. 'Deh hell I
am,' like dat. An' den I slugged 'im. See?"

With Jimmie in his company, Pete departed in a sort of blaze
of glory from the Johnson home. Maggie, leaning from the window, watched him as he walked down the street.

Here was a formidable man who disdained the strength of a
world full of fists. Here was one who had contempt for brass-
clothed power; one whose knuckles could defiantly ring against
the granite of law. He was a knight.

The two men went from under the glimmering street-lamp and
passed into shadows.

Turning, Maggie contemplated the dark, dust-stained walls,
and the scant and crude furniture of her home. A clock, in a
splintered and battered oblong box of varnished wood, she suddenly regarded as an abomination. She noted that it ticked rasp-
ingly. The almost vanished flowers in the carpet-pattern, she
conceived to be newly hideous. Some faint attempts she had
made with blue ribbon, to freshen the appearance of a dingy curtain, she now saw to be piteous.

She wondered what Pete dined on.

She reflected upon the collar and cuff factory. It began to appear to her mind as a dreary place of endless grinding. Pete's elegant occupation brought him, no doubt, into contact with people
who had money and manners. It was probable that he had a
large acquaintance of pretty girls. He must have great sums of
money to spend.

To her the earth was composed of hardships and insults. She
felt instant admiration for a man who openly defied it. She
thought that if the grim angel of death should clutch his heart,
Pete would shrug his shoulders and say: "Oh, ev'ryt'ing goes."

She anticipated that he would come again shortly. She spent some of her week's pay in the purchase of flowered cretonne for a lambrequin. She made it with infinite care and hung it to the slightly-careening mantel, over the stove, in the kitchen. She studied it with painful anxiety from different points in the room. She wanted it to look well on Sunday night when, perhaps, Jimmie's friend would come. On Sunday night, however, Pete did not appear.

Afterward the girl looked at it with a sense of humiliation. She was now convinced that Pete was superior to admiration for lambrequins.

A few evenings later Pete entered with fascinating innovations in his apparel. As she had seen him twice and he had different suits on each time, Maggie had a dim impression that his wardrobe was prodigiously extensive.

"Say, Mag," he said, "put on yer bes' duds Friday night an' I'll take yehs teh deh show. See?"

He spent a few moments in flourishing his clothes and then vanished, without having glanced at the lambrequin.

Over the eternal collars and cuffs in the factory Maggie spent the most of three days in making imaginary sketches of Pete and his daily environment. She imagined some half dozen women in love with him and thought he must lean dangerously toward an indefinite one, whom she pictured with great charms of person, but with an altogether contemptible disposition.

She thought he must live in a blare of pleasure. He had friends, and people who were afraid of him.

She saw the golden glitter of the place where Pete was to take her. An entertainment of many hues and many melodies where she was afraid she might appear small and mouse-colored.

Her mother drank whiskey all Friday morning. With lurid face and tossing hair she cursed and destroyed furniture all Friday afternoon. When Maggie came home at half-past six her mother lay asleep amidst the wreck of chairs and a table. Fragments of various household utensils were scattered about the floor. She had vented some phase of drunken fury upon the lambrequin. It lay in a bedraggled heap in the corner.

"Hah," she snorted, sitting up suddenly, "where deh hell yeh been? Why deh hell don' yeh come home earlier? Been loafin' 'round deh streets. Yer gettin' teh be a reg'lar devil."

When Pete arrived Maggie, in a worn black dress, was waiting for him in the midst of a floor strewn with wreckage. The curtain at the window had been pulled by a heavy hand and hung by one tack, dangling to and fro in the draft through the cracks at the sash. The knots of blue ribbons appeared like violated flowers. The fire in the stove had gone out. The displaced lids and open doors showed heaps of sullen grey ashes. The remnants of a meal, ghastly, like dead flesh, lay in a corner. Maggie's red mother, stretched on the floor, blasphemed and gave her daughter a bad name.

Chapter VII

An orchestra of yellow silk women and bald-headed men on an elevated stage near the centre of a great green-hued hall, played a popular waltz. The place was crowded with people grouped about little tables. A battalion of waiters slid among the throng, carrying trays of beer glasses and making change from the inexhaustible vaults of their trousers pockets. Little boys, in the costumes of French chefs, paraded up and down the irregular aisles vending fancy cakes. There was a low rumble of conversation and a subdued clinking of glasses. Clouds of tobacco smoke rolled and wavered high in air about the dull gilt of the chandeliers.

The vast crowd had an air throughout of having just quitted labor. Men with calloused hands and attired in garments that showed the wear of an endless trudge for a living, smoked their pipes contentedly and spent five, ten, or perhaps fifteen cents for beer. There was a mere sprinkling of kid-gloved men who smoked cigars purchased elsewhere. The great body of the crowd was composed of people who showed that all day they strove with their hands. Quiet Germans, with maybe their wives and two or three children, sat listening to the music, with the expressions of happy cows. An occasional party of sailors from a warship, their faces pictures of sturdy health, spent the earlier hours of the evening at the small round tables. Very infrequent tipsy men, swollen with the value of their opinions, engaged their companions in earnest and confidential conversation. In the balcony, and here and there below, shone the impassive faces of women. The nationalities of the Bowery beamed upon the stage from all directions.

Pete aggressively walked up a side aisle and took seats with Maggie at a table beneath the balcony.

"Two beehs!"

Leaning back he regarded with eyes of superiority the scene before them. This attitude affected Maggie strongly. A man who could regard such a sight with indifference must be accustomed to very great things.

It was obvious that Pete had been to this place many times before, and was very familiar with it. A knowledge of this fact made Maggie feel little and new.

He was extremely gracious and attentive. He displayed the consideration of a cultured gentleman who knew what was due.

"Say, what deh hell? Bring deh lady a big glass! What deh hell use is dat pony?"

"Don't be fresh, now," said the waiter, with some warmth, as he departed.

"Ah, git off deh eart'," said Pete, after the other's retreating form.

Maggie perceived that Pete brought forth all his elegance and all his knowledge of high-class customs for her benefit. Her heart warmed as she reflected upon his condescension.

The orchestra of yellow silk women and bald-headed men gave vent to a few bars of anticipatory music and a girl, in a pink dress with short skirts, galloped upon the stage. She smiled upon the throng as if in acknowledgment of a warm welcome, and began to walk to and fro, making profuse gesticulations and singing, in brazen soprano tones, a song, the words of which were inaudible. When she broke into the swift rattling measures of a chorus some half tipsy men near the stage joined in the rollicking refrain and glasses were pounded rhythmically upon the tables. People leaned forward to watch her and to try to catch the words of the song. When she vanished there were long rollings of applause.

Obedient to more anticipatory bars, she reappeared amidst the half-suppressed cheering of the tipsy men. The orchestra plunged into dance music and the laces of the dancer fluttered and flew in the glare of gas jets. She divulged the fact that she was attired in some half dozen skirts. It was patent that any one of them would have proved adequate for the purpose for which skirts are intended. An occasional man bent forward, intent upon the pink stockings. Maggie wondered at the splendor of the costume and lost herself in calculations of the cost of the silks and laces.

The dancer's smile of stereotyped enthusiasm was turned for ten minutes upon the faces of her audience. In the finale she fell into some of those grotesque attitudes which were at the time popular among the dancers in the theatres up-town, giving to the Bowery public the phantasies of the aristocratic theatre-going public, at reduced rates.

"Say, Pete," said Maggie, leaning forward, "dis is great."

"Sure," said Pete, with proper complacence.

A ventriloquist followed the dancer. He held two fantastic dolls on his knees. He made them sing mournful ditties and say funny things about geography and Ireland.

"Do dose little men talk?" asked Maggie.

"Naw," said Pete, "it's some damn fake. See?"

Two girls, on the bills as sisters, came forth and sang a duet that is heard occasionally at concerts given under church auspices. They supplemented it with a dance which of course can never be seen at concerts given under church auspices.

After the duettists had retired, a woman of debatable age sang a negro melody. The chorus necessitated some grotesque waddlings supposed to be an imitation of a plantation darkey, under the influence, probably, of music and the moon. The audience was just enthusiastic enough over it to have her return and sing a sorrowful lay, whose lines told of a mother's love and a sweetheart who waited and a young man who was lost at sea under the most harrowing circumstances. From the faces of a score or so in the crowd, the self-contained look faded. Many heads were bent forward with eagerness and sympathy. As the last distressing sentiment of the piece was brought forth, it was greeted by that kind of applause which rings as sincere.

As a final effort, the singer rendered some verses which described a vision of Britain being annihilated by America, and Ireland bursting her bonds. A carefully prepared crisis was reached in the last line of the last verse, where the singer threw out her arms and cried, "The star-spangled banner." Instantly a great cheer swelled from the throats of the assemblage of the masses. There was a heavy rumble of booted feet thumping the floor. Eyes gleamed with sudden fire, and calloused hands waved frantically in the air.

After a few moments' rest, the orchestra played crashingly, and a small fat man burst out upon the stage. He began to roar a song and stamp back and forth before the foot-lights, wildly waving a glossy silk hat and throwing leers, or smiles, broadcast. He made his face into fantastic grimaces until he looked like a pictured devil on a Japanese kite. The crowd laughed gleefully. His short, fat legs were never still a moment. He shouted and roared and bobbed his shock of red wig until the audience broke out in excited applause.

Pete did not pay much attention to the progress of events upon the stage. He was drinking beer and watching Maggie.

Her cheeks were blushing with excitement and her eyes were glistening. She drew deep breaths of pleasure. No thoughts of the atmosphere of the collar and cuff factory came to her.

When the orchestra crashed finally, they jostled their way to the sidewalk with the crowd. Pete took Maggie's arm and pushed a way for her, offering to fight with a man or two.

They reached Maggie's home at a late hour and stood for a moment in front of the gruesome doorway.

"Say, Mag," said Pete, "give us a kiss for takin' yeh teh deh show, will yer?"

Maggie laughed, as if startled, and drew away from him.

"Naw, Pete," she said, "dat wasn't in it."

"Ah, what deh hell?" urged Pete.

The girl retreated nervously.

"Ah, what deh hell?" repeated he.

Maggie darted into the hall, and up the stairs. She turned and smiled at him, then disappeared.

Pete walked slowly down the street. He had something of an astonished expression upon his features. He paused under a lamp-post and breathed a low breath of surprise.

"Gawd," he said, "I wonner if I've been played fer a duffer."

Chapter VIII

As thoughts of Pete came to Maggie's mind, she began to have an intense dislike for all of her dresses.

"What deh hell ails yeh? What makes yeh be allus fixin' and fussin'? Good Gawd," her mother would frequently roar at her.

She began to note, with more interest, the well-dressed women she met on the avenues. She envied elegance and soft palms. She craved those adornments of person which she saw every day on the street, conceiving them to be allies of vast importance to women.

Studying faces, she thought many of the women and girls she chanced to meet, smiled with serenity as though forever cherished and watched over by those they loved.

The air in the collar and cuff establishment strangled her. She knew she was gradually and surely shrivelling in the hot, stuffy room. The begrimed windows rattled incessantly from the passing of elevated trains. The place was filled with a whirl of noises and odors.

She wondered as she regarded some of the grizzled women in the room, mere mechanical contrivances sewing seams and grinding out, with heads bended over their work, tales of imagined or real girl-hood happiness, past drunks, the baby at home, and unpaid wages. She speculated how long her youth would endure. She began to see the bloom upon her cheeks as valuable.

She imagined herself, in an exasperating future, as a scrawny woman with an eternal grievance. Too, she thought Pete to be a very fastidious person concerning the appearance of women.

She felt she would love to see somebody entangle their fingers in the oily beard of the fat foreigner who owned the establishment. He was a detestable creature. He wore white socks with low shoes.

He sat all day delivering orations, in the depths of a cushioned chair. His pocketbook deprived them of the power of retort.

"What een hell do you sink I pie fife dolla a week for? Play? No, py damn!"

Maggie was anxious for a friend to whom she could talk about Pete. She would have liked to discuss his admirable mannerisms with a reliable mutual friend. At home, she found her mother often drunk and always raving.

It seems that the world had treated this woman very badly, and she took a deep revenge upon such portions of it as came within her reach. She broke furniture as if she were at last getting her rights. She swelled with virtuous indignation as she carried the lighter articles of household use, one by one under the shadows of the three gilt balls, where Hebrews chained them with chains of interest.

Jimmie came when he was obliged to by circumstances over which he had no control. His well-trained legs brought him staggering home and put him to bed some nights when he would rather have gone elsewhere.

Swaggering Pete loomed like a golden sun to Maggie. He took her to a dime museum where rows of meek freaks astonished her. She contemplated their deformities with awe and thought them a sort of chosen tribe.

Pete, raking his brains for amusement, discovered the Central Park Menagerie and the Museum of Arts. Sunday afternoons would sometimes find them at these places. Pete did not appear to be particularly interested in what he saw. He stood around looking heavy, while Maggie giggled in glee.

Once at the Menagerie he went into a trance of admiration before the spectacle of a very small monkey threatening to thrash a cageful because one of them had pulled his tail and he had not wheeled about quickly enough to discover who did it. Ever after Pete knew that monkey by sight and winked at him, trying to induce him to fight with other and larger monkeys.

At the Museum, Maggie said, "Dis is outa sight."

"Oh hell," said Pete, "wait till next summer an' I'll take yehs to a picnic."

While the girl wandered in the vaulted rooms, Pete occupied himself in returning stony stare for stony stare, the appalling scrutiny of the watch-dogs of the treasures. Occasionally he would remark in loud tones: "Dat jay has got glass eyes," and sentences of the sort. When he tired of this amusement he would go to the mummies and moralize over them.

Usually he submitted with silent dignity to all which he had to go through, but, at times, he was goaded into comment.

"What deh hell," he demanded once. "Look at all dese little jugs! Hundred jugs in a row! Ten rows in a case an' 'bout a t'ousand cases! What deh blazes use is dem?"

Evenings during the week he took her to see plays in which the brain-clutching heroine was rescued from the palatial home of her guardian, who is cruelly after her bonds, by the hero with the beautiful sentiments. The latter spent most of his time out at soak in pale-green snow storms, busy with a nickel-plated revolver, rescuing aged strangers from villains.

Maggie lost herself in sympathy with the wanderers swooning in snow storms beneath happy-hued church windows. And a choir within singing "Joy to the World." To Maggie and the rest of the audience this was transcendental realism. Joy always within, and they, like the actor, inevitably without. Viewing it, they hugged themselves in ecstatic pity of their imagined or real condition.

The girl thought the arrogance and granite-heartedness of the magnate of the play was very accurately drawn. She echoed the maledictions that the occupants of the gallery showered on this individual when his lines compelled him to expose his extreme selfishness.

Shady persons in the audience revolted from the pictured villainy of the drama. With untiring zeal they hissed vice and applauded virtue. Unmistakably bad men evinced an apparently sincere admiration for virtue.

The loud gallery was overwhelmingly with the unfortunate and the oppressed. They encouraged the struggling hero with cries, and jeered the villain, hooting and calling attention to his whiskers. When anybody died in the pale-green snow storms, the gallery mourned. They sought out the painted misery and hugged it as akin.

In the hero's erratic march from poverty in the first act, to wealth and triumph in the final one, in which he forgives all the enemies that he has left, he was assisted by the gallery, which applauded his generous and noble sentiments and confounded the speeches of his opponents by making irrelevant but very sharp remarks. Those actors who were cursed with villainy parts were confronted at every turn by the gallery. If one of them rendered lines containing the most subtile distinctions between right and wrong, the gallery was immediately aware if the actor meant wickedness, and denounced him accordingly.

The last act was a triumph for the hero, poor and of the masses, the representative of the audience, over the villain and the rich man, his pockets stuffed with bonds, his heart packed with tyrannical purposes, imperturbable amid suffering.

Maggie always departed with raised spirits from the showing places of the melodrama. She rejoiced at the way in which the poor and virtuous eventually surmounted the wealthy and wicked. The theater made her think. She wondered if the culture and refinement she had seen imitated, perhaps grotesquely, by the heroine on the stage, could be acquired by a girl who lived in a tenement house and worked in a shirt factory.

Chapter IX

A group of urchins were intent upon the side door of a saloon. Expectancy gleamed from their eyes. They were twisting their fingers in excitement.

"Here she comes," yelled one of them suddenly.

The group of urchins burst instantly asunder and its individual fragments were spread in a wide, respectable half circle about the point of interest. The saloon door opened with a crash, and the figure of a woman appeared upon the threshold. Her gray hair fell in knotted masses about her shoulders. Her face was crimsoned and wet with perspiration. Her eyes had a rolling glare.

"Not a damn cent more of me money will yehs ever get, not a damn cent. I spent me money here fer t'ree years an' now yehs tells me yeh'll sell me no more stuff! T'hell wid yeh, Johnnie Murckre! 'Disturbance?' Disturbance be damned! T'hell wid yeh, Johnnie—"

The door received a kick of exasperation from within and the woman lurched heavily out on the sidewalk.

The gamins in the half-circle became violently agitated. They began to dance about and hoot and yell and jeer. Wide dirty grins spread over each face.

The woman made a furious dash at a particularly outrageous cluster of little boys. They laughed delightedly and scampered off a short distance, calling out over their shoulders to her. She stood tottering on the curb-stone and thundered at them.

"Yeh devil's kids," she howled, shaking red fists. The little boys whooped in glee. As she started up the street they fell in behind and marched uproariously. Occasionally she wheeled about and made charges on them. They ran nimbly out of reach and taunted her.

In the frame of a gruesome doorway she stood for a moment cursing them. Her hair straggled, giving her crimson features a look of insanity. Her great fists quivered as she shook them madly in the air.

The urchins made terrific noises until she turned and disappeared. Then they filed quietly in the way they had come.

The woman floundered about in the lower hall of the tenement house and finally stumbled up the stairs. On an upper hall a door was opened and a collection of heads peered curiously out, watching her. With a wrathful snort the woman confronted the door, but it was slammed hastily in her face and the key was turned.

She stood for a few minutes, delivering a frenzied challenge at the panels.

"Come out in deh hall, Mary Murphy, damn yeh, if yehs want a row. Come ahn, yeh overgrown terrier, come ahn."

She began to kick the door with her great feet. She shrilly defied the universe to appear and do battle. Her cursing trebles brought heads from all doors save the one she threatened. Her eyes glared in every direction. The air was full of her tossing fists.

"Come ahn, deh hull damn gang of yehs, come ahn," she roared at the spectators. An oath or two, cat-calls, jeers and bits of facetious advice were given in reply. Missiles clattered about her feet.

"What deh hell's deh matter wid yeh?" said a voice in the gathered gloom, and Jimmie came forward. He carried a tin dinner-pail in his hand and under his arm a brown truckman's apron done in a bundle. "What deh hell's wrong?" he demanded.

"Come out, all of yehs, come out," his mother was howling. "Come ahn an' I'll stamp yer damn brains under me feet."

"Shet yer face, an' come home, yeh damned old fool," roared Jimmie at her. She strided up to him and twirled her fingers in his face. Her eyes were darting flames of unreasoning rage and her frame trembled with eagerness for a fight.

"T'hell wid yehs! An' who deh hell are yehs? I ain't givin' a snap of me fingers fer yehs," she bawled at him. She turned her huge back in tremendous disdain and climbed the stairs to the next floor.

Jimmie followed, cursing blackly. At the top of the flight he seized his mother's arm and started to drag her toward the door of their room.

"Come home, damn yeh," he gritted between his teeth.

"Take yer hands off me! Take yer hands off me," shrieked his mother.

She raised her arm and whirled her great fist at her son's face. Jimmie dodged his head and the blow struck him in the back of the neck. "Damn yeh," gritted he again. He threw out his left hand and writhed his fingers about her middle arm. The mother and the son began to sway and struggle like gladiators.

"Whoop!" said the Rum Alley tenement house. The hall filled with interested spectators.

"Hi, ol' lady, dat was a dandy!"

"T'ree to one on deh red!"

"Ah, stop yer damn scrappin'!"

The door of the Johnson home opened and Maggie looked out. Jimmie made a supreme cursing effort and hurled his mother into the room. He quickly followed and closed the door. The Rum Alley tenement swore disappointedly and retired.

The mother slowly gathered herself up from the floor. Her eyes glittered menacingly upon her children.

"Here, now," said Jimmie, "we've had enough of dis. Sit down, an' don' make no trouble."

He grasped her arm, and twisting it, forced her into a creaking chair.

"Keep yer hands off me," roared his mother again.

"Damn yer ol' hide," yelled Jimmie, madly. Maggie shrieked and ran into the other room. To her there came the sound of a storm of crashes and curses. There was a great final thump and Jimmie's voice cried: "Dere, damn yeh, stay still." Maggie opened the door now, and went warily out. "Oh, Jimmie."

He was leaning against the wall and swearing. Blood stood upon bruises on his knotty fore-arms where they had scraped against the floor or the walls in the scuffle. The mother lay screeching on the floor, the tears running down her furrowed face.

Maggie, standing in the middle of the room, gazed about her. The usual upheaval of the tables and chairs had taken place. Crockery was strewn broadcast in fragments. The stove had been disturbed on its legs, and now leaned idiotically to one side. A pail had been upset and water spread in all directions.

The door opened and Pete appeared. He shrugged his shoulders. "Oh, Gawd," he observed.

He walked over to Maggie and whispered in her ear. "Ah, what deh hell, Mag? Come ahn and we'll have a hell of a time."

The mother in the corner upreared her head and shook her tangled locks.

"Teh hell wid him and you," she said, glowering at her daughter in the gloom. Her eyes seemed to burn balefully. "Yeh've gone teh deh devil, Mag Johnson, yehs knows yehs have gone teh deh devil. Yer a disgrace teh yer people, damn yeh. An' now, git out an' go ahn wid dat doe-faced jude of yours. Go teh hell wid him, damn yeh, an' a good riddance. Go teh hell an' see how yeh likes it."

Maggie gazed long at her mother.

"Go teh hell now, an' see how yeh likes it. Git out. I won't have sech as yehs in me house! Get out, d'yeh hear! Damn yeh, git out!"

The girl began to tremble.

At this instant Pete came forward. "Oh, what deh hell, Mag, see," whispered he softly in her ear. "Dis all blows over. See?

Deh ol' woman 'ill be all right in deh mornin'. Come ahn out wid me! We'll have a hell of a time."

The woman on the floor cursed. Jimmie was intent upon his bruised fore-arms. The girl cast a glance about the room filled with a chaotic mass of debris, and at the red, writhing body of her mother.

"Go teh hell an' good riddance."

She went.

Chapter X

Jimmie had an idea it wasn't common courtesy for a friend to come to one's home and ruin one's sister. But he was not sure how much Pete knew about the rules of politeness.

The following night he returned home from work at rather a late hour in the evening. In passing through the halls he came upon the gnarled and leathery old woman who possessed the music-box. She was grinning in the dim light that drifted through dust-stained panes. She beckoned to him with a smudged forefinger.

"Ah, Jimmie, what do yehs tink I got onto las' night. It was deh funnies' ting I ever saw," she cried, coming close to him and leering. She was trembling with eagerness to tell her tale. "I was by me door las' night when yer sister and her jude feller came in late, oh, very late. An' she, the dear, she was a-cryin' as if her heart would break, she was. It was deh funnies' ting I ever saw. An' right out here by me door she asked him did he love her, did he. An' she was a-cryin' as if her heart would break, poor t'ing. An' him, I could see by deh way what he said it dat she had been askin' orften, he says: 'Oh, hell, yes,' he says, says he, 'Oh, hell, yes.' "

Storm-clouds swept over Jimmie's face, but he turned from the leathery old woman and plodded on up stairs.

"Oh, hell, yes," called she after him. She laughed a laugh that was like a prophetic croak. " 'Oh, hell, yes,' he says, says he, 'Oh, hell, yes.' "

There was no one in at home. The rooms showed that attempts had been made at tidying them. Parts of the wreckage of the day before had been repaired by an unskilful hand. A chair or two and the table, stood uncertainly upon legs. The floor had been newly swept. Too, the blue ribbons had been restored to the curtains, and the lambrequin, with its immense sheaves of yellow wheat and red roses of equal size, had been returned, in a worn and sorry state, to its position at the mantel. Maggie's jacket and hat were gone from the nail behind the door.

Jimmie walked to the window and began to look through the blurred glass. It occurred to him to vaguely wonder, for an instant, if some of the women of his acquaintance had brothers.

Suddenly, however, he began to swear.

"But he was me frien'! I brought 'im here! Dat's deh hell of it!"

He fumed about the room, his anger gradually rising to the furious pitch.

"I'll kill deh jay! Dat's what I'll do! I'll kill deh jay!"

He clutched his hat and sprang toward the door. But it opened and his mother's great form blocked the passage.

"What deh hell's deh matter wid yeh?" exclaimed she, coming into the rooms.

Jimmie gave vent to a sardonic curse and then laughed heavily.

"Well, Maggie's gone teh deh devil! Dat's what! See?"

"Eh?" said his mother.

"Maggie's gone teh deh devil! Are yehs deaf?" roared Jimmie, impatiently.

"Deh hell she has," murmured the mother, astounded.

Jimmie grunted, and then began to stare out at the window. His mother sat down in a chair, but a moment later sprang erect and delivered a maddened whirl of oaths. Her son turned to look at her as she reeled and swayed in the middle of the room, her fierce face convulsed with passion, her blotched arms raised high in imprecation.

"May Gawd curse her forever," she shrieked. "May she eat nothin' but stones an' deh dirt in deh street. May she sleep in deh gutter an' never see deh sun shine again. Deh damn—"

"Here, now," said her son. "Take a drop on yourself."

The mother raised lamenting eyes to the ceiling.

"She's deh devil's own chil', Jimmie," she whispered. "Ah, who would tink such a bad girl could grow up in our fambly, Jimmie, me son. Many deh hour I've spent in talk wid dat girl an' tol' her if she ever went on deh streets I'd see her damned. An' after all her bringin' up an' what I tol' her and talked wid her, she goes teh deh bad, like a duck teh water."

The tears rolled down her furrowed face. Her hands trembled.

"An' den when dat Sadie MacMallister next door to us was sent teh deh devil by dat feller what worked in deh soap-factory, didn't I tell our Mag dat if she—"

"Ah, dat's anudder story," interrupted the brother. "Of course, dat Sadie was nice an' all dat—but—see—it ain't dessame as if—well, Maggie was diff'ent—see—she was diff'ent."

He was trying to formulate a theory that he had always unconsciously held, that all sisters, excepting his own, could advisedly be ruined.

He suddenly broke out again. "I'll go t'ump hell outa deh mug what did her deh harm. I'll kill 'im! He tinks he kin scrap, but when he gits me a-chasin' 'im he'll fin' out where he's wrong, deh damned duffer. I'll wipe up deh street wid 'im."

In a fury he plunged out of the doorway. As he vanished the mother raised her head and lifted both hands, entreating.

"May Gawd curse her forever," she cried.

In the darkness of the hallway Jimmie discerned a knot of women talking volubly. When he strode by they paid no attention to him.

"She allus was a bold thing," he heard one of them cry in an eager voice. "Dere wasn't a feller come teh deh house but she'd try teh mash 'im. My Annie says deh shameless t'ing tried teh ketch her feller, her own feller, what we useter know his fader."

"I could a' tol' yehs dis two years ago," said a woman, in a key of triumph. "Yesir, it was over two years ago dat I says teh my ol' man, I says, 'Dat Johnson girl ain't straight,' I says. 'Oh, hell,' he says. 'Oh, hell.' 'Dat's all right,' I says, 'but I know what I knows,' I says, 'an' it'ill come out later. You wait an' see,' I says, 'you see.' "

"Anybody what had eyes could see dat dere was somethin' wrong wid dat girl. I didn't like her actions."

On the street Jimmie met a friend. "What deh hell?" asked the latter.

Jimmie explained. "An' I'll tump 'im till he can't stand."

"Oh, what deh hell," said the friend. "What's deh use! Yeh'll git pulled in! Everybody 'ill be onto it! An' ten plunks! Gee!"

Jimmie was determined. "He t'inks he kin scrap, but he'll fin' out diff'ent."

"Gee," remonstrated the friend, "What deh hell?"

Chapter XI

On a corner a glass-fronted building shed a yellow glare upon the pavements. The open mouth of a saloon called seductively to passengers to enter and annihilate sorrow or create rage.

The interior of the place was papered in olive and bronze tints of imitation leather. A shining bar of counterfeit massiveness extended down the side of the room. Behind it a great mahogany-appearing sideboard reached the ceiling. Upon its shelves rested pyramids of shimmering glasses that were never disturbed. Mirrors set in the face of the sideboard multiplied them. Lemons, oranges and paper napkins, arranged with mathematical precision, sat among the glasses. Many-hued decanters of liquor perched at regular intervals on the lower shelves. A nickel-plated cash register occupied a position in the exact center of the general effect. The elementary senses of it all seemed to be opulence and geometrical accuracy.

Across from the bar a smaller counter held a collection of plates upon which swarmed frayed fragments of crackers, slices of boiled ham, dishevelled bits of cheese, and pickles swimming in vinegar. An odor of grasping, begrimed hands and munching mouths pervaded.

Pete, in a white jacket, was behind the bar bending expectantly toward a quiet stranger. "A beeh," said the man. Pete drew a foam-topped glassful and set it dripping upon the bar.

At this moment the light bamboo doors at the entrance swung open and crashed against the siding. Jimmie and a companion entered. They swaggered unsteadily but belligerently toward the bar and looked at Pete with bleared and blinking eyes.

"Gin," said Jimmie.

"Gin," said the companion.

Pete slid a bottle and two glasses along the bar. He bended his head sideways as he assiduously polished away with a napkin at the gleaming wood. He had a look of watchfulness upon his features.

Jimmie and his companion kept their eyes upon the bartender and conversed loudly in tones of contempt.

"He's a dindy masher, ain't he, by Gawd?" laughed Jimmie.

"Oh, hell, yes," said the companion, sneering widely. "He's great, he is. Git onto deh mug on deh blokie. Dat's enough to make a feller turn hand-springs in 'is sleep."

The quiet stranger moved himself and his glass a trifle further away and maintained an attitude of oblivion.

"Gee! ain't he hot stuff!"

"Git onto his shape! Great Gawd!"

"Hey," cried Jimmie, in tones of command. Pete came along slowly, with a sullen dropping of the under lip.

"Well," he growled, "what's eatin' yehs?"

"Gin," said Jimmie.

"Gin," said the companion.

As Pete confronted them with the bottle and the glasses, they laughed in his face. Jimmie's companion, evidently overcome with merriment, pointed a grimy forefinger in Pete's direction.

"Say, Jimmie," demanded he, "what deh hell is dat behind deh bar?"

"Damned if I knows," replied Jimmie. They laughed loudly. Pete put down a bottle with a bang and turned a formidable face toward them. He disclosed his teeth and his shoulders heaved restlessly.

"You fellers can't guy me," he said. "Drink yer stuff an' git out an' don' make no trouble."

Instantly the laughter faded from the faces of the two men and expressions of offended dignity immediately came.

"Who deh hell has said anyt'ing teh you," cried they in the same breath.

The quiet stranger looked at the door calculatingly.

"Ah, come off," said Pete to the two men. "Don't pick me up for no jay. Drink yer rum an' git out an' don' make no trouble."

"Oh, deh hell," airily cried Jimmie.

"Oh, deh hell," airily repeated his companion.

"We goes when we git ready! See!" continued Jimmie.

"Well," said Pete in a threatening voice, "don' make no trouble."

Jimmie suddenly leaned forward with his head on one side. He snarled like a wild animal.

"Well, what if we does? See?" said he.

Dark blood flushed into Pete's face, and he shot a lurid glance at Jimmie.

"Well, den we'll see whose deh bes' man, you or me," he said.

The quiet stranger moved modestly toward the door.

Jimmie began to swell with valor.

"Don' pick me up fer no tenderfoot. When yeh tackles me yeh tackles one of deh bes' men in deh city. See? I'm a scrapper, I am. Ain't dat right, Billie?"

"Sure, Mike," responded his companion in tones of conviction.

"Oh, hell," said Pete, easily. "Go fall on yerself."

The two men again began to laugh.

"What deh hell is dat talkin'?" cried the companion.

"Damned if I knows," replied Jimmie with exaggerated contempt.

Pete made a furious gesture. "Git outa here now, an' don' make no trouble. See? Youse fellers er lookin' fer a scrap an' it's damn likely yeh'll fin' one if yeh keeps on shootin' off yer mout's. I know yehs! See? I kin lick better men dan yehs ever saw in yer lives. Dat's right! See? Don' pick me up fer no stuff er yeh might be jolted out in deh street before yeh knows where yeh is. When I comes from behind dis bar, I t'rows yehs boat inteh deh street. See?"

"Oh, hell," cried the two men in chorus.

The glare of a panther came into Pete's eyes. "Dat's what I said! Unnerstan'?"

He came through a passage at the end of the bar and swelled down upon the two men. They stepped promptly forward and crowded close to him.

They bristled like three roosters. They moved their heads pugnaciously and kept their shoulders braced. The nervous muscles about each mouth twitched with a forced smile of mockery.

"Well, what deh hell yer goin' teh do?" gritted Jimmie.

Pete stepped warily back, waving his hands before him to keep the men from coming too near.

"Well, what deh hell yer goin' teh do?" repeated Jimmie's ally. They kept close to him, taunting and leering. They strove to make him attempt the initial blow.

"Keep back, now! Don' crowd me," ominously said Pete.

Again they chorused in contempt. "Oh, hell!"

In a small, tossing group, the three men edged for positions like frigates contemplating battle.

"Well, why deh hell don' yeh try teh t'row us out?" cried Jimmie and his ally with copious sneers.

The bravery of bull-dogs sat upon the faces of the men. Their clenched fists moved like eager weapons.

The allied two jostled the bartender's elbows, glaring at him with feverish eyes and forcing him toward the wall.

Suddenly Pete swore redly. The flash of action gleamed from his eyes. He threw back his arm and aimed a tremendous, lightning-like blow at Jimmie's face. His foot swung a step forward and the weight of his body was behind his fist. Jimmie ducked his head, Bowery-like, with the quickness of a cat. The fierce, answering blows of him and his ally crushed on Pete's bowed head.

The quiet stranger vanished.

The arms of the combatants whirled in the air like flails. The faces of the men, at first flushed to flame-colored anger, now began to fade to the pallor of warriors in the blood and heat of a battle. Their lips curled back and stretched tightly over the gums in ghoul-like grins. Through their white, gripped teeth struggled hoarse whisperings of oaths. Their eyes glittered with murderous fire.

Each head was huddled between its owner's shoulders, and arms were swinging with marvelous rapidity. Feet scraped to and fro with a loud scratching sound upon the sanded floor. Blows left crimson blotches upon pale skin. The curses of the first quarter minute of the fight died away. The breaths of the fighters came wheezingly from their lips and the three chests were straining and heaving. Pete at intervals gave vent to low, labored hisses, that sounded like a desire to kill. Jimmie's ally gibbered at times like a wounded maniac. Jimmie was silent, fighting with the face of a sacrificial priest. The rage of fear shone in all their eyes and their blood-colored fists swirled.

At a tottering moment a blow from Pete's hand struck the ally and he crashed to the floor. He wriggled instantly to his feet and grasping the quiet stranger's beer glass from the bar, hurled it at Pete's head.

High on the wall it burst like a bomb, shivering fragments flying in all directions. Then missiles came to every man's hand. The place had heretofore appeared free of things to throw, but suddenly glass and bottles went singing through the air. They were thrown point blank at bobbing heads. The pyramid of shimmering glasses, that had never been disturbed, changed to cascades as heavy bottles were flung into them. Mirrors splintered to nothing.

The three frothing creatures on the floor buried themselves in a frenzy for blood. There followed in the wake of missiles and fists some unknown prayers, perhaps for death.

The quiet stranger had sprawled very pyrotechnically out on

the sidewalk. A laugh ran up and down the avenue for the half of a block.

"Dey've trowed a bloke inteh deh street."

People heard the sound of breaking glass and shuffling feet within the saloon and came running. A small group, bending down to look under the bamboo doors, watching the fall of glass, and three pairs of violent legs, changed in a moment to a crowd.

A policeman came charging down the sidewalk and bounced through the doors into the saloon. The crowd bended and surged in absorbing anxiety to see.

Jimmie caught first sight of the on-coming interruption. On his feet he had the same regard for a policeman that, when on his truck, he had for a fire engine. He howled and ran for the side door.

The officer made a terrific advance, club in hand. One comprehensive sweep of the long night stick threw the ally to the floor and forced Pete to a corner. With his disengaged hand he made a furious effort at Jimmie's coat-tails. Then he regained his balance and paused.

"Well, well, you are a pair of pictures. What in hell yeh been up to?"

Jimmie, with his face drenched in blood, escaped up a side street, pursued a short distance by some of the more law-loving, or excited individuals of the crowd.

Later, from a corner safely dark, he saw the policeman, the ally and the bartender emerge from the saloon. Pete locked the doors and then followed up the avenue in the rear of the crowd-encompassed policeman and his charge.

On first thoughts Jimmie, with his heart throbbing at battle heat, started to go desperately to the rescue of his friend, but he halted.

"Ah, what deh hell?" he demanded of himself.

Chapter XII

In a hall of irregular shape sat Pete and Maggie drinking beer. A submissive orchestra dictated to by a spectacled man with frowsy hair and a dress suit, industriously followed the bobs of his head and the waves of his baton. A ballad singer, in a dress of flaming scarlet, sang in the inevitable voice of brass. When she vanished, men seated at the tables near the front applauded loudly, pounding the polished wood with their beer glasses. She returned attired in less gown, and sang again. She received another enthusiastic encore. She reappeared in still less gown and danced. The deafening rumble of glasses and clapping of hands that followed her exit indicated an overwhelming desire to have her come on for the fourth time, but the curiosity of the audience was not gratified.

Maggie was pale. From her eyes had been plucked all look of self-reliance. She leaned with a dependent air toward her companion. She was timid, as if fearing his anger or displeasure. She seemed to beseech tenderness of him.

Pete's air of distinguished valor had grown upon him until it threatened stupendous dimensions. He was infinitely gracious to the girl. It was apparent to her that his condescension was a marvel.

He could appear to strut even while sitting still and he showed that he was a lion of lordly characteristics by the air with which he spat.

With Maggie gazing at him wonderingly, he took pride in commanding the waiters who were, however, indifferent or deaf.

"Hi, you, git a russle on yehs! What deh hell yeh's lookin' at? Two more beehs, d'yeh hear?"

He leaned back and critically regarded the person of a girl with a straw-colored wig who upon the stage was flinging her heels in somewhat awkward imitation of a well-known danseuse.

At times Maggie told Pete long confidential tales of her former home life, dwelling upon the escapades of the other members of the family and the difficulties she had to combat in order to obtain a degree of comfort. He responded in tones of philanthropy. He pressed her arm with an air of reassuring proprietorship.

"Dey was damn jays," he said, denouncing the mother and brother.

The sound of the music which, by the efforts of the frowsy-headed leader, drifted to her ears through the smoked-filled atmosphere, made the girl dream. She thought of her former Rum Alley environment and turned to regard Pete's strong protecting fists. She thought of the collar and cuff manufactory and the eternal moan of the proprietor: "What een hell do you sink I pie fife dolla a week for? Play? No, py damn." She contemplated Pete's man-subduing eyes and noted that wealth and prosperity was indicated by his clothes. She imagined a future, rose-tinted, because of its distance from all that she previously had experienced.

As to the present she perceived only vague reasons to be miserable. Her life was Pete's and she considered him worthy of the charge. She would be disturbed by no particular apprehensions, so long as Pete adored her as he now said he did. She did not feel like a bad woman. To her knowledge she had never seen any better.

At times men at other tables regarded the girl furtively. Pete, aware of it, nodded at her and grinned. He felt proud.

"Mag, yer a bloomin' good-looker," he remarked, studying her face through the haze. The men made Maggie fear, but she blushed at Pete's words as it became apparent to her that she was the apple of his eye.

Grey-headed men, wonderfully pathetic in their dissipation, stared at her through clouds. Smooth cheeked boys, some of them with faces of stone and mouths of sin, not nearly so pathetic as the grey heads, tried to find the girl's eyes in the smoke wreaths. Maggie considered she was not what they thought her. She confined her glances to Pete and the stage.

The orchestra played negro melodies and a versatile drummer pounded, whacked, clattered and scratched on a dozen machines to make noise.

Those glances of the men, shot at Maggie from under half-closed lids, made her tremble. She thought them all to be worse men than Pete.

"Come, let's go," she said.

As they went out Maggie perceived two women seated at a table with some men. They were painted and their cheeks had lost their roundness. As she passed them the girl, with a shrinking movement, drew back her skirts.

Chapter XIII

Jimmie did not return home for a number of days after the fight with Pete in the saloon. When he did, he approached with extreme caution.

He found his mother raving. Maggie had not returned home. The parent continually wondered how her daughter could come to such a pass. She had never considered Maggie as a pearl dropped unstained into Rum Alley from Heaven, but she could not conceive how it was possible for her daughter to fall so low as to bring disgrace upon her family. She was terrific in denunciation of the girl's wickedness.

The fact that the neighbors talked of it, maddened her. When women came in, and in the course of their conversation casually asked, "Where's Maggie dese days?" the mother shook her fuzzy head at them and appalled them with curses. Cunning hints inviting confidence she rebuffed with violence.

"An' wid all deh bringin' up she had, how could she?" moaningly she asked of her son. "Wid all deh talkin' wid her I did an' deh t'ings I tol' her to remember? When a girl is bringed up deh way I bringed up Maggie, how kin she go teh deh devil?"

Jimmie was transfixed by these questions. He could not conceive how under the circumstances his mother's daughter and his sister could have been so wicked.

His mother took a drink from a squdgy bottle that sat on the table. She continued her lament.

"She had a bad heart, dat girl did, Jimmie. She was wicked teh deh heart an' we never knowed it."

Jimmie nodded, admitting the fact.

"We lived in deh same house wid her an' I brought her up an' we never knowed how bad she was."

Jimmie nodded again.

"Wid a home like dis an' a mudder like me, she went teh deh bad," cried the mother, raising her eyes.

One day, Jimmie came home, sat down in a chair and began to wriggle about with a new and strange nervousness. At last he spoke shamefacedly.

"Well, look-a-here, dis t'ing queers us! See? We're queered! An' maybe it 'ud be better if I—well, I t'ink I kin look 'er up an'—maybe it 'ud be better if I fetched her home an—"

The mother started from her chair and broke forth into a storm of passionate anger.

"What! Let 'er come an' sleep under deh same roof wid her mudder agin! Oh, yes, I will, won't I? Sure? Shame on yehs, Jimmie Johnson, fer sayin' such a t'ing teh yer own mudder—teh yer own mudder! Little did I tink when yehs was a babby playin' about me feet dat ye'd grow up teh say sech a t'ing teh yer mudder—yer own mudder. I never taut—"

Sobs choked her and interrupted her reproaches.

"Dere ain't nottin teh raise sech hell about," said Jimmie. "I on'y says it 'ud be better if we keep dis t'ing dark, see? It queers us! See?"

His mother laughed a laugh that seemed to ring through the city and be echoed and re-echoed by countless other laughs. "Oh, yes, I will, won' I! Sure!"

"Well, yeh must take me fer a damn fool," said Jimmie, indignant at his mother for mocking him. "I didn't say we'd make 'er inteh a little tin angel, ner nottin, but deh way it is now she can queer us! Don' che see?"

"Aye, she'll git tired of deh life atter a while an' den she'll wanna be a-comin' home, won' she, deh beast! I'll let 'er in den, won' I?"

"Well, I didn' mean none of dis prod'gal bus'ness anyway," explained Jimmie.

"It wasn't no prod'gal dauter, yeh damn fool," said the mother. "It was prod'gal son, anyhow."

"I know dat," said Jimmie.

For a time they sat in silence. The mother's eyes gloated on a scene her imagination could call before her. Her lips were set in a vindictive smile.

"Aye, she'll cry, won' she, an' carry on, an' tell how Pete, or some odder feller, beats 'er an' she'll say she's sorry an' all dat an' she ain't happy, she ain't, an' she wants to come home agin, she does."

With grim humor, the mother imitated the possible wailing notes of the daughter's voice.

"Den I'll take 'er in, won't I, deh beast. She kin cry 'er two eyes out on deh stones of deh street before I'll dirty deh place wid her. She abused an' ill-treated her own mudder—her own mudder what loved her an' she'll never git anodder chance dis side of hell."

Jimmie thought he had a great idea of women's frailty, but he could not understand why any of his kin should be victims.

"Damn her," he fervidly said.

Again he wondered vaguely if some of the women of his acquaintance had brothers. Nevertheless, his mind did not for an instant confuse himself with those brothers nor his sister with theirs. After the mother had, with great difficulty, suppressed the neighbors, she went among them and proclaimed her grief. "May Gawd forgive dat girl," was her continual cry. To attentive ears she recited the whole length and breadth of her woes.

"I bringed 'er up deh way a dauter oughta be bringed up an' dis is how she served me! She went teh deh devil deh first chance she got! May Gawd forgive her."

When arrested for drunkenness she used the story of her daughter's downfall with telling effect upon the police justices. Finally one of them said to her, peering down over his spectacles: "Mary, the records of this and other courts show that you are the mother of forty-two daughters who have been ruined. The case is unparalleled in the annals of this court, and this court thinks—"

The mother went through life shedding large tears of sorrow. Her red face was a picture of agony.

Of course Jimmie publicly damned his sister that he might appear on a higher social plane. But, arguing with himself, stumbling about in ways that he knew not, he, once, almost came to a conclusion that his sister would have been more firmly good had she better known why. However, he felt that he could not hold such a view. He threw it hastily aside.

Chapter XIV

In a hilarious hall there were twenty-eight tables and twenty-eight women and a crowd of smoking men. Valiant noise was made on a stage at the end of the hall by an orchestra composed of men who looked as if they had just happened in. Soiled waiters ran to and fro, swooping down like hawks on the unwary in the throng; clattering along the aisles with trays covered with glasses; stumbling over women's skirts and charging two prices for everything but beer, all with a swiftness that blurred the view of the cocoanut palms and dusty monstrosities painted upon the walls of the room. A bouncer, with an immense load of business upon his hands, plunged about in the crowd, dragging bashful strangers to prominent chairs, ordering waiters here and there and quarreling furiously with men who wanted to sing with the orchestra.

The usual smoke cloud was present, but so dense that heads and arms seemed entangled in it. The rumble of conversation was replaced by a roar. Plenteous oaths heaved through the air. The room rang with the shrill voices of women bubbling o'er with drink-laughter. The chief element in the music of the orchestra was speed. The musicians played in intent fury. A woman was singing and smiling upon the stage, but no one took notice of her. The rate at which the piano, cornet and violins were going, seemed to impart wildness to the half-drunken crowd. Beer glasses were emptied at a gulp and conversation became a rapid chatter. The smoke eddied and swirled like a shadowy river hurrying toward some unseen falls. Pete and Maggie entered the hall and took chairs at a table near the door. The woman who was seated there made an attempt to occupy Pete's attention and, failing, went away.

Three weeks had passed since the girl had left home. The air of spaniel-like dependence had been magnified and showed its direct effect in the peculiar off-handedness and ease of Pete's ways toward her.

She followed Pete's eyes with hers, anticipating with smiles gracious looks from him.

A woman of brilliance and audacity, accompanied by a mere boy, came into the place and took seats near them.

At once Pete sprang to his feet, his face beaming with glad surprise.

"By Gawd, there's Nellie," he cried.

He went over to the table and held out an eager hand to the woman.

"Why, hello, Pete, me boy, how are you," said she, giving him her fingers.

Maggie took instant note of the woman. She perceived that her black dress fitted her to perfection. Her linen collar and cuffs were spotless. Tan gloves were stretched over her well-shaped hands. A hat of a prevailing fashion perched jauntily upon her dark hair. She wore no jewelry and was painted with no apparent paint. She looked clear-eyed through the stares of the men.

"Sit down, and call your lady-friend over," she said cordially to Pete. At his beckoning Maggie came and sat between Pete and the mere boy.

"I thought yeh were gone away fer good," began Pete, at once. "When did yeh git back? How did dat Buff'lo bus'ness turn out?"

The woman shrugged her shoulders. "Well, he didn't have as many stamps as he tried to make out, so I shook him, that's all."

"Well, I'm glad teh see yehs back in deh city," said Pete, with awkward gallantry.

He and the woman entered into a long conversation, exchanging reminiscences of days together. Maggie sat still, unable to formulate an intelligent sentence upon the conversation and painfully aware of it.

She saw Pete's eyes sparkle as he gazed upon the handsome stranger. He listened smilingly to all she said. The woman was familiar with all his affairs, asked him about mutual friends, and knew the amount of his salary.

She paid no attention to Maggie, looking toward her once or twice and apparently seeing the wall beyond.

The mere boy was sulky. In the beginning he had welcomed with acclamations the additions.

"Let's all have a drink! What'll you take, Nell? And you, Miss what's-your-name. Have a drink, Mr. ——, you, I mean."

He had shown a sprightly desire to do the talking for the company and tell all about his family. In a loud voice he declaimed on various topics. He assumed a patronizing air toward Pete. As Maggie was silent, he paid no attention to her. He made a great show of lavishing wealth upon the woman of brilliance and audacity.

"Do keep still, Freddie! You gibber like an ape, dear," said the woman to him. She turned away and devoted her attention to Pete.

"We'll have many a good time together again, eh?"

"Sure, Mike," said Pete, enthusiastic at once.

"Say," whispered she, leaning forward, "let's go over to Billie's and have a heluva time."

"Well, it's dis way! See?" said Pete. "I got dis lady frien' here."

"Oh, t'hell with her," argued the woman.

Pete appeared disturbed.

"All right," said she, nodding her head at him. "All right for you! We'll see the next time you ask me to go anywheres with you."

Pete squirmed.

"Say," he said, beseechingly, "come wid me a minit an' I'll tell yer why."

The woman waved her hand.

"Oh, that's all right, you needn't explain, you know. You wouldn't come merely because you wouldn't come, that's all there is of it."

To Pete's visible distress she turned to the mere boy, bringing him speedily from a terrific rage. He had been debating whether it would be the part of a man to pick a quarrel with Pete, or would he be justified in striking him savagely with his beer glass without warning. But he recovered himself when the woman turned to renew her smilings. He beamed upon her with an expression that was somewhat tipsy and inexpressibly tender.

"Say, shake that Bowery jay," requested he, in a loud whisper.

"Freddie, you are so droll," she replied.

Pete reached forward and touched the woman on the arm.

"Come out a minit while I tells yeh why I can't go wid yer. Yer doin' me dirt, Nell! I never taut ye'd do me dirt, Nell. Come on, will yer?" He spoke in tones of injury.

"Why, I don't see why I should be interested in your explanations," said the woman, with a coldness that seemed to reduce Pete to a pulp.

His eyes pleaded with her. "Come out a minit while I tells yeh."

The woman nodded slightly at Maggie and the mere boy, "Scuse me."

The mere boy interrupted his loving smile and turned a shriveling glare upon Pete. His boyish countenance flushed and he spoke, in a whine, to the woman:

"Oh, I say, Nellie, this ain't a square deal, you know. You aren't goin' to leave me and go off with that duffer, are you? I should think—"

"Why, you dear boy, of course I'm not," cried the woman, affectionately. She bended over and whispered in his ear. He smiled again and settled in his chair as if resolved to wait patiently.

As the woman walked down between the rows of tables, Pete was at her shoulder talking earnestly, apparently in explanation. The woman waved her hands with studied airs of indifference. The doors swung behind them, leaving Maggie and the mere boy seated at the table.

Maggie was dazed. She could dimly perceive that something stupendous had happened. She wondered why Pete saw fit to remonstrate with the woman, pleading for forgiveness with his eyes. She thought she noted an air of submission about her leonine Pete. She was astounded.

The mere boy occupied himself with cock-tails and a cigar. He was tranquilly silent for half an hour. Then he bestirred himself and spoke.

"Well," he said, sighing, "I knew this was the way it would be." There was another stillness. The mere boy seemed to be musing.

"She was pulling m'leg. That's the whole amount of it," he said, suddenly. "It's a bloomin' shame the way that girl does. Why, I've spent over two dollars in drinks to-night. And she goes off with that plug-ugly who looks as if he had been hit in the face with a coin dye. I call it rocky treatment for a fellah like me. Here, waiter, bring me a cock-tail and make it damned strong."

Maggie made no reply. She was watching the doors. "It's a mean piece of business," complained the mere boy. He explained to her how amazing it was that anybody should treat him in such a manner. "But I'll get square with her, you bet. She won't get far ahead of yours truly, you know," he added, winking. "I'll tell her plainly that it was bloomin' mean business. And she won't come it over me with any of her 'now-Freddie-dears.' She thinks my name is Freddie, you know, but of course it ain't. I always tell these people some name like that, because if they got onto your right name they might use it sometime. Understand? Oh, they don't fool me much."

Maggie was paying no attention, being intent upon the doors. The mere boy relapsed into a period of gloom, during which he exterminated a number of cock-tails with a determined air, as if replying defiantly to fate. He occasionally broke forth into sentences composed of invectives joined together in a long string.

The girl was still staring at the doors. After a time the mere boy began to see cobwebs just in front of his nose. He spurred himself into being agreeable and insisted upon her having a charlotte-russe and a glass of beer.

"They's gone," he remarked, "they's gone." He looked at her through the smoke wreaths. "Shay, lil' girl, we mightish well make bes' of it. You ain't such bad lookin' girl, y'know. Not half bad. Can't come up to Nell, though. No, can't do it! Well, I should shay not! Nell fine-lookin' girl! F—i—n—ine. You look damn bad longsider her, but by y'self ain't so bad. Have to do anyhow. Nell gone. O'ny you left. Not half bad, though."

Maggie stood up.

"I'm going home," she said.

The mere boy started.

"Eh? What? Home," he cried, struck with amazement. "I beg pardon, did hear say home?"

"I'm going home," she repeated.

"Great Gawd, what hava struck," demanded the mere boy of himself, stupefied.

In a semi-comatose state he conducted her on board an uptown car, ostentatiously paid her fare, leered kindly at her through the rear window and fell off the steps.

Chapter XV

A forlorn woman went along a lighted avenue. The street was filled with people desperately bound on missions. An endless crowd darted at the elevated station stairs and the horse cars were thronged with owners of bundles.

The pace of the forlorn woman was slow. She was apparently searching for some one. She loitered near the doors of saloons and watched men emerge from them. She scanned furtively the faces in the rushing stream of pedestrians. Hurrying men, bent on catching some boat or train, jostled her elbows, failing to notice her, their thoughts fixed on distant dinners.

The forlorn woman had a peculiar face. Her smile was no smile. But when in repose her features had a shadowy look that was like a sardonic grin, as if some one had sketched with cruel forefinger indelible lines about her mouth.

Jimmie came strolling up the avenue. The woman encountered him with an aggrieved air.

"Oh, Jimmie, I've been lookin' all over fer yehs—," she began.

Jimmie made an impatient gesture and quickened his pace.

"Ah, don't bodder me! Good Gawd!" he said, with the savageness of a man whose life is pestered.

The woman followed him along the sidewalk in somewhat the manner of a suppliant.

"But, Jimmie," she said, "yehs told me ye'd—"

Jimmie turned upon her fiercely as if resolved to make a last stand for comfort and peace.

"Say, fer Gawd's sake, Hattie, don' foller me from one end of deh city teh deh odder. Let up, will yehs! Give me a minute's res', can't yehs? Yehs makes me tired, allus taggin' me. See? Ain' yehs got no sense? Do yehs want people teh get onto me? Go chase yerself, fer Gawd's sake."

The woman stepped closer and laid her fingers on his arm. "But, look-a here—"

Jimmie snarled. "Oh, go teh hell."

He darted into the front door of a convenient saloon and a moment later came out into the shadows that surrounded the side door. On the brilliantly lighted avenue he perceived the forlorn woman dodging about like a scout. Jimmie laughed with an air of relief and went away.

When he arrived home he found his mother clamoring. Maggie had returned. She stood shivering beneath the torrent of her mother's wrath.

"Well, I'm damned," said Jimmie in greeting.

His mother, tottering about the room, pointed a quivering fore-finger.

"Lookut her, Jimmie, lookut her. Dere's yer sister, boy. Dere's yer sister. Lookut her! Lookut her!"

She screamed in scoffing laughter.

The girl stood in the middle of the room. She edged about as if unable to find a place on the floor to put her feet.

"Ha, ha, ha," bellowed the mother. "Dere she stands! Ain' she purty? Lookut her! Ain' she sweet, deh beast? Lookut her! Ha, ha, lookut her!"

She lurched forward and put her red and seamed hands upon her daughter's face. She bent down and peered keenly up into the eyes of the girl.

"Oh, she's jes' dessame as she ever was, ain' she? She's her mudder's purty darlin' yit, ain' she? Lookut her, Jimmie! Come here, fer Gawd's sake, and lookut her."

The loud, tremendous sneering of the mother brought the denizens of the Rum Alley tenement to their doors. Women came in the hall-ways. Children scurried to and fro.

"What's up? Dat Johnson party on anudder tear?"

"Naw! Young Mag's come home!"

"Deh hell yeh say?"

Through the open doors curious eyes stared in at Maggie. Children ventured into the room and ogled her, as if they formed the front row at a theatre. Women, without, bended toward each other and whispered, nodding their heads with airs of profound philosophy. A baby, overcome with curiosity concerning this object at which all were looking, sidled forward and touched her dress, cautiously, as if investigating a red-hot stove. Its mother's voice rang out like a warning trumpet. She rushed forward and grabbed her child, casting a terrible look of indignation at the girl.

Maggie's mother paced to and fro, addressing the doorful of eyes, expounding like a glib showman at a museum. Her voice rang through the building.

"Dere she stands," she cried, wheeling suddenly and pointing with dramatic finger. "Dere she stands! Lookut her! Ain' she a dindy? An' she was so good as to come home teh her mudder, she was! Ain' she a beaut'? Ain' she a dindy? Fer Gawd's sake!"

The jeering cries ended in another burst of shrill laughter.

The girl seemed to awaken. "Jimmie—"

He drew hastily back from her.

"Well, now, yer a hell of a t'ing, ain' yeh?" he said, his lips curling in scorn. Radiant virtue sat upon his brow and his repelling hands expressed horror of contamination.

Maggie turned and went.

The crowd at the door fell back precipitately. A baby falling down in front of the door, wrenched a scream like a wounded animal from its mother. Another woman sprang forward and picked it up, with a chivalrous air, as if rescuing a human being from an oncoming express train.

As the girl passed down through the hall, she went before open doors framing more eyes strangely microscopic, and sending broad beams of inquisitive light into the darkness of her path. On the second floor she met the gnarled old woman who possessed the music box.

"So," she cried, " 'ere yehs are back again, are yehs? An' dey've kicked yehs out? Well, come in an' stay wid me teh-night. I ain' got no moral standin'."

From above came an unceasing babble of tongues, over all of which rang the mother's derisive laughter.

Chapter XVI

Pete did not consider that he had ruined Maggie. If he had thought that her soul could never smile again, he would have believed the mother and brother, who were pyrotechnic over the affair, to be responsible for it.

Besides, in his world, souls did not insist upon being able to smile. "What deh hell?"

He felt a trifle entangled. It distressed him. Revelations and scenes might bring upon him the wrath of the owner of the saloon, who insisted upon respectability of an advanced type.

"What deh hell do dey wanna' raise such a smoke about it fer?" demanded he of himself, disgusted with the attitude of the family. He saw no necessity for anyone's losing their equilibrium merely because their sister or their daughter had stayed away from home.

Searching about in his mind for possible reasons for their conduct, he came upon the conclusion that Maggie's motives were correct, but that the two others wished to snare him. He felt pursued.

The woman of brilliance and audacity whom he had met in the hilarious hall showed a disposition to ridicule him.

"A little pale thing with no spirit," she said. "Did you note the expression of her eyes? There was something in them about pumpkin pie and virtue. That is a peculiar way the left corner of her mouth has of twitching, isn't it? Dear, dear, my cloud-compelling Pete, what are you coming to?"

Pete asserted at once that he never was very much interested in the girl. The woman interrupted him, laughing.

"Oh, it's not of the slightest consequence to me, my dear young man. You needn't draw maps for my benefit. Why should I be concerned about it?"

But Pete continued with his explanations. If he was laughed at for his tastes in women, he felt obliged to say that they were only temporary or indifferent ones.

The morning after Maggie had departed from home, Pete stood behind the bar. He was immaculate in white jacket and apron and his hair was plastered over his brow with infinite correctness. No customers were in the place. Pete was twisting his napkined fist slowly in a beer glass, softly whistling to himself and occasionally holding the object of his attention between his eyes and a few weak beams of sunlight that had found their way over the thick screens and into the shaded room.

With lingering thoughts of the woman of brilliance and audacity, the bartender raised his head and stared through the varying cracks between the swaying bamboo doors. Suddenly the whistling pucker faded from his lips. He saw Maggie walking slowly past. He gave a great start, fearing for the previously-mentioned eminent respectability of the place.

He threw a swift, nervous glance about him, all at once feeling guilty. No one was in the room.

He went hastily over to the side door. Opening it and looking out, he perceived Maggie standing, as if undecided, on the corner. She was searching the place with her eyes.

As she turned her face toward him Pete beckoned to her hurriedly, intent upon returning with speed to a position behind the bar and to the atmosphere of respectability upon which the proprietor insisted.

Maggie came to him, the anxious look disappearing from her face and a smile wreathing her lips.

"Oh, Pete—," she began brightly.

The bartender made a violent gesture of impatience.

"Oh, my Gawd," cried he, vehemently. "What deh hell do yeh wanna hang aroun' here fer? Do yeh wanna git me inteh trouble?" he demanded with an air of injury.

Astonishment swept over the girl's features. "Why, Pete! yehs tol' me—"

Pete glanced profound irritation. His countenance reddened with the anger of a man whose respectability is being threatened.

"Say, yehs makes me tired. See? What deh hell deh yeh wanna tag aroun' atter me fer? Yeh'll git me inteh trouble wid deh ol' man an' dey'll be hell teh pay! If he sees a woman roun' here he'll go crazy an' I'll lose me job! See? Ain' yehs got no sense? Don' be allus bodderin' me. See? Yer brudder come in here an' raised hell an' deh ol' man hada put up fer it! An' now I'm done! See? I'm done."

The girl's eyes stared into his face. "Pete, don' yeh remem—"

"Oh, hell," interrupted Pete, anticipating.

The girl seemed to have a struggle with herself. She was apparently bewildered and could not find speech. Finally she asked in a low voice: "But where kin I go?"

The question exasperated Pete beyond the powers of endurance. It was a direct attempt to give him some responsibility in a matter that did not concern him. In his indignation he volunteered information.

"Oh, go teh hell," cried he. He slammed the door furiously and returned, with an air of relief, to his respectability.

Maggie went away.

She wandered aimlessly for several blocks. She stopped once and asked aloud a question of herself: "Who?"

A man who was passing near her shoulder, humorously took the questioning word as intended for him.

"Eh? What? Who? Nobody! I didn't say anything," he laughingly said, and continued his way.

Soon the girl discovered that if she walked with such apparent aimlessness, some men looked at her with calculating eyes. She quickened her step, frightened. As a protection, she adopted a demeanor of intentness as if going somewhere.

After a time she left rattling avenues and passed between rows of houses with sternness and stolidity stamped upon their features. She hung her head for she felt their eyes grimly upon her.

Suddenly she came upon a stout gentleman in a silk hat and a chaste black coat, whose decorous row of buttons reached from his chin to his knees. The girl had heard of the Grace of God and she decided to approach this man.

His beaming, chubby face was a picture of benevolence and kind-heartedness. His eyes shone good-will.

But as the girl timidly accosted him, he gave a convulsive movement and saved his respectability by a vigorous side-step. He did not risk it to save a soul. For how was he to know that there was a soul before him that needed saving?

Chapter XVII

Upon a wet evening, several months after the last chapter, two interminable rows of cars, pulled by slipping horses, jangled along a prominent side-street. A dozen cabs, with coat-enshrouded drivers, clattered to and fro. Electric lights, whirring softly, shed a blurred radiance. A flower dealer, his feet tapping impatiently, his nose and his wares glistening with rain-drops, stood behind an array of roses and chrysanthemums. Two or three theatres emptied a crowd upon the storm-swept pavements. Men pulled their hats over their eyebrows and raised their collars to their ears. Women shrugged impatient shoulders in their warm cloaks and stopped to arrange their skirts for a walk through the storm. People having been comparatively silent for two hours burst into a roar of conversation, their hearts still kindling from the glowings of the stage.

The pavements became tossing seas of umbrellas. Men stepped forth to hail cabs or cars, raising their fingers in varied forms of polite request or imperative demand. An endless procession wended toward elevated stations. An atmosphere of pleasure and prosperity seemed to hang over the throng, born, perhaps, of good clothes and of having just emerged from a place of forget-fulness.

In the mingled light and gloom of an adjacent park, a handful of wet wanderers, in attitudes of chronic dejection, was scattered among the benches.

A girl of the painted cohorts of the city went along the street. She threw changing glances at men who passed her, giving smiling invitations to men of rural or untaught pattern and usually seeming sedately unconscious of the men with a metropolitan seal upon their faces.

Crossing glittering avenues, she went into the throng emerging from the places of forgetfulness. She hurried forward through the crowd as if intent upon reaching a distant home, bending forward in her handsome cloak, daintily lifting her skirts and picking for her well-shod feet the dryer spots upon the pavements.

The restless doors of saloons, clashing to and fro, disclosed animated rows of men before bars and hurrying barkeepers.

A concert hall gave to the street faint sounds of swift, machine-like music, as if a group of phantom musicians were hastening.

A tall young man, smoking a cigarette with a sublime air, strolled near the girl. He had on evening dress, a moustache, a chrysanthemum, and a look of ennui, all of which he kept carefully under his eye. Seeing the girl walk on as if such a young man as he was not in existence, he looked back transfixed with interest. He stared glassily for a moment, but gave a slight convulsive start when he discerned that she was neither new, Parisian, nor theatrical. He wheeled about hastily and turned his stare into the air, like a sailor with a search-light.

A stout gentleman, with pompous and philanthropic whiskers, went stolidly by, the broad of his back sneering at the girl.

A belated man in business clothes, and in haste to catch a car, bounced against her shoulder. "Hi, there, Mary, I beg your pardon! Brace up, old girl." He grasped her arm to steady her, and then was away running down the middle of the street.

The girl walked on out of the realm of restaurants and saloons. She passed more glittering avenues and went into darker blocks than those where the crowd travelled.

A young man in light overcoat and derby hat received a glance shot keenly from the eyes of the girl. He stopped and looked at her, thrusting his hands in his pockets and making a mocking smile curl his lips. "Come, now, old lady," he said, "you don't mean to tell me that you sized me up for a farmer?"

A laboring man marched along with bundles under his arms. To her remarks, he replied: "It's a fine evenin', ain't it?"

She smiled squarely into the face of a boy who was hurrying by with his hands buried in his overcoat, his blonde locks bobbing on his youthful temples, and a cheery smile of unconcern upon his lips. He turned his head and smiled back at her, waving his hands.

"Not this eve—some other eve!"

A drunken man, reeling in her pathway, began to roar at her. "I ain' ga no money, dammit," he shouted, in a dismal voice. He lurched on up the street, wailing to himself, "Dammit, I ain' ga no money. Damn ba' luck. Ain' ga no more money."

The girl went into gloomy districts near the river, where the tall black factories shut in the street and only occasional broad beams of light fell across the pavements from saloons. In front of one of these places, from whence came the sound of a violin vigorously scraped, the patter of feet on boards and the ring of loud laughter, there stood a man with blotched features.

"Ah, there," said the girl.

"I've got a date," said the man.

Further on in the darkness she met a ragged being with shifting, blood-shot eyes and grimey hands. "Ah, what deh hell? Tink I'm a millionaire?"

She went into the blackness of the final block. The shutters of the tall buildings were closed like grim lips. The structures seemed to have eyes that looked over her, beyond her, at other things. Afar off the lights of the avenues glittered as if from an impossible distance. Street car bells jingled with a sound of merriment.

When almost to the river the girl saw a great figure. On going forward she perceived it to be a huge fat man in torn and greasy garments. His grey hair straggled down over his forehead. His small, bleared eyes, sparkling from amidst great rolls of red fat, swept eagerly over the girl's upturned face. He laughed, his brown, disordered teeth gleaming under a grey, grizzled moustache from which beer-drops dripped. His whole body gently quivered and shook like that of a dead jelly fish. Chuckling and leering, he followed the girl of the crimson legions.

At their feet the river appeared a deathly black hue. Some hidden factory sent up a yellow glare, that lit for a moment the waters lapping oilily against timbers. The varied sounds of life, made joyous by distance and seeming unapproachableness, came faintly and died away to a silence.

Chapter XVIII

In a partitioned-off section of a saloon sat a man with a half dozen women, gleefully laughing, hovering about him. The man had arrived at that stage of drunkenness where affection is felt for the universe.

"I'm good f'ler, girls," he said, convincingly. "I'm damn good f'ler. An'body treats me right, I allus trea's zem right! See?"

The women nodded their heads approvingly. "To be sure," they cried in hearty chorus. "You're the kind of a man we like, Pete. You're outa sight! What yeh goin' to buy this time, dear?"

"An'thin' yehs wants, damn it," said the man in an abandonment of good will. His countenance shone with the true spirit of benevolence. He was in the proper mode of missionaries. He would have fraternized with obscure Hottentots. And above all, he was overwhelmed in tenderness for his friends, who were all illustrious.

"An'thing yehs wants, damn it," repeated he, waving his hands with beneficent recklessness. "I'm good f'ler, girls, an' if an'body treats me right I—here," called he through an open door to a waiter, "bring girls drinks, damn it. What 'ill yehs have, girls? An'thing yehs want, damn it!"

The waiter glanced in with the disgusted look of the man who serves intoxicants for the man who takes too much of them. He nodded his head shortly at the order from each individual, and went.

"Damn it," said the man, "we're havin' heluva time. I like you girls! Damn'd if I don't! Yer right sort! See?"

He spoke at length and with feeling, concerning the excellencies of his assembled friends.

"Don' try pull man's leg, but have a heluva time! Das right! Das way teh do! Now, if I sawght yehs tryin' work me fer drinks, wouldn' buy damn t'ing! But yer right sort, damn it! Yehs know how ter treat a f'ler, an' I stays by yehs 'til spen' las' cent! Das right! I'm good f'ler an' I knows when an'body treats me right!"

Between the times of the arrival and departure of the waiter, the man discoursed to the women on the tender regard he felt for all living things. He laid stress upon the purity of his motives in all dealings with men in the world and spoke of the fervor of his friendship for those who were amiable. Tears welled slowly from his eyes. His voice quavered when he spoke to them.

Once when the waiter was about to depart with an empty tray, the man drew a coin from his pocket and held it forth.

"Here," said he, quite magnificently, "here's quar'."

The waiter kept his hands on his tray.

"I don' want yer money," he said.

The other put forth the coin with tearful insistence.

"Here, damn it," cried he, "tak't! Yer damn goo' f'ler an' I wan' yehs tak't!"

"Come, come, now," said the waiter, with the sullen air of a man who is forced into giving advice. "Put yer mon in yer pocket! Yer loaded an' yehs on'y makes a damn fool of yerself."

As the latter passed out of the door the man turned pathetically to the women.

"He don' know I'm damn goo' f'ler," cried he, dismally.

"Never you mind, Pete, dear," said a woman of brilliance and audacity, laying her hand with great affection upon his arm. "Never you mind, old boy! We'll stay by you, dear!"

"Das ri'," cried the man, his face lighting up at the soothing tones of the woman's voice. "Das ri', I'm damn goo' f'ler an' w'en anyone trea's me ri', I treats zem ri'! Shee!"

"Sure!" cried the women. "And we're not goin' back on you, old man."

The man turned appealing eyes to the woman of brilliance and audacity. He felt that if he could be convicted of a contemptible action he would die.

"Shay, Nell, damn it, I allus trea's yehs shquare, didn' I? I allus been goo' f'ler wi' yehs, ain't I, Nell?"

"Sure you have, Pete," assented the woman. She delivered an oration to her companions. "Yessir, that's a fact. Pete's a square fellah, he is. He never goes back on a friend. He's the right kind an' we stay by him, don't we, girls?"

"Sure," they exclaimed. Looking lovingly at him they raised their glasses and drank his health.

"Girlsh," said the man, beseechingly, "I allus trea's yehs ri', didn' I? I'm goo' f'ler, ain' I, girlsh?"

"Sure," again they chorused.

"Well," said he finally, "le's have nozzer drink, zen."

"That's right," hailed a woman, "that's right. Yer no bloomin' jay! Yer spends yer money like a man. Dat's right."

The man pounded the table with his quivering fists.

"Yessir," he cried, with deep earnestness, as if someone disputed him. "I'm damn goo' f'ler, an' w'en anyone trea's me ri', I allus trea's—le's have nozzer drink."

He began to beat the wood with his glass.

"Shay," howled he, growing suddenly impatient. As the waiter did not then come, the man swelled with wrath.

"Shay," howled he again.

The waiter appeared at the door.

"Bringsh drinksh," said the man.

The waiter disappeared with the orders.

"Zat f'ler dam fool," cried the man. "He insul' me! I'm ge'-man! Can' stan' be insul'! I'm goin' lickim when comes!"

"No, no," cried the women, crowding about and trying to subdue him. "He's all right! He didn't mean anything! Let it go! He's a good fellah!"

"Din' he insul' me?" asked the man earnestly.

"No," said they. "Of course he didn't! He's all right!"

"Sure he didn' insul' me?" demanded the man, with deep anxiety in his voice.

"No, no! We know him! He's a good fellah. He didn't mean anything."

"Well, zen," said the man, resolutely, "I'm go' 'pol'gize!"

When the waiter came, the man struggled to the middle of the floor.

"Girlsh shed you insul' me! I shay damn lie! I 'pol'gize!"

"All right," said the waiter.

The man sat down. He felt a sleepy but strong desire to straighten things out and have a perfect understanding with everybody.

"Nell, I allus trea's yeh shquare, din I? Yeh likes me, don' yehs, Nell? I'm goo' f'ler?"

"Sure," said the woman of brilliance and audacity.

"Yeh knows I'm stuck on yehs, don' yehs, Nell?"

"Sure," she repeated, carelessly.

Overwhelmed by a spasm of drunken adoration, he drew two or three bills from his pocket, and, with the trembling fingers of an offering priest, laid them on the table before the woman.

"Yehs knows, damn it, yehs kin have all got, 'cause I'm stuck on yehs, Nell, damn't, I—I'm stuck on yehs, Nell—buy drinksh—damn't—we're havin' heleva time—w'en anyone trea's me ri'—I—damn't, Nell—we're havin' heluva—time."

Shortly he went to sleep with his swollen face fallen forward on his chest.

The women drank and laughed, not heeding the slumbering man in the corner. Finally he lurched forward and fell groaning to the floor.

The women screamed in disgust and drew back their skirts.

"Come ahn," cried one, starting up angrily, "let's get out of here."

The woman of brilliance and audacity stayed behind, taking

up the bills and stuffing them into a deep, irregularly-shaped pocket. A guttural snore from the recumbent man caused her to turn and look down at him.

She laughed. "What a damn fool," she said, and went.

The smoke from the lamps settled heavily down in the little compartment, obscuring the way out. The smell of oil, stifling in its intensity, pervaded the air. The wine from an overturned glass dripped softly down upon the blotches on the man's neck.

Chapter XIX

In a room a woman sat at a table eating like a fat monk in a picture.

A soiled, unshaven man pushed open the door and entered.

"Well," said he, "Mag's dead."

"What?" said the woman, her mouth filled with bread.

"Mag's dead," repeated the man.

"Deh hell she is," said the woman. She continued her meal. When she finished her coffee she began to weep.

"I kin remember when her two feet was no bigger dan yer tumb, and she weared worsted boots," moaned she.

"Well, whata dat?" said the man.

"I kin remember when she weared worsted boots," she cried.

The neighbors began to gather in the hall, staring in at the weeping woman as if watching the contortions of a dying dog. A dozen women entered and lamented with her. Under their busy hands the rooms took on that appalling appearance of neatness and order with which death is greeted.

Suddenly the door opened and a woman in a black gown rushed in with outstretched arms. "Ah, poor Mary," she cried, and tenderly embraced the moaning one.

"Ah, what ter'ble affliction is dis," continued she. Her vocabulary was derived from mission churches. "Me poor Mary, how I feel fer yehs! Ah, what a ter'ble affliction is a disobed'ent chile."

Her good, motherly face was wet with tears. She trembled in

eagerness to express her sympathy. The mourner sat with bowed head, rocking her body heavily to and fro, and crying out in a high, strained voice that sounded like a dirge on some forlorn pipe.

"I kin remember when she weared worsted boots an' her two feets was no bigger dan yer tumb an' she weared worsted boots, Miss Smith," she cried, raising her streaming eyes.

"Ah, me poor Mary," sobbed the woman in black. With low, coddling cries, she sank on her knees by the mourner's chair, and put her arms about her. The other women began to groan in different keys.

"Yer poor misguided chil' is gone now, Mary, an' let us hope it's fer deh bes'. Yeh'll fergive her now, Mary, won't yehs, dear, all her disobed'ence? All her tankless behavior to her mudder an' all her badness? She's gone where her ter'ble sins will be judged."

The woman in black raised her face and paused. The inevitable sunlight came streaming in at the windows and shed a ghastly cheerfulness upon the faded hues of the room. Two or three of the spectators were sniffling, and one was loudly weeping. The mourner arose and staggered into the other room. In a moment she emerged with a pair of faded baby shoes held in the hollow of her hand.

"I kin remember when she used to wear dem," cried she. The women burst anew into cries as if they had all been stabbed. The mourner turned to the soiled and unshaven man.

"Jimmie, boy, go git yer sister! Go git yer sister an' we'll put deh boots on her feets!"

"Dey won't fit her now, yeh damn fool," said the man.

"Go git yer sister, Jimmie," shrieked the woman, confronting him fiercely.

The man swore sullenly. He went over to a corner and slowly began to put on his coat. He took his hat and went out, with a dragging, reluctant step.

The woman in black came forward and again besought the mourner.

"Yeh'll fergive her, Mary! Yeh'll fergive yer bad, bad chil'! Her life was a curse an' her days were black an' yeh'll fergive yer bad girl? She's gone where her sins will be judged."

"She's gone where her sins will be judged," cried the other women, like a choir at a funeral.

"Deh Lord gives and deh Lord takes away," said the woman in black, raising her eyes to the sunbeams.

"Deh Lord gives and deh Lord takes away," responded the others.

"Yeh'll fergive her, Mary!" pleaded the woman in black. The mourner essayed to speak but her voice gave way. She shook her great shoulders frantically, in an agony of grief. Hot tears seemed to scald her quivering face. Finally her voice came and arose like a scream of pain.

"Oh, yes, I'll fergive her! I'll fergive her!"

GEORGE'S MOTHER

Chapter I

In the swirling rain that came at dusk the broad avenue glistened with that deep bluish tint which is so widely condemned when it is put into pictures. There were long rows of shops, whose fronts shone with full, golden light. Here and there, from druggists' windows, or from the red street-lamps that indicated the positions of fire-alarm boxes, a flare of uncertain, wavering crimson was thrown upon the wet pavements.

The lights made shadows, in which the buildings loomed with a new and tremendous massiveness, like castles and fortresses. There were endless processions of people, mighty hosts, with umbrellas waving, banner-like, over them. Horse-cars, aglitter with new paint, rumbled in steady array between the pillars that supported the elevated railroad. The whole street resounded with the tinkle of bells, the roar of iron-shod wheels on the cobbles, the ceaseless trample of the hundreds of feet. Above all, too, could be heard the loud screams of the tiny newsboys, who scurried in all directions. Upon the corners, standing in from the dripping eaves, were many loungers, descended from the world that used to prostrate itself before pageantry.

A brown young man went along the avenue. He held a tin lunch-pail under his arm in a manner that was evidently uncomfortable. He was puffing at a corn-cob pipe. His shoulders had a self-reliant poise, and the hang of his arms and the raised veins of his hands showed him to be a man who worked with his muscles.

As he passed a street-corner a man in old clothes gave a shout of surprise, and rushing impetuously forward, grasped his hand.

"Hello, Kelcey, ol' boy," cried the man in old clothes. "How's th' boy, anyhow? Where in thunder yeh been fer th' last seventeen years? I'll be hanged if you ain't th' last man I ever expected t' see."

The brown youth put his pail to the ground and grinned. "Well, if it ain't ol' Charley Jones," he said, ecstatically shaking hands. "How are yeh, anyhow? Where yeh been keepin' yerself? I ain't seen yeh fer a year!"

"Well, I should say so! Why, th' last time I saw you was up in Handyville!"

"Sure! On Sunday, we——"

"Sure! Out at Bill Sickles's place. Let's go get a drink!"

They made toward a little glass-fronted saloon that sat blinking jovially at the crowds. It engulfed them with a gleeful motion of its two widely smiling lips.

"What'll yeh take, Kelcey?"

"Oh, I guess I'll take a beer."

"Gimme little whiskey, John."

The two friends leaned against the bar and looked with enthusiasm upon each other.

"Well, well, I'm thunderin' glad t' see yeh," said Jones.

"Well, I guess," replied Kelcey. "Here's to yeh, ol' man."

"Let 'er go."

They lifted their glasses, glanced fervidly at each other, and drank.

"Yeh ain't changed much, on'y yeh've growed like th' devil," said Jones, reflectively, as he put down his glass. "I'd know yeh anywheres!"

"Certainly yeh would," said Kelcey. "An' I knew you, too, th' minute I saw yeh. Yer changed, though!"

"Yes," admitted Jones, with some complacency, "I s'pose I am." He regarded himself in the mirror that multiplied the bottles on the shelf back of the bar. He should have seen a grinning face with a rather pink nose. His derby was perched carelessly on the back part of his head. Two wisps of hair straggled down over his hollow temples. There was something very worldly and wise about him. Life did not seem to confuse him. Evidently he understood its complications. His hand thrust into his trousers' pocket, where he jingled keys, and his hat perched back on his head expressed a young man of vast knowledge. His extensive acquaintance with bartenders aided him materially in this habitual expression of wisdom.

Having finished he turned to the barkeeper. "John, has any of th' gang been in t'-night yet?"

"No—not yet," said the barkeeper. "Ol' Bleecker was aroun' this afternoon about four. He said if I seen any of th' boys t' tell 'em he'd be up t'-night if he could get away. I saw Connor an' that other fellah goin' down th' avenyeh about an hour ago. I guess they'll be back after awhile."

"This is th' hang-out fer a great gang," said Jones, turning to Kelcey. "They're a great crowd, I tell yeh. We own th' place when we get started. Come aroun' some night. Any night, almost. T'-night, b' jiminy. They'll almost all be here, an' I'd like t' interduce yeh. They're a great gang! Gre-e-at!"

"I'd like teh," said Kelcey.

"Well, come ahead, then," cried the other, cordially. "Yeh'd like t' know 'em. It's an outa sight crowd. Come aroun' t'-night!"

"I will if I can."

"Well, yeh ain't got anything t' do, have yeh?" demanded Jones. "Well, come along, then. Yeh might just as well spend yer time with a good crowd 'a fellahs. An' it's a great gang. Great! Gre-e-at!"

"Well, I must make fer home now, anyhow," said Kelcey. "It's late as blazes. What'll yeh take this time, ol' man?"

"Gimme little more whiskey, John!"

"Guess I'll take another beer!"

Jones emptied the whiskey into his large mouth and then put

the glass upon the bar. "Been in th' city long?" he asked. "Um—well, three years is a good deal fer a slick man. Doin' well? Oh, well, nobody's doin' well these days." He looked down mournfully at his shabby clothes. "Father's dead, ain't 'ee? Yeh don't say so? Fell off a scaffoldin', didn't 'ee? I heard it somewheres. Mother's livin', of course? I thought she was. Fine ol' lady—fi-i-ne. Well, you're th' last of her boys. Was five of yeh onct, wasn't there? I knew four m'self. Yes, five! I thought so. An' all gone but you, hey? Well you'll have t' brace up an' be a comfort t' th' ol' mother. Well, well, well, who would 'a thought that on'y you'd be left out 'a all that mob 'a tow-headed kids. Well, well, well, it's a queer world, ain't it?"

A contemplation of this thought made him sad. He sighed and moodily watched the other sip beer.

"Well, well, it's a queer world—a damn queer world."

"Yes," said Kelcey, "I'm th' on'y one left!" There was an accent of discomfort in his voice. He did not like this dwelling upon a sentiment that was connected with himself.

"How is th' ol' lady, anyhow?" continued Jones. "Th' last time I remember she was as spry as a little ol' cricket, an' was helpeltin' aroun' the country lecturin' before W.C.T.U.'s an' one thing an' another."

"Oh, she's pretty well," said Kelcey.

"An' outa five boys you're th' on'y one she's got left? Well, well—have another drink before yeh go."

"Oh, I guess I've had enough."

A wounded expression came into Jones's eyes. "Oh, come on," he said.

"Well, I'll take another beer!"

"Gimme little more whiskey, John!"

When they had concluded this ceremony, Jones went with his friend to the door of the saloon. "Good-by, ol' man," he said, genially. His homely features shone with friendliness. "Come aroun', now, sure. T'-night! See? They're a great crowd. Gre-e-at!"

Chapter II

A man with a red, mottled face put forth his head from a window and cursed violently. He flung a bottle high across two backyards at a window of the opposite tenement. It broke against the bricks of the house and the fragments fell crackling upon the stones below. The man shook his fist.

A bare-armed woman, making an array of clothes on a line in one of the yards, glanced casually up at the man and listened to his words. Her eyes followed his to the other tenement. From a distant window, a youth with a pipe, yelled some comments upon the poor aim. Two children, being in the proper yard, picked up the bits of broken glass and began to fondle them as new toys.

From the window at which the man raged came the sound of an old voice, singing. It quavered and trembled out into the air as if a sound-spirit had a broken wing.

> "Should I be car-reed tew th' skies
>   O-on flow'ry be-eds of ee-ease,
>   While others fought tew win th' prize
>   An' sailed through blood-ee seas."

The man in the opposite window was greatly enraged. He continued to swear.

A little old woman was the owner of the voice. In a fourth-story room of the red and black tenement she was trudging on a journey. In her arms she bore pots and pans, and sometimes a broom and dust-pan. She wielded them like weapons. Their weight seemed to have bended her back and crooked her arms until she walked with difficulty. Often she plunged her hands into water at a sink. She splashed about, the dwindled muscles working to and fro under the loose skin of her arms. She came from the sink, steaming and bedraggled as if she had crossed a flooded river.

There was the flurry of a battle in this room. Through the clouded dust or steam one could see the thin figure dealing mighty blows. Always her way seemed beset. Her broom was continually poised, lance-wise, at dust demons. There came clashings and clangings as she strove with her tireless foes.

It was a picture of indomitable courage. And as she went on her way her voice was often raised in a long cry, a strange war-chant, a shout of battle and defiance, that rose and fell in harsh screams, and exasperated the ears of the man with the red, mottled face.

"Should I be car-reed tew th' skies
O-on flow'ry be-eds of ee-ease——"

Finally she halted for a moment. Going to the window she sat down and mopped her face with her apron. It was a lull, a moment of respite. Still it could be seen that she even then was planning skirmishes, charges, campaigns. She gazed thoughtfully about the room and noted the strength and position of her enemies. She was very alert.

At last, she turned to the mantel. "Five o'clock," she murmured, scrutinizing a little, swaggering, nickel-plated clock.

She looked out at chimneys growing thickly on the roofs. A man at work on one seemed like a bee. In the intricate yards below, vine-line lines had strange leaves of cloth. To her ears there came the howl of the man with the red, mottled face. He was engaged in a furious altercation with the youth who had called attention to his poor aim. They were like animals in a jungle.

In the distance an enormous brewery towered over the other buildings. Great gilt letters advertised a brand of beer. Thick smoke came from funnels and spread near it like vast and powerful wings. The structure seemed a great bird, flying. The letters of the sign made a chain of gold hanging from its neck. The little old woman looked at the brewery. It vaguely interested her, for a moment, as a stupendous affair, a machine of mighty strength.

Presently she sprang from her rest and began to buffet with her shrivelled arms. In a moment the battle was again in full swing. Terrific blows were given and received. There arose the clattering uproar of a new fight. The little intent warrior never hesitated nor faltered. She fought with a strong and relentless will. Beads and lines of perspiration stood upon her forehead.

Three blue plates were leaning in a row on the shelf back of the stove. The little old woman had seen it done somewhere. In front of them swaggered the round nickel-plated clock. Her son had stuck many cigarette pictures in the rim of a looking-glass that hung near. Occasional chromos were tacked upon the yellowed walls of the room. There was one in a gilt frame. It was quite an affair, in reds and greens. They all seemed like trophies.

It began to grow dark. A mist came winding. Rain plashed softly upon the window-sill. A lamp had been lighted in the opposite tenement; the strong orange glare revealed the man with a red, mottled face. He was seated by a table, smoking and reflecting.

The little old woman looked at the clock again. "Quarter 'a six."

She had paused for a moment, but she now hurled herself fiercely at the stove that lurked in the gloom, red-eyed, like a dragon. It hissed, and there was renewed clangor of blows. The little old woman dashed to and fro.

Chapter III

As it grew toward seven o'clock the little old woman became nervous. She often would drop into a chair and sit staring at the little clock.

"I wonder why he don't come," she continually repeated. There was a small, curious note of despair in her voice. As she sat thinking and staring at the clock the expressions of her face changed swiftly. All manner of emotions flickered in her eyes and about her lips. She was evidently perceiving in her imagination the journey of a loved person. She dreamed for him mishaps and obstacles. Something tremendous and irritating was hindering him from coming to her.

She had lighted an oil-lamp. It flooded the room with vivid yellow glare. The table, in its oil-cloth covering, had previously appeared like a bit of bare, brown desert. It now was a white garden, growing the fruits of her labor.

"Seven o'clock," she murmured, finally. She was aghast.

Then suddenly she heard a step upon the stair. She sprang up and began to bustle about the room. The little fearful emotions passed at once from her face. She seemed now to be ready to scold.

Young Kelcey entered the room. He gave a sigh of relief, and dropped his pail in a corner. He was evidently greatly wearied by a hard day of toil.

The little old woman hobbled over to him and raised her wrinkled lips. She seemed on the verge of tears and an outburst of reproaches.

"Hello!" he cried, in a voice of cheer. "Been gettin' anxious?"

"Yes," she said, hovering about him. "Where yeh been, George? What made yeh so late? I've been waitin' th' longest while. Don't throw your coat down there. Hang it up behind th' door."

The son put his coat on the proper hook, and then went to splatter water in a tin wash-basin at the sink.

"Well, yeh see, I met Jones—you remember Jones? Ol' Handyville fellah. An' we had t' stop an' talk over ol' times. Jones is quite a boy."

The little old woman's mouth set in a sudden straight line. "Oh, that Jones," she said. "I don't like him."

The youth interrupted a flurry of white towel to give a glance of irritation. "Well, now, what's th' use of talkin' that way?" he said to her. "What do yeh know 'bout 'im? Ever spoke to 'im in yer life?"

"Well, I don't know as I ever did since he grew up," replied the little old woman. "But I know he ain't th' kind 'a man I'd like t' have you go around with. He ain't a good man. I'm sure he ain't. He drinks."

Her son began to laugh. "Th' dickens he does?" He seemed amazed, but not shocked at this information.

She nodded her head with the air of one who discloses a dreadful thing. "I'm sure of it! Once I saw 'im comin' outa Simpson's Hotel, up in Handyville, an' he could hardly walk. He drinks! I'm sure he drinks!"

"Holy smoke!" said Kelcey.

They sat down at the table and began to wreck the little white garden. The youth leaned back in his chair, in the manner of a man who is paying for things. His mother bended alertly forward, apparently watching each mouthful. She perched on the edge of her chair, ready to spring to her feet and run to the closet or the stove for anything that he might need. She was as anxious as a young mother with a babe. In the careless and comfortable attitude of the son there was denoted a great deal of dignity.

"Yeh ain't eatin' much t'-night, George?"

"Well, I ain't very hungry, t' tell th' truth."

"Don't yeh like yer supper, dear? Yeh must eat somethin', chile. Yeh mustn't go without."

"Well, I'm eatin' somethin', ain't I?"

He wandered aimlessly through the meal. She sat over behind the little blackened coffee-pot and gazed affectionately upon him.

After a time she began to grow agitated. Her worn fingers were gripped. It could be seen that a great thought was within her. She was about to venture something. She had arrived at a supreme moment. "George," she said, suddenly, "come t' prayer-meetin' with me t'-night."

The young man dropped his fork. "Say, you must be crazy," he said, in amazement.

"Yes, dear," she continued, rapidly, in a small pleading voice, "I'd like t' have yeh go with me onct in a while. Yeh never go with me any more, dear, an' I'd like t' have yeh go. Yeh ain't been anywheres at all with me in th' longest while."

"Well," he said, "well, but what th' blazes——"

"Ah, come on," said the little old woman. She went to him and put her arms about his neck. She began to coax him with caresses.

The young man grinned. "Thunderation!" he said, "what would I do at a prayer-meetin'?"

The mother considered him to be consenting. She did a little antique caper.

"Well, yeh can come an' take care 'a yer mother," she cried, gleefully. "It's such a long walk every Thursday night alone, an' don't yeh s'pose that when I have such a big, fine, strappin' boy, I want 'im t' beau me aroun' some? Ah, I knew ye'd come."

He smiled for a moment, indulgent of her humor. But presently his face turned a shade of discomfort. "But——" he began, protesting.

"Ah, come on," she continually repeated.

He began to be vexed. He frowned into the air. A vision came to him of dreary blackness arranged in solemn rows. A mere dream of it was depressing.

"But—" he said again. He was obliged to make great search for an argument. Finally he concluded, "But what th' blazes would I do at prayer-meetin'?"

In his ears was the sound of a hymn, made by people who tilted their heads at a prescribed angle of devotion. It would be too apparent that they were all better than he. When he entered they would turn their heads and regard him with suspicion. This would be an enormous aggravation, since he was certain that he was as good as they.

"Well, now, y' see," he said, quite gently, "I don't wanta go, an' it wouldn't do me no good t' go if I didn't wanta go."

His mother's face swiftly changed. She breathed a huge sigh, the counterpart of ones he had heard upon like occasions. She put a tiny black bonnet on her head, and wrapped her figure in an old shawl. She cast a martyr-like glance upon her son and went mournfully away. She resembled a limited funeral procession.

The young man writhed under it to an extent. He kicked moodily at a table-leg. When the sound of her footfalls died away he felt distinctly relieved.

Chapter IV

That night, when Kelcey arrived at the little smiling saloon, he found his friend Jones standing before the bar engaged in a violent argument with a stout man.

"Oh, well," this latter person was saying, "you can make a lot of noise, Charlie, for a man that never says anything—let's have a drink!"

Jones was waving his arms and delivering splintering blows upon some distant theories. The stout man chuckled fatly and winked at the bartender.

The orator ceased for a moment to say, "Gimme little whiskey, John." At the same time he perceived young Kelcey. He sprang forward with a welcoming cry. "Hello, ol' man, didn't much think ye'd come." He led him to the stout man.

"Mr. Bleecker—my friend Mr. Kelcey!"

"How d'yeh do!"

"Mr. Kelcey, I'm happy to meet you, sir; have a drink."

They drew up in line and waited. The busy hands of the bartender made glasses clink. Mr. Bleecker, in a very polite way, broke the waiting silence.

"Never been here before, I believe, have you, Mr. Kelcey?"

The young man felt around for a high-bred reply. "Er—no— I've never had that—er—pleasure," he said.

After a time the strained and wary courtesy of their manners wore away. It became evident to Bleecker that his importance slightly dazzled the young man. He grew warmer. Obviously, the youth was one whose powers of perception were developed. Directly, then, he launched forth into a tale of by-gone days, when the world was better. He had known all the great men of that age. He reproduced his conversations with them. There were traces of pride and of mournfulness in his voice. He rejoiced at the glory of the world of dead spirits. He grieved at the youth and flippancy of the present one. He lived with his head in the clouds of the past, and he seemed obliged to talk of what he saw there.

Jones nudged Kelcey ecstatically in the ribs. "You've got th' ol' man started in great shape," he whispered.

Kelcey was proud that the prominent character of the place talked at him, glancing into his eyes for appreciation of fine points.

Presently they left the bar, and going into a little rear room, took seats about a table. A gas-jet with a colored globe shed a crimson radiance. The polished wood of walls and furniture gleamed with faint rose-colored reflections. Upon the floor saw-dust was thickly sprinkled.

Two other men presently came. By the time Bleecker had told three tales of the grand past, Kelcey was slightly acquainted with everybody.

He admired Bleecker immensely. He developed a brotherly feeling for the others, who were all gentle-spoken. He began to feel that he was passing the happiest evening of his life. His companions were so jovial and good-natured; and everything they did was marked by such courtesy.

For a time the two men who had come in late did not presume to address him directly. They would say: "Jones, won't your friend have so and so, or so and so?" And Bleecker would begin his orations: "Now, Mr. Kelcey, don't you think——"

Presently he began to believe that he was a most remarkably fine fellow, who had at last found his place in a crowd of most remarkably fine fellows.

Jones occasionally breathed comments into his ear.

"I tell yeh, Bleecker's an ol'-timer. He was a husky guy in his day, yeh can bet. He was one 'a th' best known men in N' York onct. Yeh ought to hear him tell about——"

Kelcey listened intently. He was profoundly interested in these intimate tales of men who had gleamed in the rays of old suns.

"That O'Connor's a damn fine fellah," interjected Jones once, referring to one of the others. "He's one 'a th' best fellahs I ever knowed. He's always on th' dead level. An' he's always jest th' same as yeh see 'im now—good-natured an' grinnin'."

Kelcey nodded. He could well believe it.

When he offered to buy drinks there came a loud volley of protests. "No, no, Mr. Kelcey," cried Bleecker, "no, no. To-night you are our guest. Some other time——"

"Here," said O'Connor, "it's my turn now."

He called and pounded for the bartender. He then sat with a coin in his hand warily eying the others. He was ready to frustrate them if they offered to pay.

After a time Jones began to develop qualities of great eloquence and wit. His companions laughed. "It's the whiskey talking now," said Bleecker.

He grew earnest and impassioned. He delivered speeches on various subjects. His lectures were to him very imposing. The force of his words thrilled him. Sometimes he was overcome.

The others agreed with him in all things. Bleecker grew almost tender, and considerately placed words here and there for his use. As Jones became fiercely energetic the others became more docile in agreeing. They soothed him with friendly interjections.

His mood changed directly. He began to sing popular airs with enthusiasm. He congratulated his companions upon being in his society. They were excited by his frenzy. They began to fraternize in jovial fashion. It was understood that they were true and tender spirits. They had come away from a grinding world filled with men who were harsh.

When one of them chose to divulge some place where the

world had pierced him, there was a chorus of violent sympathy. They rejoiced at their temporary isolation and safety.

Once a man, completely drunk, stumbled along the floor of the saloon. He opened the door of the little room and made a show of entering. The men sprang instantly to their feet. They were ready to throttle any invader of their island. They elbowed each other in rivalry as to who should take upon himself the brunt of an encounter.

"Oh!" said the drunken individual, swaying on his legs and blinking at the party, "oh! thish private room?"

"That's what it is, Willie," said Jones. "An' you git outa here er we'll throw yeh out."

"That's what we will," said the others.

"Oh," said the drunken man. He blinked at them aggrievedly for an instant and then went away.

They sat down again. Kelcey felt, in a way, that he would have liked to display his fidelity to the others by whipping the intruder.

The bartender came often. "Gee, you fellahs er tanks," he said, in a jocular manner, as he gathered empty glasses and polished the table with his little towel.

Through the exertions of Jones the little room began to grow clamorous. The tobacco-smoke eddied about the forms of the men in ropes and wreaths. Near the ceiling there was a thick gray cloud.

Each man explained, in his way, that he was totally out of place in the before-mentioned world. They were possessed of various virtues which were unappreciated by those with whom they were commonly obliged to mingle; they were fitted for a tree-shaded land, where everything was peace. Now that five of them had congregated it gave them happiness to speak their inmost thoughts without fear of being misunderstood.

As he drank more beer Kelcey felt his breast expand with manly feeling. He knew that he was capable of sublime things. He wished that some day one of his present companions would come to him for relief. His mind pictured a little scene. In it he was magnificent in his friendship.

He looked upon the beaming faces and knew that if at that instant there should come a time for a great sacrifice he would blissfully make it. He would pass tranquilly into the unknown, or into bankruptcy, amid the ejaculations of his companions upon his many virtues.

They had no bickerings during the evening. If one chose to momentarily assert himself, the others instantly submitted.

They exchanged compliments. Once old Bleecker stared at Jones for a few moments. Suddenly he broke out: "Jones, you're one of the finest fellows I ever knew!" A flush of pleasure went over the other's face, and then he made a modest gesture, the protest of an humble man. "Don't flim-flam me, ol' boy," he said, with earnestness. But Bleecker roared that he was serious about it. The two men arose and shook hands emotionally. Jones bunted against the table and knocked off a glass.

Afterward a general hand-shaking was inaugurated. Brotherly sentiments flew about the room. There was an uproar of fraternal feeling.

Jones began to sing. He beat time with precision and dignity. He gazed into the eyes of his companions, trying to call music from their souls. O'Connor joined in heartily, but with another tune. Off in a corner old Bleecker was making a speech.

The bartender came to the door. "Gee, you fellahs er making a row. It's time fer me t' shut up th' front th' place, an' you mugs better sit on yerselves. It's one o'clock."

They began to argue with him. Kelcey, however, sprang to his feet. "One o'clock," he said. "Holy smoke, I mus' be flyin'!"

There came protesting howls from Jones. Bleecker ceased his oration. "My dear boy—" he began. Kelcey searched for his hat. "I've gota go t' work at seven," he said.

The others watched him with discomfort in their eyes. "Well," said O'Connor, "if one goes we might as well all go." They sadly took their hats and filed out.

The cold air of the street filled Kelcey with vague surprise. It made his head feel hot. As for his legs, they were like willow-twigs.

A few yellow lights blinked. In front of an all-night restaurant a huge red electric lamp hung and sputtered. Horse-car bells jingled far down the street. Overhead a train thundered on the elevated road.

On the sidewalk the men took fervid leave. They clutched hands with extraordinary force and proclaimed, for the last time, ardent and admiring friendships.

When he arrived at his home Kelcey proceeded with caution. His mother had left a light burning low. He stumbled once in his voyage across the floor. As he paused to listen he heard the sound of little snores coming from her room.

He lay awake for a few moments and thought of the evening. He had a pleasurable consciousness that he had made a good impression upon those fine fellows. He felt that he had spent the most delightful evening of his life.

Chapter V

Kelcey was cross in the morning. His mother had been obliged to shake him a great deal, and it had seemed to him a most unjust thing. Also, when he, blinking his eyes, had entered the kitchen, she had said: "Yeh left th' lamp burnin' all night last night, George. How many times must I tell yeh never t' leave th' lamp burnin'?"

He ate the greater part of his breakfast in silence, moodily stirring his coffee and glaring at a remote corner of the room with eyes that felt as if they had been baked. When he moved his eyelids there was a sensation that they were cracking. In his mouth there was a singular taste. It seemed to him that he had been sucking the end of a wooden spoon. Moreover, his temper was rampant within him. It sought something to devour.

Finally he said, savagely: "Damn these early hours!"

His mother jumped as if he had flung a missile at her. "Why, George—" she began.

Kelcey broke in again. "Oh, I know all that—but this gettin' up in th' mornin' so early makes me sick. Jest when a man is gettin' his mornin' nap he's gota get up. I——"

"George, dear," said his mother, "yeh know how I hate yeh t' swear, dear. Now please don't." She looked beseechingly at him.

He made a swift gesture. "Well, I ain't swearin', am I?" he demanded. "I was on'y sayin' that this gettin'-up business gives me a pain, wasn't I?"

"Well, yeh know how swearin' hurts me," protested the little old woman. She seemed about to sob. She gazed off retrospectively. She apparently was recalling persons who had never been profane.

"I don't see where yeh ever caught this way a' swearin' out at everything," she continued, presently. "Fred, ner John, ner Willie never swore a bit. Ner Tom neither, except when he was real mad."

The son made another gesture. It was directed into the air, as if he saw there a phantom injustice. "Oh, good thunder," he said, with an accent of despair. Thereupon, he relapsed into a mood of silence. He sombrely regarded his plate.

This demeanor speedily reduced his mother to meekness. When she spoke again it was in a conciliatory voice. "George, dear, won't yeh bring some sugar home t'-night?" It could be seen that she was asking for a crown of gold.

Kelcey aroused from his semi-slumber. "Yes, if I kin remember it," he said.

The little old woman arose to stow her son's lunch into the pail. When he had finished his breakfast he stalked for a time about the room in a dignified way. He put on his coat and hat, and taking his lunch-pail went to the door. There he halted, and without turning his head, stiffly said: "Well, good-by!"

The little old woman saw that she had offended her son. She did not seek an explanation. She was accustomed to these phenomena. She made haste to surrender.

"Ain't yeh goin' t' kiss me good-by," she asked in a little woful voice.

The youth made a pretence of going on, deaf-heartedly. He wore the dignity of an injured monarch.

Then the little old woman called again in forsaken accents: "George—George—ain't yeh goin' t' kiss me good-by?" When he moved he found that she was hanging to his coat-tails.

He turned eventually with a murmur of a sort of tenderness. "Why, 'a course I am," he said. He kissed her. Withal there was an undertone of superiority in his voice, as if he were granting an astonishing suit. She looked at him with reproach and gratitude and affection.

She stood at the head of the stairs and watched his hand sliding along the rail as he went down. Occasionally she could see his arm and part of his shoulder. When he reached the first floor she called to him: "Good-by!"

The little old woman went back to her work in the kitchen with a frown of perplexity upon her brow. "I wonder what was th' matter with George this mornin'," she mused. "He didn't seem a bit like himself!"

As she trudged to and fro at her labor she began to speculate. She was much worried. She surmised in a vague way that he was a sufferer from a great internal disease. It was something no doubt that devoured the kidneys or quietly fed upon the lungs. Later, she imagined a woman, wicked and fair, who had fascinated him and was turning his life into a bitter thing. Her mind created many wondrous influences that were swooping like green dragons at him. They were changing him to a morose man, who suffered silently. She longed to discover them, that she might go bravely to the rescue of her heroic son. She knew that he, generous in his pain, would keep it from her. She racked her mind for knowledge.

However, when he came home at night he was extraordinarily blithe. He seemed to be a lad of ten. He capered all about the room. When she was bringing the coffee-pot from the stove to the table, he made show of waltzing with her so that she spilled some of the coffee. She was obliged to scold him.

All through the meal he made jokes. She occasionally was compelled to laugh, despite the fact that she believed that she should not laugh at her own son's jokes. She uttered reproofs at times, but he did not regard them.

"Golly," he said once, "I feel fine as silk. I didn't think I'd get over feelin' bad so quick. It——" He stopped abruptly.

During the evening he sat content. He smoked his pipe and read from an evening paper. She bustled about at her work. She seemed utterly happy with him there, lazily puffing out little clouds of smoke and giving frequent brilliant dissertations upon the news of the day. It seemed to her that she must be a model mother to have such a son, one who came home to her at night and sat contented, in a languor of the muscles after a good day's toil. She pondered upon the science of her management.

The week thereafter, too, she was joyous, for he stayed at home each night of it, and was sunny-tempered. She became convinced that she was a perfect mother, rearing a perfect son. There came often a love-light into her eyes. The wrinkled, yellow face frequently warmed into a smile of the kind that a maiden bestows upon him who to her is first and perhaps last.

Chapter VI

The little old woman habitually discouraged all outbursts of youthful vanity upon the part of her son. She feared that he would get to think too much of himself, and she knew that nothing could do more harm. Great self-esteem was always passive, she thought, and if he grew to regard his qualities of mind as forming a dazzling constellation, he would tranquilly sit still and not do those wonders she expected of him. So she was constantly on the alert to suppress even a shadow of such a thing. As for him he ruminated with the savage, vengeful bitterness of a young man, and decided that she did not comprehend him.

But despite her precautions he often saw that she believed him to be the most marvellous young man on the earth. He had only to look at those two eyes that became lighted with a glow from her heart whenever he did some excessively brilliant thing. On these occasions he could see her glance triumphantly at a neighbor, or whoever happened to be present. He grew to plan for these glances. And then he took a vast satisfaction in detecting and appropriating them.

Nevertheless, he could not understand why, directly after a scene of this kind, his mother was liable to call to him to hang his coat on the hook under the mantel, her voice in a key of despair as if he were negligent and stupid in what was, after all, the only important thing in life.

"If yeh'll only get in the habit of doin' it, it'll be jest as easy as throwin' it down anywheres," she would say to him. "When yeh pitch it down anywheres, somebody's got t' pick it up, an' that'll most likely be your poor ol' mother. Yeh can hang it up yerself, if yeh'll on'y think." This was intolerable. He usually went then and hurled his coat savagely at the hook. The correctness of her position was maddening.

It seemed to him that anyone who had a son of his glowing attributes should overlook the fact that he seldom hung up his coat. It was impossible to explain this situation to his mother. She was unutterably narrow. He grew sullen.

There came a time, too, that, even in all his mother's tremendous admiration for him, he did not entirely agree with her. He was delighted that she liked his great wit. He spurred himself to new and flashing effort because of this appreciation. But for the greater part he could see that his mother took pride in him in quite a different way from that in which he took pride in himself. She rejoiced at qualities in him that indicated that he was going to become a white and looming king among men. From these she made pictures in which he appeared as a benign personage, blessed by the filled hands of the poor, one whose brain could hold massive thoughts and awe certain men about whom she had read. She was fêted as the mother of this enormous man. These dreams were her solace. She spoke of them to no one because she knew that, worded, they would be ridiculous. But she dwelt with them, and they shed a radiance of gold upon her long days, her sorry labor. Upon the dead altars of her life she had builded the little fires of hope for another.

He had a complete sympathy for as much as he understood of these thoughts of his mother. They were so wise that he admired her foresight. As for himself, however, most of his dreams were of a nearer time. He had many of the distant future when he would be a man with a cloak of coldness concealing his gentleness and his faults, and of whom the men and, more particularly, the women, would think with reverence. He agreed with his mother that at that time he would go through the obstacles to other men like a flung stone. And then he would have power and he would enjoy having his bounty and his wrath alike fall swiftly upon those below. They would be awed. And above all he would mystify them.

But then his nearer dreams were a multitude. He had begun to look at the great world revolving near to his nose. He had a vast curiosity concerning this city in whose complexities he was buried. It was an impenetrable mystery, this city. It was a blend of many enticing colors. He longed to comprehend it completely, that he might walk understandingly in its greatest marvels, its mightiest march of life, its sin. He dreamed of a comprehension whose pay was the admirable attitude of a man of knowledge. He remembered Jones. He could not help but admire a man who knew so many bartenders.

Chapter VII

An indefinite woman was in all of Kelcey's dreams. As a matter of fact it was not he whom he pictured as wedding her. It was a vision of himself greater, finer, more terrible. It was himself as he expected to be. In scenes which he took mainly from pictures, this vision conducted a courtship, strutting, posing, and lying through a drama which was magnificent from glow of purple. In it he was icy, self-possessed; but she, the dream-girl, was consumed by wild, torrential passion. He went to the length of having her display it before the people. He saw them wonder at his tranquillity. It amazed them infinitely to see him remain cold before the glory of this peerless woman's love. She was to him as beseeching for affection as a pet animal, but still he controlled appearances and none knew of his deep abiding love. Some day, at the critical romantic time, he was going to divulge it. In these long dreams there were accessories of castle-like houses, wide lands, servants, horses, clothes.

They began somewhere in his childhood. When he ceased to see himself as a stern general pointing a sword at the nervous and abashed horizon, he became this sublime king of a vague woman's heart. Later when he had read some books, it all achieved clearer expression. He was told in them that there was a goddess in the world whose business it was to wait until he should exchange a glance with her. It became a creed, subtly powerful. It saved discomfort for him and for several women who flitted by him. He used her as a standard.

Often he saw the pathos of her long wait, but his faith did not falter. The world was obliged to turn gold in time. His life was to be fine and heroic, else he would not have been born. He believed that the common-place lot was the sentence, the doom of certain people who did not know how to feel. His blood was a tender current of life. He thought that the usual should fall to others whose nerves were of lead. Occasionally he wondered how fate was going to begin in making an enormous figure of him; but he had no doubt of the result. A chariot of pink clouds was coming for him. His faith was his reason for existence. Meanwhile he could dream of the indefinite woman and the fragrance of roses that came from her hair.

One day he met Maggie Johnson on the stairs. She had a pail of beer in one hand and a brown-paper parcel under her arm. She glanced at him. He discovered that it would wither his heart to see another man signally successful in the smiles of her. And the glance that she gave him was so indifferent and so unresponsive to the sudden vivid admiration in his own eyes that he immediately concluded that she was magnificent in two ways.

As she came to the landing, the light from a window passed in a silver gleam over the girlish roundness of her cheek. It was a thing that he remembered.

He was silent for the most part at supper that night. He was particularly unkind when he did speak. His mother, observing him apprehensively, tried in vain to picture the new terrible catastrophe. She eventually concluded that he did not like the beef-stew. She put more salt in it.

He saw Maggie quite frequently after the meeting upon the stairs. He reconstructed his dreams and placed her in the full glory of that sun. The dream-woman, the goddess, pitched from her pedestal, lay prostrate, unheeded, save when he brought her forth to call her insipid and childish in the presence of his new religion.

He was relatively happy sometimes when Maggie's mother would get drunk and make terrific uproars. He used then to sit in the dark and make scenes in which he rescued the girl from her hideous environment.

He laid clever plans by which he encountered her in the halls, at the door, on the street. When he succeeded in meeting her he was always overcome by the thought that the whole thing was obvious to her. He could feel the shame of it burn his face and neck. To prove to her that she was mistaken he would turn away his head or regard her with a granite stare.

After a time he became impatient of the distance between them. He saw looming princes who would aim to seize her. Hours of his leisure and certain hours of his labor he spent in contriving. The shade of this girl was with him continually. With her he built his grand dramas so that he trod in clouds, the matters of his daily life obscured and softened by a mist.

He saw that he need only break down the slight conventional barriers and she would soon discover his noble character. Sometimes he could see it all in his mind. It was very skilful. But then his courage flew away at the supreme moment. Perhaps the whole affair was humorous to her. Perhaps she was watching his mental contortions. She might laugh. He felt that he would then die or kill her. He could not approach the dread moment. He sank often from the threshold of knowledge. Directly after these occasions, it was his habit to avoid her to prove that she was a cipher to him.

He reflected that if he could only get a chance to rescue her from something, the whole tragedy would speedily unwind.

He met a young man in the halls one evening who said to him: "Say, me frien', where d' d' Johnson birds live in heh? I can't fin' me feet in dis bloomin' joint. I been battin' round heh fer a half-hour."

"Two flights up," said Kelcey stonily. He had felt a sudden quiver of his heart. The grandeur of the clothes, the fine worldly air, the experience, the self-reliance, the courage that shone in the

countenance of this other young man made him suddenly sink to
the depths of woe. He stood listening in the hall, flushing and
ashamed of it, until he heard them coming down-stairs together.
He slunk away then. It would have been a horror to him if she
had discovered him there. She might have felt sorry for him.

They were going out to a show, perhaps. That pig of the world
in his embroidered cloak was going to dazzle her with splendor.
He mused upon how unrighteous it was for other men to dazzle
women with splendor.

As he appreciated his handicap he swore with savage, vengeful bitterness. In his home his mother raised her voice in a high
key of monotonous irritability. "Hang up yer coat, can't yeh,
George?" she cried at him. "I can't go round after yeh all th'
time. It's jest as easy t' hang it up as it is t' throw it down that
way. Don't yeh ever git tired 'a hearin' me yell at yeh!"

"Yes," he exploded. In this word he put a profundity of sudden anger. He turned toward his mother a face, red, seamed,
hard with hate and rage. They stared a moment in silence. Then
she turned and staggered toward her room. Her hip struck violently against the corner of the table during this blind passage. A
moment later the door closed.

Kelcey sank down in a chair with his legs thrust out straight
and his hands deep in his trousers' pockets. His chin was forward
upon his breast and his eyes stared before him. There swept over
him all the self-pity that comes when the soul is turned back from
a road.

Chapter VIII

During the next few days Kelcey suffered from his first gloomy conviction that the earth was not grateful to him for his presence upon it. When sharp words were said to him, he interpreted them with what seemed to be a lately acquired insight. He could now perceive that the universe hated him. He sank to the most sublime depths of despair.

One evening of this period he met Jones. The latter rushed upon him with enthusiasm. "Why, yer jest th' man I wanted t' see! I was comin' round t' your place t'-night. Lucky I met yeh! Ol' Bleecker's goin' t' give a blow-out t'-morrah night. Anything yeh want t' drink! All th' boys'll be there an' everything. He tol' me expressly that he wanted yeh t' be there. Great time! Great! Can yeh come?"

Kelcey grasped the other's hand with fervor. He felt now that there was some solacing friendship in space. "You bet I will, ol' man," he said, huskily. "I'd like nothin' better in th' world!"

As he walked home he thought that he was a very grim figure. He was about to taste the delicious revenge of a partial self-destruction. The universe would regret its position when it saw him drunk.

He was a little late in getting to Bleecker's lodging. He was delayed while his mother read aloud a letter from an old uncle, who wrote in one place: "God bless the boy! Bring him up to be the man his father was." Bleecker lived in an old three-storied house on a side-street. A Jewish tailor lived and worked in the front parlor, and old Bleecker lived in the back parlor. A German, whose family took care of the house, occupied the basement. Another German, with a wife and eight children, rented the dining-room. The two upper floors were inhabited by tailors, dressmakers, a pedler, and mysterious people who were seldom seen. The door of the little hall-bedroom, at the foot of the second flight, was always open, and in there could be seen two bended men who worked at mending opera-glasses. The German woman in the dining-room was not friends with the little dressmaker in the rear room of the third floor, and frequently they yelled the vilest names up and down between the balusters. Each part of the woodwork was scratched and rubbed by the contact of innumerable persons. In one wall there was a long slit with chipped edges, celebrating the time when a man had thrown a hatchet at his wife. In the lower hall there was an eternal woman, with a rag and a pail of suds, who knelt over the worn oil-cloth. Old Bleecker felt that he had quite respectable and high-class apartments. He was glad to invite his friends.

Bleecker met Kelcey in the hall. He wore a collar that was cleaner and higher than his usual one. It changed his appearance greatly. He was now formidably aristocratic. "How are yeh, ol' man?" he shouted. He grasped Kelcey's arm, and, babbling jovially, conducted him down the hall and into the ex-parlor.

A group of standing men made vast shadows in the yellow glare of the lamp. They turned their heads as the two entered. "Why, hello, Kelcey, ol' man," Jones exclaimed, coming rapidly forward. "Good fer you! Glad yeh come! Yeh know O'Connor, 'a course! An' Schmidt! an' Woods! Then there's Zeusentell! Mr. Zeusentell—my friend Mr. Kelcey! Shake hands—both good fellows, damnitall! Then here is—oh, gentlemen, my friend Mr. Kelcey! A good fellow, he is, too! I've known 'im since I was a kid! Come, have a drink!" Everybody was excessively amiable. Kelcey felt that he had social standing. The strangers were cautious and respectful.

"By all means," said old Bleecker. "Mr. Kelcey, have a drink! An' by th' way, gentlemen, while we're about it, let's all have a drink!" There was much laughter. Bleecker was so droll at times.

With mild and polite gesturing they marched up to the table. There were upon it a keg of beer, a long row of whiskey bottles, a little heap of corn-cob pipes, some bags of tobacco, a box of cigars, and a mighty collection of glasses, cups, and mugs. Old Bleecker had arranged them so deftly that they resembled a primitive bar. There was considerable scuffling for possession of the cracked cups. Jones politely but vehemently insisted upon drinking from the worst of the assortment. He was quietly opposed by others. Everybody showed that they were awed by Bleecker's lavish hospitality. Their demeanors expressed their admiration at the cost of this entertainment.

Kelcey took his second mug of beer away to a corner and sat down with it. He wished to socially reconnoitre. Over in a corner a man was telling a story, in which at intervals he grunted like a pig. A half dozen men were listening. Two or three others sat alone in isolated places. They looked expectantly bright, ready to burst out cordially if anyone should address them. The row of bottles made quaint shadows upon the table, and upon a sidewall the keg of beer created a portentous black figure that reared toward the ceiling, hovering over the room and its inmates with spectral stature. Tobacco-smoke lay in lazy cloud-banks overhead.

Jones and O'Connor stayed near the table, occasionally being affable in all directions. Kelcey saw old Bleecker go to them and heard him whisper: "Come, we must git th' thing started. Git th' thing started." Kelcey saw that the host was fearing that all were not having a good time. Jones conferred with O'Connor and then O'Connor went to the man named Zeusentell. O'Connor evidently proposed something. Zeusentell refused at once. O'Connor beseeched. Zeusentell remained implacable. At last O'Connor broke off his argument, and going to the centre of the room, held up his hand. "Gentlemen," he shouted loudly, "we will now have a recitation by Mr. Zeusentell, entitled

'Patrick Clancy's Pig'!" He then glanced triumphantly at Zeusentell and said: "Come on!" Zeusentell had been twisting and making pantomimic appeals. He said, in a reproachful whisper: "You son of a gun."

The men turned their heads to glance at Zeusentell for a moment and then burst into a sustained clamor. "Hurray! Let 'er go! Come—give it t' us! Spring it! Spring it! Let it come!" As Zeusentell made no advances, they appealed personally. "Come, ol' man, let 'er go! Whatter yeh 'fraid of? Let 'er go! Go ahn! Hurry up!"

Zeusentell was protesting with almost frantic modesty. O'Connor took him by the lapel and tried to drag him; but he leaned back, pulling at his coat and shaking his head. "No, no, I don't know it, I tell yeh! I can't! I don't know it! I tell yeh I don't know it! I've forgotten it, I tell yeh! No—no—no—no. Ah, say, looka-here, le' go me, can't yeh? What's th' matter with yeh? I tell yeh I don't know it!" The men applauded violently. O'Connor did not relent. A little battle was waged until all of a sudden Zeusentell was seen to grow wondrously solemn. A hush fell upon the men. He was about to begin. He paused in the middle of the floor and nervously adjusted his collar and cravat. The audience became grave. " 'Patrick Clancy's Pig,' " announced Zeusentell in a shrill, dry, unnatural tone. And then he began in rapid sing-song:

"Patrick Clancy had a pig
Th' pride uv all th' nation,
The half uv him was half as big
As half uv all creation——"

When he concluded the others looked at each other to convey their appreciation. They then wildly clapped their hands or tinkled their glasses. As Zeusentell went toward his seat a man leaned over and asked: "Can yeh tell me where I kin git that." He had made a great success. After an enormous pressure he was induced to recite two more tales. Old Bleecker finally led him forward and pledged him in a large drink. He declared that they were the best things he had ever heard.

The efforts of Zeusentell imparted a gayety to the company. The men having laughed together were better acquainted, and there was now a universal topic. Some of the party, too, began to be quite drunk.

The invaluable O'Connor brought forth a man who could play the mouth-organ. The latter, after wiping his instrument upon his coat-sleeve, played all the popular airs. The men's heads swayed to and fro in the clouded smoke. They grinned and beat time with their feet. A valor, barbaric and wild, began to show in their poses and in their faces, red and glistening from perspiration. The conversation resounded in a hoarse roar. The beer would not run rapidly enough for Jones, so he remained behind to tilt the keg. This caused the black shadow on the wall to retreat and advance, sinking mystically to loom forward again with sudden menace, a huge dark figure controlled, as by some unknown emotion. The glasses, mugs, and cups travelled swift and regular, catching orange reflections from the lamp-light. Two or three men were grown so careless that they were continually spilling their drinks. Old Bleecker, cackling with pleasure, seized time to glance triumphantly at Jones. His party was going to be a success.

Chapter IX

Of a sudden Kelcey felt the buoyant thought that he was having a good time. He was all at once an enthusiast, as if he were at a festival of a religion. He felt that there was something fine and thrilling in this affair isolated from a stern world, and from which the laughter arose like incense. He knew that old sentiment of brotherly regard for those about him. He began to converse tenderly with them. He was not sure of his drift of thought, but he knew that he was immensely sympathetic. He rejoiced at their faces, shining red and wrinkled with smiles. He was capable of heroisms.

His pipe irritated him by going out frequently. He was too busy in amiable conversations to attend to it. When he arose to go for a match he discovered that his legs were a trifle uncertain under him. They bended and did not precisely obey his intent. At the table he lit a match and then, in laughing at a joke made near him, forgot to apply it to the bowl of his pipe. He succeeded with the next match after annoying trouble. He swayed so that the match would appear first on one side of the bowl and then on the other. At last he happily got it directly over the tobacco. He had burned his fingers. He inspected them, laughing vaguely.

Jones came and slapped him on the shoulder. "Well, ol' man, let's take a drink fer ol' Handyville's sake!"

Kelcey was deeply affected. He looked at Jones with moist

eyes. "I'll go yeh," he said. With an air of profound melancholy, Jones poured out some whiskey. They drank reverently. They exchanged a glistening look of tender recollections and then went over to where Bleecker was telling a humorous story to a circle of giggling listeners. The old man sat like a fat, jolly god. "—and just at that moment th' old woman put her head out of th' window an' said: 'Mike, yez lezy divil, fer phwat do yez be slapin' in me new geranium bid?' An' Mike woke up an' said: 'Domn a washwoman thot do niver wash her own bidclues. Here do I be slapin' in nothin' but dhirt an' wades.' " The men slapped their knees, roaring loudly. They begged him to tell another. A clamor of comment arose concerning the anecdote, so that when old Bleecker began a fresh one nobody was heeding.

It occurred to Jones to sing. Suddenly he burst forth with a ballad that had a rippling waltz movement, and seizing Kelcey, made a furious attempt to dance. They sprawled over a pair of outstretched legs and pitched headlong. Kelcey fell with a yellow crash. Blinding lights flashed before his vision. But he arose immediately, laughing. He did not feel at all hurt. The pain in his head was rather pleasant.

Old Bleecker, O'Connor, and Jones, who now limped and drew breath through his teeth, were about to lead him with much care and tenderness to the table for another drink, but he laughingly pushed them away and went unassisted. Bleecker told him: "Great Gawd, your head struck hard enough t' break a trunk."

He laughed again, and with a show of steadiness and courage he poured out an extravagant portion of whiskey. With cold muscles he put it to his lips and drank it. It chanced that this addition dazed him like a powerful blow. A moment later it affected him with blinding and numbing power. Suddenly unbalanced, he felt the room sway. His blurred sight could only distinguish a tumbled mass of shadow through which the beams from the light ran like swords of flame. The sound of the many voices was to him like the roar of a distant river. Still, he felt that if he could only annul the force of these million winding fingers that

gripped his senses, he was capable of most brilliant and enter-
taining things.

He was at first of the conviction that his feelings were only
temporary. He waited for them to pass away, but the mental and
physical pause only caused a new reeling and swinging of the
room. Chasms with inclined approaches were before him; peaks
leaned toward him. And withal he was blind and numb with surprise. He understood vaguely in his stupefaction that it would
disgrace him to fall down a chasm.

At last he perceived a shadow, a form, which he knew to be
Jones. The adorable Jones, the supremely wise Jones, was walking in this strange land without fear or care, erect and tranquil.
Kelcey murmured in admiration and affection, and fell toward
his friend. Jones's voice sounded as from the shores of the unknown. "Come, come, ol' man, this will never do. Brace up." It
appeared after all that Jones was not wholly wise. "Oh, I'm—all
ri' Jones! I'm all ri'! I wan' shing song! Tha's all! I wan' shing
song!"

Jones was stupid. "Come now, sit down an' shut up."

It made Kelcey burn with fury. "Jones, le' me alone, I tell yeh!
Le' me alone! I wan' shing song er te' story! G'l'm'n, I lovsh girl
live down my shtreet. Thash reason 'm drunk, 'tis! She——"

Jones seized him and dragged him toward a chair. He heard
him laugh. He could not endure these insults from his friend. He
felt a blazing desire to strangle his companion. He threw out his
hand violently, but Jones grappled him close and he was no more
than a dried leaf. He was amazed to find that Jones possessed the
strength of twenty horses. He was forced skilfully to the floor.

As he lay, he reflected in great astonishment upon Jones's mus-
cle. It was singular that he had never before discovered it. The
whole incident had impressed him immensely. An idea struck him
that he might denounce Jones for it. It would be a sage thing.
There would be a thrilling and dramatic moment in which he
would dazzle all the others. But at this moment he was assailed
by a mighty desire to sleep. Sombre and soothing clouds of slum-

ber were heavily upon him. He closed his eyes with a sigh that was yet like that of a babe.

When he awoke, there was still the battleful clamor of the revel. He half arose with a plan of participating, when O'Connor came and pushed him down again, throwing out his chin in affectionate remonstrance and saying, "Now, now," as to a child.

The change that had come over these men mystified Kelcey in a great degree. He had never seen anything so vastly stupid as their idea of his state. He resolved to prove to them that they were dealing with one whose mind was very clear. He kicked and squirmed in O'Connor's arms, until, with a final wrench, he scrambled to his feet and stood tottering in the middle of the room. He would let them see that he had a strangely lucid grasp of events. "G'l'm'n, I lovsh girl! I ain' drunker'n yeh all are! She——"

He felt them hurl him to a corner of the room and pile chairs and tables upon him until he was buried beneath a stupendous mountain. Far above, as up a mine's shaft, there were voices, lights, and vague figures. He was not hurt physically, but his feelings were unutterably injured. He, the brilliant, the good, the sympathetic had been thrust fiendishly from the party. They had had the comprehension of red lobsters. It was an unspeakable barbarism. Tears welled piteously from his eyes. He planned long diabolical explanations!

Chapter X

At first the gray lights of dawn came timidly into the room, remaining near the windows, afraid to approach certain sinister corners. Finally, mellow streams of sunshine poured in, undraping the shadows to disclose the putrefaction, making pitiless revelation. Kelcey awoke with a groan of undirected misery. He tossed his stiffened arms about his head for a moment and then leaning heavily upon his elbow stared blinking at his environment. The grim truthfulness of the day showed disaster and death. After the tumults of the previous night the interior of this room resembled a decaying battle-field. The air hung heavy and stifling with the odors of tobacco, men's breaths, and beer half filling forgotten glasses. There was ruck of broken tumblers, pipes, bottles, spilled tobacco, cigar stumps. The chairs and tables were pitched this way and that way, as after some terrible struggle. In the midst of it all lay old Bleecker stretched upon a couch in deepest sleep, as abandoned in attitude, as motionless, as ghastly as if it were a corpse that had been flung there.

A knowledge of the thing came gradually into Kelcey's eyes. He looked about him with an expression of utter woe, regret, and loathing. He was compelled to lie down again. A pain above his eyebrows was like that from an iron-clamp.

As he lay pondering, his bodily condition created for him a bitter philosophy, and he perceived all the futility of a red existence.

He saw his life problems confronting him like granite giants and he was no longer erect to meet them. He had made a calamitous retrogression in his war. Spectres were to him now as large as clouds.

Inspired by the pitiless ache in his head, he was prepared to reform and live a white life. His stomach informed him that a good man was the only being who was wise. But his perception of his future was hopeless. He was aghast at the prospect of the old routine. It was impossible. He trembled before its exactions.

Turning toward the other way, he saw that the gold portals of vice no longer enticed him. He could not hear the strains of alluring music. The beckoning sirens of drink had been killed by this pain in his head. The desires of his life suddenly lay dead like mullein stalks. Upon reflection, he saw, therefore, that he was perfectly willing to be virtuous if somebody would come and make it easy for him.

When he stared over at old Bleecker, he felt a sudden contempt and dislike for him. He considered him to be a tottering old beast. It was disgusting to perceive aged men so weak in sin. He dreaded to see him awaken lest he should be required to be somewhat civil to him.

Kelcey wished for a drink of water. For some time he had dreamed of the liquid, deliciously cool. It was an abstract, uncontained thing that poured upon him and tumbled him, taking away his pain like a kind of surgery. He arose and staggered slowly toward a little sink in a corner of the room. He understood that any rapid movement might cause his head to split.

The little sink was filled with a chaos of broken glass and spilled liquids. A sight of it filled him with horror, but he rinsed a glass with scrupulous care, and filling it, took an enormous drink. The water was an intolerable disappointment. It was insipid and weak to his scorched throat and not at all cool. He put down the glass with a gesture of despair. His face became fixed in the stony and sullen expression of a man who waits for the recuperative power of morrows.

Old Bleecker awakened. He rolled over and groaned loudly. For awhile he thrashed about in a fury of displeasure at his bodily stiffness and pain. Kelcey watched him as he would have watched a death agony. "Good Gawd," said the old man, "beer an' whiskey make th' devil of a mix. Did yeh see th' fight?"

"No," said Kelcey, stolidly.

"Why, Zeusentell an' O'Connor had a great old mill. They were scrappin' all over th' place. I thought we were all goin' t' get pulled. Thompson, that fellah over in th' corner, though, he sat down on th' whole business. He was a dandy! He had t' poke Zeusentell! He was a bird! Lord, I wish I had a Manhattan!"

Kelcey remained in bitter silence while old Bleecker dressed. "Come an' get a cocktail," said the latter briskly. This was part of his aristocracy. He was the only man of them who knew much about cocktails. He perpetually referred to them. "It'll brace yeh right up! Come along! Say, you get full too soon. You oughter wait until later, me boy! You're too speedy!" Kelcey wondered vaguely where his companion had lost his zeal for polished sentences, his iridescent mannerisms.

"Come along," said Bleecker.

Kelcey made a movement of disdain for cocktails, but he followed the other to the street. At the corner they separated. Kelcey attempted a friendly parting smile and then went on up the street. He had to reflect to know that he was erect and using his own muscles in walking. He felt like a man of paper, blown by the winds. Withal, the dust of the avenue was galling to his throat, eyes, and nostrils, and the roar of traffic cracked his head. He was glad, however, to be alone, to be rid of old Bleecker. The sight of him had been as the contemplation of a disease.

His mother was not at home. In his little room he mechanically undressed and bathed his head, arms, and shoulders. When he crawled between the two white sheets he felt a first lifting of his misery. His pillow was soothingly soft. There was an effect that was like the music of tender voices.

When he awoke again his mother was bending over him giving

vent to alternate cries of grief and joy. Her hands trembled so
that they were useless to her. "Oh, George, George, where have
yeh been? What has happened t' yeh? Oh, George, I've been so
worried! I didn't sleep a wink all night."

Kelcey was instantly wide awake. With a moan of suffering
he turned his face to the wall before he spoke. "Never mind,
mother, I'm all right. Don't fret now! I was knocked down by a
truck last night in th' street, an' they took me t' th' hospital; but
it's all right now. I got out jest a little while ago. They told me I'd
better go home an' rest up."

His mother screamed in pity, horror, joy, and self-reproach for
something unknown. She frenziedly demanded the details. He
sighed with unutterable weariness. "Oh—wait—wait—wait," he
said shutting his eyes as from the merciless monotony of a pain.
"Wait—wait—please wait. I can't talk now. I want t' rest."

His mother condemned herself with a little cry. She adjusted
his pillow, her hands shaking with love and tenderness. "There,
there, don't mind, dearie! But yeh can't think how worried I
was—an' crazy. I was near frantic. I went down t' th' shop, an'
they said they hadn't seen anything 'a yeh there. The foreman
was awful good t' me. He said he'd come up this afternoon t' see
if yeh had come home yet. He tol' me not t' worry. Are yeh sure
yer all right? Ain't there anythin' I kin git fer yeh? What did th'
docter say?"

Kelcey's patience was worn. He gestured, and then spoke
querulously. "Now—now—mother, it's all right, I tell yeh! All I
need is a little rest an' I'll be as well as ever. But it makes it all th'
worse if yeh stand there an' ask me questions an' make me think.
Jest leave me alone fer a little while, an' I'll be as well as ever.
Can't yeh do that?"

The little old woman puckered her lips funnily. "My, what an
old bear th' boy is!" She kissed him blithely. Presently she went
out, upon her face a bright and glad smile that must have been a
reminiscence of some charming girlhood.

Chapter XI

At one time Kelcey had a friend who was struck in the head by the pole of a truck and knocked senseless. He was taken to the hospital, from which he emerged in the morning an astonished man, with rather a dim recollection of the accident. He used to hold an old brier-wood pipe in his teeth in a manner peculiar to himself, and, with a brown derby hat tilted back on his head, recount his strange sensations. Kelcey had always remembered it as a bit of curious history. When his mother cross-examined him in regard to the accident, he told this story with barely a variation. Its truthfulness was incontestable.

At the shop he was welcomed on the following day with considerable enthusiasm. The foreman had told the story and there were already jokes created concerning it. Mike O'Donnell, whose wit was famous, had planned a humorous campaign, in which he made charges against Kelcey, which were, as a matter of fact, almost the exact truth. Upon hearing it, Kelcey looked at him suddenly from the corners of his eyes, but otherwise remained imperturbable. O'Donnell eventually despaired. "Yez can't goiy that kid! He tekes ut all loike mate an' dhrink." Kelcey often told the story, his pipe held in his teeth peculiarly, and his derby tilted back on his head.

He remained at home for several evenings, content to read the papers and talk with his mother. She began to look around for the tremendous reason for it. She suspected that his nearness to death in the recent accident had sobered his senses and made him think of high things. She mused upon it continually. When he sat moodily pondering she watched him. She said to herself that she saw the light breaking in upon his spirit. She felt that it was a very critical period of his existence. She resolved to use all her power and skill to turn his eyes toward the lights in the sky. Accordingly she addressed him one evening. "Come, go t' prayer-meetin' t'-night with me, will yeh, George?" It sounded more blunt than she intended.

He glanced at her in sudden surprise. "Huh?"

As she repeated her request, her voice quavered. She felt that it was a supreme moment. "Come, go t' prayer-meetin' t'-night, won't yeh?"

He seemed amazed. "Oh, I don't know," he began. He was fumbling in his mind for a reason for refusing. "I don't wanta go. I'm tired as th' dickens!" His obedient shoulders sank down languidly. His head mildly drooped.

The little old woman, with a quick perception of her helplessness, felt a motherly rage at her son. It was intolerable that she could not impart motion to him in a chosen direction. The waves of her desires were puny against the rocks of his indolence. She had a great wish to beat him. "I don't know what I'm ever goin' t' do with yeh," she told him, in a choking voice. "Yeh won't do anything I ask yeh to. Yeh never pay th' least bit 'a attention t' what I say. Yeh don't mind me any more than yeh would a fly. Whatever am I goin' t' do with yeh?" She faced him in a battleful way, her eyes blazing with a sombre light of despairing rage.

He looked up at her ironically. "I don't know," he said, with calmness. "What are yeh?" He had traced her emotions and seen her fear of his rebellion. He thrust out his legs in the easy scorn of a rapier-bravo. "What are yeh?"

The little old woman began to weep. They were tears without a shame of grief. She allowed them to run unheeded down her cheeks. As she stared into space her son saw her regarding there the powers and influences that she had held in her younger life. She was in some way acknowledging to fate that she was now but withered grass, with no power but the power to feel the winds. He was smitten with a sudden shame. Besides, in the last few days he had gained quite a character for amiability. He saw something grand in relenting at this point. "Well," he said, trying to remove a sulky quality from his voice, "well, if yer bound t' have me go, I s'pose I'll have t' go."

His mother, with strange, immobile face, went to him and kissed him on the brow. "All right, George!" There was in her wet eyes an emotion which he could not fathom.

She put on her bonnet and shawl, and they went out together. She was unusually silent, and made him wonder why she did not appear gleeful at his coming. He was resentful because she did not display more appreciation of his sacrifice. Several times he thought of halting and refusing to go farther, to see if that would not wring from her some acknowledgment.

In a dark street the little chapel sat humbly between two towering apartment-houses. A red street-lamp stood in front. It threw a marvelous reflection upon the wet pavements. It was like the death-stain of a spirit. Farther up the brilliant lights of an avenue made a span of gold across the black street. A roar of wheels and a clangor of bells came from this point, interwoven into a sound emblematic of the life of the city. It seemed somehow to affront this solemn and austere little edifice. It suggested an approaching barbaric invasion. The little church, pierced, would die with a fine, illimitable scorn for its slayers.

When Kelcey entered with his mother he felt a sudden quaking. His knees shook. It was an awesome place to him. There was a menace in the red padded carpet and the leather doors, studded with little brass tacks that penetrated his soul with their pitiless glances. As for his mother, she had acquired such a new air that he would have been afraid to address her. He felt completely alone and isolated at this formidable time.

There was a man in the vestibule who looked at them blandly.

From within came the sound of singing. To Kelcey there was a million voices. He dreaded the terrible moment when the doors should swing back. He wished to recoil, but at that instant the bland man pushed the doors aside and he followed his mother up the centre aisle of the little chapel. To him there was a riot of lights that made him transparent. The multitudinous pairs of eyes that turned toward him were implacable in their cool valuations.

They had just ceased singing. He who conducted the meeting motioned that the services should wait until the new-comers found seats. The little old woman went slowly on toward the first rows. Occasionally she paused to scrutinize vacant places, but they did not seem to meet her requirements. Kelcey was in agony. He thought the moment of her decision would never come. In his unspeakable haste he walked a little faster than his mother. Once she paused to glance in her calculating way at some seats and he forged ahead. He halted abruptly and returned, but by that time she had resumed her thoughtful march up the aisle. He could have assassinated her. He felt that everybody must have seen his torture, during which his hands were to him like monstrous swollen hides. He was wild with a rage in which his lips turned slightly livid. He was capable of doing some furious, unholy thing.

When the little old woman at last took a seat, her son sat down beside her slowly and stiffly. He was opposing his strong desire to drop.

When from the mists of his shame and humiliation the scene came before his vision, he was surprised to find that all eyes were not fastened upon his face. The leader of the meeting seemed to be the only one who saw him. He stared gravely, solemnly, re-gretfully. He was a pale-faced, but plump young man in a black coat that buttoned to his chin. It was evident to Kelcey that his mother had spoken of him to the young clergyman, and that the latter was now impressing upon him the sorrow caused by the contemplation of his sin. Kelcey hated the man.

A man seated alone over in a corner began to sing. He closed his eyes and threw back his head. Others, scattered sparsely throughout the innumerable light-wood chairs, joined him as they caught the air. Kelcey heard his mother's frail, squeaking soprano. The chandelier in the centre was the only one lighted, and far at the end of the room one could discern the pulpit swathed in gloom, solemn and mystic as a bier. It was surrounded by vague shapes of darkness on which at times was the glint of brass, or of glass that shone like steel, until one could feel there the presence of the army of the unknown, possessors of the great eternal truths, and silent listeners at this ceremony. High up, the stained-glass windows loomed in leaden array like dull-hued banners, merely catching occasional splashes of dark wine-color from the lights. Kelcey fell to brooding concerning this indefinable presence which he felt in a church.

One by one people arose and told little tales of their religious faith. Some were tearful and others calm, emotionless, and convincing. Kelcey listened closely for a time. These people filled him with a great curiosity. He was not familiar with their types.

At last the young clergyman spoke at some length. Kelcey was amazed, because, from the young man's appearance, he would not have suspected him of being so glib; but the speech had no effect on Kelcey, excepting to prove to him again that he was damned.

Chapter XII

Kelcey sometimes wondered whether he liked beer. He had been obliged to cultivate a talent for imbibing it. He was born with an abhorrence which he had steadily battled until it had come to pass that he could drink from ten to twenty glasses of beer without the act of swallowing causing him to shiver. He understood that drink was an essential to joy, to the coveted position of a man of the world and of the streets. The saloons contained the mystery of a street for him. When he knew its saloons he comprehended the street. Drink and its surroundings were the eyes of a superb green dragon to him. He followed a fascinating glitter, and the glitter required no explanation.

Directly after old Bleecker's party he almost reformed. He was tired and worn from the tumult of it, and he saw it as one might see a skeleton emerged from a crimson cloak. He wished then to turn his face away. Gradually, however, he recovered his mental balance. Then he admitted again by his point of view that the thing was not so terrible. His headache had caused him to exaggerate. A drunk was not the blight which he had once remorsefully named it. On the contrary, it was a mere unpleasant incident. He resolved, however, to be more cautious.

When prayer-meeting night came again his mother approached him hopefully. She smiled like one whose request is already granted. "Well, will yeh go t' prayer-meetin' with me t'-night again?"

He turned toward her with eloquent suddenness, and then riveted his eyes upon a corner of the floor. "Well, I guess not," he said.

His mother tearfully tried to comprehend his state of mind. "What has come over yeh?" she said, tremblingly. "Yeh never used t' be this way, George. Yeh never used t' be so cross an' mean t' me—"

"Oh, I ain't cross an' mean t' yeh," he interpolated, exasperated and violent.

"Yes, yeh are, too! I ain't hardly had a decent word from yeh in ever so long. Yer as cross an' as mean as yeh can be. I don't know what t' make of it. It can't be—" There came a look in her eyes that told that she was going to shock and alarm him with her heaviest sentence—"it can't be that yeh've got t' drinkin'."

Kelcey grunted with disgust at the ridiculous thing. "Why, what an old goose yer gettin' t' be."

She was compelled to laugh a little, as a child laughs between tears at a hurt. She had not been serious. She was only trying to display to him how she regarded his horrifying mental state. "Oh, of course, I didn't mean that, but I think yeh act jest as bad as if yeh did drink. I wish yeh would do better, George!"

She had grown so much less frigid and stern in her censure that Kelcey seized the opportunity to try to make a joke of it. He laughed at her, but she shook her head and continued: "I do wish yeh would do better. I don't know what's t' become 'a yeh, George. Yeh don't mind what I say no more'n if I was th' wind in th' chimbly. Yeh don't care about nothin' 'cept goin' out nights. I can't ever get yeh t' prayer-meetin' ner church; yeh never go out with me anywheres unless yeh can't get out of it; yeh swear an' take on sometimes like everything, yeh never——"

He gestured wrathfully in interruption. "Say, lookahere, can't yeh think 'a something I do?"

She ended her oration then in the old way. "An' I don't know what's goin' t' become 'a yeh."

She put on her bonnet and shawl and then came and stood

near him, expectantly. She imparted to her attitude a subtle threat of unchangeableness. He pretended to be engrossed in his newspaper. The little swaggering clock on the mantel became suddenly evident, ticking with loud monotony. Presently she said, firmly: "Well, are yeh comin'?"

He was reading.

"Well, are yeh comin'?"

He threw his paper down, angrily. "Oh, why don't yeh go on an' leave me alone?" he demanded in supreme impatience. "What do yeh wanta pester me fer? Yeh'd think there was robbers. Why can't yeh go alone er else stay home? You wanta go an' I don't wanta go, an' yeh keep all time tryin' t' drag me. Yeh know I don't wanta go." He concluded in a last defiant wounding of her. "What do I care 'bout those ol' bags-'a-wind anyhow? They gimme a pain!"

His mother turned her face and went from him. He sat staring with a mechanical frown. Presently he went and picked up his newspaper.

Jones told him that night that everybody had had such a good time at old Bleecker's party that they were going to form a club. They waited at the little smiling saloon, and then amid much enthusiasm all signed a membership-roll. Old Bleecker, late that night, was violently elected president. He made speeches of thanks and gratification during the remainder of the meeting. Kelcey went home rejoicing. He felt that at any rate he would have true friends. The dues were a dollar for each week.

He was deeply interested. For a number of evenings he fairly gobbled his supper in order that he might be off to the little smiling saloon to discuss the new organization. All the men were wildly enthusiastic. One night the saloon-keeper announced that he would donate half the rent of quite a large room over his saloon. It was an occasion for great cheering. Kelcey's legs were like whalebone when he tried to go up-stairs upon his return home, and the edge of each step was moved curiously forward.

His mother's questions made him snarl. "Oh, nowheres!" At

other times he would tell her: "Oh, t' see some friends 'a mine! Where d' yeh s'pose?"

Finally, some of the women of the tenement concluded that the little old mother had a wild son. They came to condole with her. They sat in the kitchen for hours. She told them of his wit, his cleverness, his kind heart.

Chapter XIII

At a certain time Kelcey discovered that some young men who stood in the cinders between a brick wall and the pavement, and near the side-door of a corner saloon, knew more about life than other people. They used to lean there smoking and chewing, and comment upon events and persons. They knew the neighborhood extremely well. They debated upon small typical things that transpired before them until they had extracted all the information that existence contained. They sometimes inaugurated little fights with foreigners or well-dressed men. It was here that Sapristi Glielmi, the pedler, stabbed Pete Brady to death, for which he got a life-sentence. Each patron of the saloon was closely scrutinized as he entered the place. Sometimes they used to throng upon the heels of a man and in at the bar assert that he had asked them in to drink. When he objected, they would claim with one voice that it was too deep an insult and gather about to thrash him. When they had caught chance customers and absolute strangers, the barkeeper had remained in stolid neutrality, ready to serve one or seven, but two or three times they had encountered the wrong men. Finally, the proprietor had come out one morning and told them, in the fearless way of his class, that their pastime must cease. "It quits right here! See? Right here! Th' nex' time yeh try t' work it, I come with th' bung-starter, an' th' mugs I miss with it git pulled. See? It quits!" Infrequently, however, men did ask them in to drink.

The policeman of that beat grew dignified and shrewd whenever he approached this corner. Sometimes he stood with his hands behind his back and cautiously conversed with them. It was understood on both sides that it was a good thing to be civil.

In winter this band, a trifle diminished in numbers, huddled in their old coats and stamped little flat places in the snow, their faces turned always toward the changing life in the streets. In the summer they became more lively. Sometimes, then, they walked out to the curb to look up and down the street. Over in a trampled vacant lot, surrounded by high tenement-houses, there was a sort of a den among some bowlders. An old truck was made to form a shelter. The small hoodlums of that vicinity all avoided the spot. So many of them had been thrashed upon being caught near it. It was the summer-time lounging-place of the band from the corner.

They were all too clever to work. Some of them had worked, but these used their experiences as stores from which to draw tales. They were like veterans with their wars. One lad in particular used to recount how he whipped his employer, the proprietor of a large grain and feed establishment. He described his victim's features and form and clothes with minute exactness. He bragged of his wealth and social position. It had been a proud moment of the lad's life. He was like a savage who had killed a great chief.

Their feeling for contemporaneous life was one of contempt. Their philosophy taught that in a large part the whole thing was idle and a great bore. With fine scorn they sneered at the futility of it. Work was done by men who had not the courage to stand still and let the skies clap together if they willed.

The vast machinery of the popular law indicated to them that there were people in the world who wished to remain quiet. They awaited the moment when they could prove to them that a riotous upheaval, a cloud-burst of destruction would be a delicious thing. They thought of their fingers buried in the lives of these people. They longed dimly for a time when they could run through decorous streets with crash and roar of war, an army of revenge for pleasures long possessed by others, a wild sweeping compensation for their years without crystal and gilt, women and wine. This thought slumbered in them, as the image of Rome might have lain small in the hearts of the barbarians.

Kelcey respected these youths so much that he ordinarily used the other side of the street. He could not go near to them, because if a passer-by minded his own business he was a disdainful prig and had insulted them; if he showed that he was aware of them they were likely to resent his not minding his own business and prod him into a fight if the opportunity were good. Kelcey longed for their acquaintance and friendship, for with it came social safety and ease; they were respected so universally.

Once in another street Fidsey Corcoran was whipped by a short, heavy man. Fidsey picked himself up, and in the fury of defeat hurled pieces of brick at his opponent. The short man dodged with skill and then pursued Fidsey for over a block. Sometimes he got near enough to punch him. Fidsey raved in maniacal fury. The moment the short man would attempt to resume his own affairs, Fidsey would turn upon him again, tears and blood upon his face, with the lashed rage of a vanquished animal. The short man used to turn about, swear madly, and make little dashes. Fidsey always ran and then returned as pursuit ceased. The short man apparently wondered if this maniac was ever going to allow him to finish whipping him. He looked helplessly up and down the street. People were there who knew Fidsey, and they remonstrated with him; but he continued to confront the short man, gibbering like a wounded ape, using all the eloquence of the street in his wild oaths.

Finally the short man was exasperated to black fury. He decided to end the fight. With low snarls, ominous as death, he plunged at Fidsey.

Kelcey happened there then. He grasped the short man's shoulder. He cried out in the peculiar whine of the man who interferes. "Oh, hol' on! Yeh don't wanta hit 'im any more! Yeh've done enough to 'im now! Leave 'im be!"

The short man wrenched and tugged. He turned his face until

his teeth were almost at Kelcey's cheek: "Le' go me! Le' go me, you——" The rest of his sentence was screamed curses.

Kelcey's face grew livid from fear, but he somehow managed to keep his grip. Fidsey, with but an instant's pause, plunged into the new fray.

They beat the short man. They forced him against a high board-fence where for a few seconds their blows sounded upon his head in swift thuds. A moment later Fidsey descried a running policeman. He made off, fleet as a shadow. Kelcey noted his going. He ran after him.

Three or four blocks away they halted. Fidsey said: "I'd 'a licked dat big stuff in 'bout a minute more," and wiped the blood from his eyes.

At the gang's corner, they asked: "Who soaked yeh, Fidsey?" His description was burning. Everybody laughed. "Where is 'e now?" Later they began to question Kelcey. He recited a tale in which he allowed himself to appear prominent and redoubtable. They looked at him then as if they thought he might be quite a man.

Once when the little old woman was going out to buy something for her son's supper, she discovered him standing at the side-door of the saloon engaged intimately with Fidsey and the others. She slunk away, for she understood that it would be a terrible thing to confront him and his pride there with youths who were superior to mothers.

When he arrived home he threw down his hat with a weary sigh, as if he had worked long hours, but she attacked him before he had time to complete the falsehood. He listened to her harangue with a curled lip. In defence he merely made a gesture of supreme exasperation. She never understood the advanced things in life. He felt the hopelessness of ever making her comprehend. His mother was not modern.

Chapter XIV

The little old woman arose early and bustled in the preparation of breakfast. At times she looked anxiously at the clock. An hour before her son should leave for work she went to his room and called him in the usual tone of sharpness, "George! George!"

A sleepy growl came to her.

"Come, come it's time t' git up," she continued. "Come now, git right up!"

Later she went again to the door. "George, are yeh gittin' up?"

"Huh?"

"Are yeh gittin' up?"

"Yes, I'll git right up!" He had introduced a valor into his voice which she detected to be false. She went to his bedside and took him by the shoulder. "George—George—git up!"

From the mist-lands of sleep he began to protest incoherently. "Oh, le' me be, won' yeh? 'M sleepy!"

She continued to shake him. "Well, it's time t' git up. Come—come—come on, now."

Her voice, shrill with annoyance, pierced his ears in a slender, piping thread of sound. He turned over on the pillow to bury his head in his arms. When he expostulated, his tones came half-smothered. "Oh le' me be, can't yeh? There's plenty 'a time! Jest fer ten minutes! 'M sleepy!"

She was implacable. "No, yeh must git up now! Yeh ain't got more'n time enough t' eat yer breakfast an' git t' work."

Eventually he arose, sullen and grumbling. Later he came to his breakfast, blinking his dry eyelids, his stiffened features set in a mechanical scowl.

Each morning his mother went to his room, and fought a battle to arouse him. She was like a soldier. Despite his pleadings, his threats, she remained at her post, imperturbable and unyielding. These affairs assumed large proportions in his life. Sometimes he grew beside himself with a bland, unformulated wrath. The whole thing was a consummate imposition. He felt that he was being cheated of his sleep. It was an injustice to compel him to arise morning after morning with bitter regularity, before the sleep-gods had at all loosened their grasp. He hated that unknown force which directed his life.

One morning he swore a tangled mass of oaths, aimed into the air, as if the injustice poised there. His mother flinched at first; then her mouth set in the little straight line. She saw that the momentous occasion had come. It was the time of the critical battle. She turned upon him valorously. "Stop your swearin', George Kelcey. I won't have yeh talk so before me! I won't have it! Stop this minute! Not another word! Do yeh think I'll allow yeh t' swear b'fore me like that? Not another word! I won't have it! I declare I won't have it another minute!"

At first her projected words had slid from his mind as if striking against ice, but at last he heeded her. His face grew sour with passion and misery. He spoke in tones dark with dislike. "Th' 'ell yeh won't? Whatter yeh goin' t' do 'bout it?" Then, as if he considered that he had not been sufficiently impressive, he arose and slowly walked over to her. Having arrived at point-blank range he spoke again. "Whatter yeh goin' t' do 'bout it?" He regarded her then with an unaltering scowl, albeit his mien was as dark and cowering as that of a condemned criminal.

She threw out her hands in the gesture of an impotent one. He was acknowledged victor. He took his hat and slowly left her.

For three days they lived in silence. He brooded upon his mother's agony and felt a singular joy in it. As opportunity offered, he did little despicable things. He was going to make her abject. He was now uncontrolled, ungoverned; he wished to be an emperor. Her suffering was all a sort of compensation for his own dire pains.

She went about with a gray, impassive face. It was as if she had survived a massacre in which all that she loved had been torn from her by the brutality of savages.

One evening at six he entered and stood looking at his mother as she peeled potatoes. She had hearkened to his coming listlessly, without emotion, and at his entrance she did not raise her eyes.

"Well, I'm fired," he said, suddenly.

It seemed to be the final blow. Her body gave a convulsive movement in the chair. When she finally lifted her eyes, horror possessed her face. Her under jaw had fallen. "Fired? Outa work? Why—George?" He went over to the window and stood with his back to her. He could feel her gray stare upon him.

"Yep! Fired!"

At last she said, "Well—whatter yeh goin' t' do?"

He tapped the pane with his finger-nail. He answered in a tone made hoarse and unnatural by an assumption of gay carelessness, "Oh, nothin'!"

She began, then, her first weeping. "Oh—George—George— George——"

He looked at her scowling. "Ah, whatter yeh givin' us? Is this all I git when I come home f'm being fired? Anybody 'ud think it was my fault. I couldn't help it."

She continued to sob in a dull, shaking way. In the pose of her head there was an expression of her conviction that comprehension of her pain was impossible to the universe. He paused for a moment, and then, with his usual tactics, went out, slamming the door. A pale flood of sunlight, imperturbable at its vocation, streamed upon the little old woman, bowed with pain, forlorn in her chair.

Chapter XV

Kelcey was standing on the corner next day when three little boys came running. Two halted some distance away, and the other came forward. He halted before Kelcey, and spoke importantly.

"Hey, your ol' woman's sick."

"What?"

"Your ol' woman's sick."

"Git out!"

"She is, too!"

"Who tol' yeh?"

"Mis' Callahan. She said fer me t' run an' tell yeh. Dey want yeh."

A swift dread struck Kelcey. Like flashes of light little scenes from the past shot through his brain. He had thoughts of a vengeance from the clouds. As he glanced about him the familiar view assumed a meaning that was ominous and dark. There was prophecy of disaster in the street, the buildings, the sky, the people. Something tragic and terrible in the air was known to his nervous, quivering nostrils. He spoke to the little boy in a tone that quavered. "All right!"

Behind him he felt the sudden contemplative pause of his companions of the gang. They were watching him. As he went rapidly up the street he knew that they had come out to the middle of the walk and were staring after him. He was glad that they could not see his face, his trembling lips, his eyes wavering in fear. He stopped at the door of his home and stared at the panel as if he saw written thereon a word. A moment later he entered. His eye comprehended the room in a frightened glance.

His mother sat gazing out at the opposite walls and windows. She was leaning her head upon the back of the chair. Her face was overspread with a singular pallor, but the glance of her eyes was strong and the set of her lips was tranquil.

He felt an unspeakable thrill of thanksgiving at seeing her seated there calmly. "Why, mother, they said yeh was sick," he cried, going toward her impetuously. "What's th' matter?"

She smiled at him. "Oh, it ain't nothin'! I on'y got kinda dizzy, that's all." Her voice was sober and had the ring of vitality in it.

He noted her common-place air. There was no alarm or pain in her tones, but the misgivings of the street, the prophetic twinges of his nerves made him still hesitate. "Well—are you sure it ain't? They scared me 'bout t' death."

"No, it ain't anything, o'ny some sorta dizzy feelin'. I fell down b'hind th' stove. Missis Callahan, she came an' picked me up. I must 'a laid there fer quite a while. Th' docter said he guessed I'd be all right in a couple 'a hours. I don't feel nothin'!"

Kelcey heaved a great sigh of relief. "Lord, I was scared." He began to beam joyously, since he was escaped from his fright. "Why, I couldn't think what had happened," he told her.

"Well, it ain't nothin'," she said.

He stood about awkwardly, keeping his eyes fastened upon her in a sort of surprise, as if he had expected to discover that she had vanished. The reaction from his panic was a thrill of delicious contentment. He took a chair and sat down near her, but presently he jumped up to ask: "There ain't nothin' I can git fer yeh, is ther?" He looked at her eagerly. In his eyes shone love and joy. If it were not for the shame of it he would have called her endearing names.

"No, ther ain't nothin'," she answered. Presently she continued, in a conversational way, "Yeh ain't found no work yit, have yeh?"

The shadow of his past fell upon him then and he became suddenly morose. At last he spoke in a sentence that was a vow, a declaration of change. "No, I ain't, but I'm goin' t' hunt fer it hard, you bet."

She understood from his tone that he was making peace with her. She smiled at him gladly. "Yer a good boy, George!" A radiance from the stars lit her face.

Presently she asked, "D' yeh think yer old boss would take yeh on ag'in if I went t' see him?"

"No," said Kelcey, at once. "It wouldn't do no good! They got all th' men they want. There ain't no room there. It wouldn't do no good." He ceased to beam for a moment as he thought of certain disclosures. "I'm goin' t' try to git work everywheres. I'm goin' t' make a wild break t' git a job, an' if there's one anywheres I'll git it."

She smiled at him again. "That's right, George!"

When it came supper-time he dragged her in her chair over to the table and then scurried to and fro to prepare a meal for her. She laughed gleefully at him. He was awkward and densely ignorant. He exaggerated his helplessness sometimes until she was obliged to lean back in her chair to laugh. Afterward they sat by the window. Her hand rested upon his hair.

Chapter XVI

When Kelcey went to borrow money from old Bleecker, Jones and the others, he discovered that he was below them in social position. Old Bleecker said gloomily that he did not see how he could loan money at that time. When Jones asked him to have a drink, his tone was careless. O'Connor recited at length some bewildering financial troubles of his own. In them all he saw that something had been reversed. They remained silent upon many occasions, when they might have grunted in sympathy for him.

As he passed along the street near his home he perceived Fidsey Corcoran and another of the gang. They made eloquent signs. "Are yeh wid us?"

He stopped and looked at them. "What's wrong with yeh?"

"Are yeh wid us er not," demanded Fidsey. "New barkeep'! Big can! We got it over in d' lot. Big can, I tell yeh." He drew a picture in the air, so to speak, with his enthusiastic fingers.

Kelcey turned dejectedly homeward. "Oh, I guess not, this roun'."

"What's d' matter wi'che?" said Fidsey. "Yer gittin' t' be a reg'lar willie! Come ahn, I tell yeh! Youse gits one smoke at d' can b'cause yeh b'longs t' d' gang, an' yeh don't wanta give it up widout er scrap! See? Some udder john'll git yer smoke. Come ahn!"

When they arrived at the place among the bowlders in the vacant lot, one of the band had a huge and battered tin-pail tilted afar up. His throat worked convulsively. He was watched keenly and anxiously by five or six others. Their eyes followed carefully each fraction of distance that the pail was lifted. They were very silent.

Fidsey burst out violently as he perceived what was in progress. "Heh, Tim, yeh big sojer, le' go d' can! What 'a yeh tink! Wese er in dis! Le' go dat!"

He who was drinking made several angry protesting contortions of his throat. Then he put down the pail and swore. "Who's a big sojer? I ain't gittin' more'n me own smoke! Yer too bloomin' swift! Yeh'd tink yeh was d' on'y mug what owned dis can! Close yer face while I gits me smoke!"

He took breath for a moment and then returned the pail to its tilted position. Fidsey went to him and worried and clamored. He interfered so seriously with the action of drinking that the other was obliged to release the pail again for fear of choking.

Fidsey grabbed it and glanced swiftly at the contents. "Dere! Dat's what I was hollerin' at! Lookut d' beer! Not 'nough t' wet yer t'roat! Yehs can't have not'in' on d' level wid youse damn' tanks! Youse was a reg'lar resevoiy, Tim Connigan! Look what yeh lef' us! Ah, say, youse was a dandy! What 'a yeh tink we ah? Willies? Don' we want no smoke? Say, lookut dat can! It's drier'n hell! What 'a yeh tink?"

Tim glanced in at the beer. Then he said: "Well, d' mug what come b'fore me, he on'y lef' me dat much. Blue Billee, he done d' swallerin'! I on'y had a tas'e!"

Blue Billie, from his seat near, called out in wrathful protest: "Yeh lie, Tim. I never had more'n a mouf-ful!" An inspiration evidently came to him then, for his countenance suddenly brightened, and, arising, he went toward the pail. "I ain't had me reg'lar smoke yit! Guess I come in aheader Fidsey, don' I?"

Fidsey, with a sardonic smile, swung the pail behind him. "I guess nit! Not dis minnet! Youse hadger smoke. If yeh ain't, yeh don't git none. See?"

Blue Billie confronted Fidsey determinedly. "D' 'ell I don't!"

"Nit," said Fidsey.

Billie sat down again.

Fidsey drank his portion. Then he manoeuvred skilfully before the crowd until Kelcey and the other youth took their shares. "Youse er a mob 'a tanks," he told the gang. "Nobody 'ud git not'in' if dey wasn't on t' yehs!"

Blue Billie's soul had been smouldering in hate against Fidsey. "Ah, shut up! Youse ain't gota take care 'a dose two mugs, dough. Youse hadger smoke, ain't yeh? Den yer tr'u. G' home!"

"Well, I hate t' see er bloke use 'imself fer a tank," said Fidsey. "But youse don't wanta go jollyin' 'round 'bout d' can, Blue, er youse'll git done."

"Who'll do me?" demanded Blue Billie, casting his eye about him.

"Kel' will," said Fidsey, bravely.

"D' 'ell he will?"

"Dat's what he will!"

Blue Billie made the gesture of a warrior. "He never saw d' day 'a his life dat he could do me little finger. If 'e says much t' me, I'll push 'is face all over d' lot."

Fidsey called to Kelcey. "Say, Kel', hear what dis mug is chewin'?"

Kelcey was apparently deep in other matters. His back was half-turned.

Blue Billie spoke to Fidsey in a battleful voice. "Did 'e ever say 'e could do me?"

Fidsey said: "Soitenly 'e did. Youse is dead easy, 'e says. He says he kin punch holes in you, Blue!"

"When did 'e say it?"

"Oh—any time. Youse is a cinch, Kel' says."

Blue Billie walked over to Kelcey. The others of the band followed him exchanging joyful glances.

"Did youse say yeh could do me?"

Kelcey slowly turned, but he kept his eyes upon the ground. He heard Fidsey darting among the others telling of his prowess, preparing them for the downfall of Blue Billie. He stood heavily on one foot and moved his hands nervously. Finally he said, in a low growl, "Well, what if I did?"

The sentence sent a happy thrill through the band. It was the formidable question. Blue Billie braced himself. Upon him came the responsibility of the next step. The gang fell back a little upon all sides. They looked expectantly at Blue Billie.

He walked forward with a deliberate step until his face was close to Kelcey.

"Well, if you did," he said, with a snarl between his teeth, "I'm goin' t' t'ump d' life outa yeh right heh!"

A little boy, wild of eye and puffing, came down the slope as from an explosion. He burst out in a rapid treble, "Is dat Kelcey feller here? Say, yeh ol' woman's sick again. Dey want yeh! Yehs better run! She's awful sick!"

The gang turned with loud growls. "Ah, git outa here!" Fidsey threw a stone at the little boy and chased him a short distance, but he continued to clamor, "Youse better come, Kelcey feller! She's awful sick! She was hollerin'! Dey been lookin' fer yeh over'n hour!" In his eagerness he returned part way, regardless of Fidsey!

Kelcey had moved away from Blue Billie. He said: "I guess I'd better go!" They howled at him. "Well," he continued, "I can't— I don't wanta—I don't wanta leave me mother be—she—"

His words were drowned in the chorus of their derision. "Well, lookahere"—he would begin and at each time their cries and screams ascended. They dragged at Blue Billie. "Go fer 'im, Blue! Slug 'im! Go ahn!"

Kelcey went slowly away while they were urging Blue Billie to do a decisive thing. Billie stood fuming and blustering and explaining himself. When Kelcey had achieved a considerable distance from him, he stepped forward a few paces and hurled a terrible oath. Kelcey looked back darkly.

Chapter XVII

When he entered the chamber of death, he was brooding over the recent encounter and devising extravagant revenges upon Blue Billie and the others.

The little old woman was stretched upon her bed. Her face and hands were of the hue of the blankets. Her hair, seemingly of a new and wondrous grayness, hung over her temples in whips and tangles. She was sickeningly motionless, save for her eyes, which rolled and swayed in maniacal glances.

A young doctor had just been administering medicine. "There," he said, with a great satisfaction, "I guess that'll do her good!" As he went briskly toward the door he met Kelcey. "Oh," he said. "Son?"

Kelcey had that in his throat which was like fur. When he forced his voice, the words came first low and then high as if they had broken through something. "Will she—will she——"

The doctor glanced back at the bed. She was watching them as she would have watched ghouls, and muttering. "Can't tell," he said. "She's wonderful woman! Got more vitality than you and I together! Can't tell! May—may not! Good-day! Back in two hours."

In the kitchen Mrs. Callahan was feverishly dusting the furniture, polishing this and that. She arranged everything in decorous rows. She was preparing for the coming of death. She looked at the floor as if she longed to scrub it.

The doctor paused to speak in an undertone to her, glancing at the bed. When he departed she labored with a renewed speed.

Kelcey approached his mother. From a little distance he called to her. "Mother—mother——" He proceeded with caution lest this mystic being upon the bed should clutch at him.

"Mother—mother—don't yeh know me?" He put forth apprehensive, shaking fingers and touched her hand.

There were two brilliant steel-colored points upon her eyeballs. She was staring off at something sinister.

Suddenly she turned to her son in a wild babbling appeal. "Help me! Help me! Oh, help me! I see them coming."

Kelcey called to her as to a distant place. "Mother! Mother!" She looked at him, and then there began within her a struggle to reach him with her mind. She fought with some implacable power whose fingers were in her brain. She called to Kelcey in stammering, incoherent cries for help.

Then she again looked away. "Ah, there they come! There they come! Ah, look—look—loo—" She arose to a sitting posture without the use of her arms.

Kelcey felt himself being choked. When her voice pealed forth in a scream he saw crimson curtains moving before his eyes. "Mother—oh, mother—there's nothin'—there's nothin'——"

She was at a kitchen-door with a dish-cloth in her hand. Within there had just been a clatter of crockery. Down through the trees of the orchard she could see a man in a field ploughing. "Bill—o-o-oh, Bill—have yeh seen Georgie? Is he out there with you? Georgie! Georgie! Come right here this minnet! Right—this—minnet!"

She began to talk to some people in the room. "I want t' know what yeh want here! I want yeh t' git out! I don't want yeh here! I don't feel good t'-day, an' I don't want yeh here! I don't feel good t'-day! I want yeh t' git out!" Her voice became peevish. "Go away! Go away! Go away!"

Kelcey lay in a chair. His nerveless arms allowed his fingers to sweep the floor. He became so that he could not hear the chatter from the bed, but he was always conscious of the ticking of the little clock out on the kitchen shelf.

When he aroused, the pale-faced but plump young clergyman was before him.

"My poor lad——" began this latter.

The little old woman lay still with her eyes closed. On the table at the head of the bed was a glass containing a water-like medicine. The reflected lights made a silver star on its side. The two men sat side by side, waiting. Out in the kitchen Mrs. Callahan had taken a chair by the stove and was waiting.

Kelcey began to stare at the wall-paper. The pattern was clusters of brown roses. He felt them like hideous crabs crawling upon his brain.

Through the door-way he saw the oil-cloth covering of the table catching a glimmer from the warm afternoon sun. The window disclosed a fair, soft sky, like blue enamel, and a fringe of chimneys and roofs, resplendent here and there. An endless roar, the eternal trample of the marching city, came mingled with vague cries. At intervals the woman out by the stove moved restlessly and coughed.

Over the transom from the hall-way came two voices.

"Johnnie!"

"Wot!"

"You come right here t' me! I want yehs t' go t' d' store fer me!"

"Ah, ma, send Sally!"

"No, I will not! You come right here!"

"All right, in a minnet!"

"Johnnie!"

"In a minnet, I tell yeh!"

"Johnnie——" There was the sound of a heavy tread, and later a boy squealed. Suddenly the clergyman started to his feet. He rushed forward and peered. The little old woman was dead.

TALES OF NEW YORK

The Broken-Down Van

The gas lamps had just been lit and the two great red furniture vans with impossible landscapes on their sides rolled and plunged slowly along the street. Each was drawn by four horses, and each almost touched the roaring elevated road above. They were on the uptown track of the surface road—indeed the street was so narrow that they must be on one track or the other.

They tossed and pitched and proceeded slowly, and a horse car with a red light came up behind. The car was red, and the bulls-eye light was red, and the driver's hair was red. He blew his whistle shrilly and slapped the horse's lines impatiently. Then he whistled again. Then he pounded on the red dash board with his car-hook till the red light trembled. Then a car with a green light crept up behind the car with the red light; and the green driver blew his whistle and pounded on his dash board; and the conductor of the red car seized his strap from his position on the rear platform and rung such a rattling tattoo on the gong over the red driver's head that the red driver became frantic and stood up on his toes and puffed out his cheeks as if he were playing the trombone in a German street-band and blew his whistle till an imaginative person could see slivers flying from it, and pounded his red dash board till the metal was dented in and the car-hook was bent. And just as the driver of a newly-come car with a blue light began to blow his whistle and pound his dash board and the green conductor began to ring his bell like a demon which drove the green driver mad and made him rise up and blow and pound as no man ever blew or pounded before, which made the red conductor lose the last vestige of control of himself and caused him to bounce up and down on his bell strap as he grasped it with both hands in a wild, maniacal dance, which of course served to drive uncertain Reason from her tottering throne in the red driver, who dropped his whistle and his hook and began to yell, and ki-yi, and whoop harder than the worst personal devil encountered by the sternest of Scotch Presbyterians ever yelled and ki-yied and whooped on the darkest night after the good man had drunk the most hot Scotch whiskey; just then the left-hand forward wheel on the rear van fell off and the axle went down. The van gave a mighty lurch and then swayed and rolled and rocked and stopped; the red driver applied his brake with a jerk and his horses turned out to keep from being crushed between car and van; the other drivers applied their brakes with a jerk and their horses turned out; the two cliff-dwelling men on the shelf half-way up the front of the stranded van began to shout loudly to their brother cliff-dwellers on the forward van; a girl, six years old, with a pail of beer crossed under the red car horses' necks; a boy, eight years old, mounted the red car with the sporting extras of the evening papers; a girl, ten years old, went in front of the van horses with two pails of beer; an unclassified boy poked his finger in the black grease in the hub of the right-hand hind van wheel and began to print his name on the red landscape on the van's side; a boy with a little head and big ears examined the white rings on the martingales of the van leaders with a view of stealing them in the confusion; a sixteen-year-old girl without any hat and with a roll of half-finished vests under her arm crossed the front platform of the green car. As she stepped up on to the sidewalk a barber from a ten-cent shop said "Ah! there!" and she answered "smarty!" with withering scorn and went down a side street. A few drops of warm summer rain began to fall.

Well, the van was wrecked and something had got to be done. It was on the busiest car track on Manhattan Island. The cliff-dwellers got down in some mysterious way—probably on a rope ladder. Their brethren drove their van down a side street and came back to see what was the matter.

"The nut is off," said the captain of the wrecked van.

"Yes," said the first mate, "the nut is off."

"Hah," said the captain of the other van, "the nut is off."

"Yer right," said his first mate, "the nut is off."

The driver of the red car came up, hot and irritated. But he had regained his reason. "The nut is off," he said.

The drivers of the green and of the blue car came along. "The nut," they said in chorus, "is off."

The red, green and blue conductors came forward. They examined the situation carefully as became men occupying a higher position. Then they made this report through the chairman, the red conductor:

"The nut is gone."

"Yes," said the driver of the crippled van, who had spoken first, "yes, the damned nut is lost."

Then the driver of the other van swore, and the two assistants swore, and the three car drivers swore and the three car conductors used some polite but profane expressions. Then a strange man, an unknown man and an outsider, with his trousers held up by a trunk-strap, who stood at hand, swore harder than any of the rest. The others turned and looked at him inquiringly and savagely. The man wriggled nervously.

"You wanter tie it up," he said at last.

"Wot yo' goin' to tie it to, you cussed fool?" asked the assistant of the head van scornfully, "a berloon?"

"Ha, ha!" laughed the others.

"Some folks make me tired," said the second van driver.

"Go and lose yourself with the nut," said the red conductor, severely.

"That's it," said the others. "Git out, 'fore we t'row you out."

The officiously profane stranger slunk away.

The crisis always produces the man.

In this crisis the man was the first van driver.

"Bill," said the first van driver, "git some candles." Bill vanished.

A car with a white light, a car with a white and red light, a car with a white light and a green bar across it, a car with a blue light and a white circle around it, another car with a red bullseye light and one with a red flat light had come up and stopped. More were coming to extend the long line. The elevated trains thundered overhead, and made the street tremble. A dozen horse cars went down on the other track, and the drivers made derisive noises, rather than speaking derisive words at their brother van-bound drivers. Each delayed car was full of passengers, and they craned their necks and peppery old gentlemen inquired what the trouble was, and a happy individual who had been to Coney Island began to sing.

Trucks, mail-wagons and evening paper carts crowded past. A jam was imminent. A Chatham Square cab fought its way along with a man inside wearing a diamond like an arc-light. A hundred people stopped on either sidewalk; ten per cent of them whistled "Boom-de-ay." A half dozen small boys managed to just miss being killed by passing teams. Four Jews looked out of four different pawnshops. Pullers-in for three clothing stores were alert. The ten-cent barber eyed a Division-st. girl who was a millinery puller-in and who was chewing gum with an earnest, almost fierce, motion of the jaw. The ever-forward flowing tide of the growlers flowed on. The men searched under the slanting rays of the electric light for the lost nut, back past a dozen cars; scattering drops of rain continued to fall and a hand-organ came up and began an overture.

Just then Bill rose up from somewhere with four candles. The leader lit them and each van man took one and they continued the search for the nut. The humorous driver on a blue car asked them why they didn't get a fire-fly; the equally playful driver of a white car advised them of the fact that the moon would be up in the course of two or three hours. Then a gust of wind came and blew out the candles. The hand-organ man played on. A dozen newsboys arrived with evening paper extras about the Presidential nomination. The passengers bought the extras and found that they contained nothing new. A man with a stock of suspenders on his arm began to look into the trade situation. He might have made a sale to the profane man with the trunk-strap but he had disappeared. The leader again asserted himself.

"Bill," he shouted, "you git a lager beer-keg." Bill was gone in an instant.

"Jim," continued the leader, in a loud voice, as if Jim were up at the sharp end of the mainmast and the leader was on the deck, "Jim, unhitch them hosses and take out the pole."

Jim started to obey orders. A policeman came and walked around the van, looked at the prostrated wheel, started to say something, concluded not to, made the hand-organ man move on, and then went to the edge of the sidewalk and began talking to the Division-st. girl with the gum, to the infinite disgust of the cheap barber. The trunk-strap man came out of a restaurant with a sign of "Breakfast, 13 cents; Dinner, 15 cents," where he had been hidden and slunk into the liquor store next door with a sign of "Hot spiced rum, 6 cents; Sherry with a Big Egg in it, 5 cents." At the door he almost stepped on a small boy with a pitcher of beer so big that he had to set it down and rest every half block.

Bill was now back with the keg. "Set it right there," said the leader. "Now you, Jim, sock that pole under the axle and we'll h'ist 'er up and put the keg under."

One of the horses began kicking the front of the van. "Here, there!" shouted the leader and the horse subsided. "Six or seven o' you fellers git under that pole," commanded the leader, and he was obeyed. "Now all together!" The axle slowly rose and Bill slipped under the chime of the keg. But it was not high enough to allow the wheel to go on. "Git a paving block," commanded the leader to Bill. Just then a truck loaded with great, noisy straps of

iron tried to pass. The wheels followed the car track too long, the
truck struck the rear of the van and the axle went down with a
crash while the keg rolled away into the gutter. Even great leaders lose their self-control sometimes; Washington swore at the
Battle of Long Island; so this van leader now swore. His language
was plain and scandalous. The truckman offered to lick the van
man till he couldn't walk. He stopped his horses to get down to
do it. But the policeman left the girl and came and made the
truckman give over his warlike movement, much to the disgust of
the crowd. Then he punched the suspender man in the back with
the end of his club and went back to the girl. But the second de-
lay was too much for the driver of the green car, and he turned
out his horses and threw his car from the track. It pitched like a
skiff in the swell of a steamer. It staggered and rocked and as it
went past the van plunged into the gutter and made the crowd
stand back, but the horses strained themselves and finally
brought it up and at last it blundered on to its track and rolled
away at a furious rate with the faces of the passengers wreathed
in smiles and the conductor looking proudly back. Two other
cars followed the example of the green and went lumbering past
on the stones.

"Tell them fellers we'll be out of their way now in a minute,"
said the leader to the red conductor. Bill had arrived with the
paving block. "Up with 'er, now," called the leader. The axle
went up again and the keg with the stone on top of it went under.
The leader seized the wheel himself and slipped it on. "Hitch on
them hosses!" he commanded, and it was done. "Now, pull slow
there, Bill," and Bill pulled slow. The great red car with the impossible landscape gave a preliminary rock and roll, the wheel
which had made the trouble dropped down an inch or two from
the keg and the van moved slowly forward. There was nothing to
hold the wheel on and the leader walked close to it and watched
it anxiously. But it stayed on to the corner, and around the corner, and into the side street. The red driver gave a triumphant
ki-yi and his horses plunged forward in their collars eagerly. The

other drivers gave glad ki-yis and the other horses plunged ahead. Twenty cars rolled past at a fast gait. "Now, youse fellys, move on!" said the policeman, and the crowd broke up. The cheap barber was talking to a girl with one black eye, but he retreated to his shop with the sign which promised "bay rum and a clean towel to every customer." Inside the liquor store the trunk-strap man was telling a man with his sleeves rolled up how two good men could have put their shoulders under the van and h'isted it up while a ten-year-old boy put on the wheel.

An Ominous Baby

A baby was wandering in a strange country. He was a tattered child with a frowsled wealth of yellow hair. His dress, of a checked stuff, was soiled and showed the marks of many conflicts like the chain-shirt of a warrior. His sun-tanned knees shone above wrinkled stockings which he pulled up occasionally with an impatient movement when they entangled his feet. From a gaping shoe there appeared an array of tiny toes.

He was toddling along an avenue between rows of stolid, brown houses. He went slowly, with a look of absorbed interest on his small, flushed face. His blue eyes stared curiously. Carriages went with a musical rumble over the smooth asphalt. A man with a chrysanthemum was going up steps. Two nursery maids chatted as they walked slowly, while their charges hob-nobbed amiably between perambulators. A truck wagon roared thunderously in the distance.

The child from the poor district made way along the brown street filled with dull gray shadows. High up, near the roofs, glancing sun-rays changed cornices to blazing gold and silvered the fronts of windows. The wandering baby stopped and stared at the two children laughing and playing in their carriages among the heaps of rugs and cushions. He braced his legs apart in an at-titude of earnest attention. His lower jaw fell and disclosed his small, even teeth. As they moved on, he followed the carriages with awe in his face as if contemplating a pageant. Once one of the babies, with twittering laughter, shook a gorgeous rattle at him. He smiled jovially in return.

Finally a nursery maid ceased conversation and, turning, made a gesture of annoyance.

"Go 'way, little boy," she said to him. "Go 'way. You're all dirty."

He gazed at her with infant tranquillity for a moment and then went slowly off, dragging behind him a bit of rope he had acquired in another street. He continued to investigate the new scenes. The people and houses struck him with interest as would flowers and trees. Passengers had to avoid the small, absorbed figure in the middle of the sidewalk. They glanced at the intent baby face covered with scratches and dust as with scars and powder smoke.

After a time, the wanderer discovered upon the pavement, a pretty child in fine clothes playing with a toy. It was a tiny fire engine painted brilliantly in crimson and gold. The wheels rattled as its small owner dragged it uproariously about by means of a string. The babe with his bit of rope trailing behind him paused and regarded the child and the toy. For a long while he remained motionless, save for his eyes, which followed all movements of the glittering thing.

The owner paid no attention to the spectator but continued his joyous imitations of phases of the career of a fire engine. His gleeful baby laugh rang against the calm fronts of the houses. After a little, the wandering baby began quietly to sidle nearer. His bit of rope, now forgotten, dropped at his feet. He removed his eyes from the toy and glanced expectantly at the other child.

"Say," he breathed, softly.

The owner of the toy was running down the walk at top speed. His tongue was clanging like a bell and his legs were galloping. An iron post on the corner was all ablaze. He did not look around at the coaxing call from the small, tattered figure on the curb.

The wandering baby approached still nearer and, presently, spoke again. "Say," he murmured, "le' me play wif it?"

The other child interrupted some shrill tootings. He bended his head and spoke disdainfully over his shoulder.

"No," he said.

The wanderer retreated to the curb. He failed to notice the bit of rope, once treasured. His eyes followed as before the winding course of the engine, and his tender mouth twitched.

"Say," he ventured at last, "is dat yours?"

"Yes," said the other, tilting his round chin. He drew his property suddenly behind him as if it were menaced. "Yes," he repeated, "it's mine."

"Well, le' me play wif it?" said the wandering baby, with a trembling note of desire in his voice.

"No," cried the pretty child with determined lips. "It's mine! My ma-ma buyed it."

"Well, tan't I play wif it?" His voice was a sob. He stretched forth little, covetous hands.

"No," the pretty child continued to repeat. "No, it's mine."

"Well, I want to play wif it," wailed the other. A sudden, fierce frown mantled his baby face. He clenched his thin hands and advanced with a formidable gesture. He looked some wee battler in a war.

"It's mine! It's mine!" cried the pretty child, his voice in the treble of outraged rights.

"I want it," roared the wanderer.

"It's mine! It's mine!"

"I want it!"

"It's mine!"

The pretty child retreated to the fence, and there paused at bay. He protected his property with outstretched arms. The small vandal made a charge. There was a short scuffle at the fence. Each grasped the string to the toy and tugged. Their faces were wrinkled with baby rage, the verge of tears.

Finally, the child in tatters gave a supreme tug and wrenched the string from the other's hands. He set off rapidly down the street, bearing the toy in his arms. He was weeping with the air of a wronged one who has at last succeeded in achieving his rights. The other baby was squalling lustily. He seemed quite helpless. He wrung his chubby hands and railed.

After the small barbarian had got some distance away, he paused and regarded his booty. His little form curved with pride. A soft, gleeful smile loomed through the storm of tears. With great care, he prepared the toy for travelling. He stopped a moment on a corner and gazed at the pretty child whose small figure was quivering with sobs. As the latter began to show signs of beginning pursuit, the little vandal turned and vanished down a dark side street as into a swallowing cavern.

A Great Mistake

An Italian kept a fruit stand on a corner where he had good aim
at the people who came down from the elevated station and at
those who went along two thronged streets. He sat most of the
day in a backless chair that was placed strategically.

There was a babe living hard by, up five flights of stairs, who
regarded this Italian as a tremendous being. The babe had inves-
tigated this fruit stand. It had thrilled him as few things he had
met with in his travels had thrilled him. The sweets of the world
laid there in dazzling rows, tumbled in luxurious heaps. When he
gazed at this Italian seated amid such splendid treasure, his lower
lip hung low and his eyes raised to the vendor's face were filled
with deep respect, worship, as if he saw omnipotence.

The babe came often to this corner. He hovered about the
stand and watched each detail of the business. He was fascinated
by the tranquility of the vendor, the majesty of power and possession. At times, he was so engrossed in his contemplation that
people, hurrying, had to use care to avoid bumping him down.

He had never ventured very near to the stand. It was his habit
to hang warily about the curb. Even there he resembled a babe
who looks unbidden at a feast of gods.

One day, however, as the baby was thus staring, the vendor
arose and going along the front of the stand, began to polish oranges with a red pocket-handkerchief. The breathless spectator

moved across the sidewalk until his small face almost touched the vendor's sleeve. His fingers were gripped in a fold of his dress.

At last, the Italian finished with the oranges and returned to his chair. He drew a newspaper printed in his language from behind a bunch of bananas. He settled himself in a comfortable position and began to glare savagely at the print. The babe was left face to face with the massed joys of the world.

For a time he was a simple worshipper at this golden shrine. Then tumultuous desires began to shake him. His dreams were of conquest. His lips moved. Presently into his head there came a little plan.

He sidled nearer, throwing swift and cunning glances at the Italian. He strove to maintain his conventional manner, but the whole plot was written upon his countenance.

At last he had come near enough to touch the fruit. From the tattered skirt came slowly his small dirty hand. His eyes were still fixed upon the vendor. His features were set, save for the under lip, which had a faint fluttering movement. The hand went forward.

Elevated trains thundered to the station and the stairway poured people upon the sidewalks. There was a deep sea roar from feet and wheels going ceaselessly. None seemed to perceive the babe engaged in the great venture.

The Italian turned his paper. Sudden panic smote the babe. His hand dropped and he gave vent to a cry of dismay. He remained for a moment staring at the vendor. There was evidently a great debate in his mind. His infant intellect had defined the Italian. The latter was undoubtedly a man who would eat babes that provoked him. And the alarm in him when the vendor had turned his newspaper brought vividly before him the consequences if he were detected.

But at this moment, the vendor gave a blissful grunt and tilting his chair against a wall, closed his eyes. His paper dropped unheeded.

The babe ceased his scrutiny and again raised his hand. It was moved with supreme caution toward the fruit. The fingers were bent, claw-like, in the manner of great heart-shaking greed.

Once he stopped and chattered convulsively because the vendor moved in his sleep. The babe with his eyes still upon the Italian again put forth his hand and the rapacious fingers closed over a round bulb.

And it was written that the Italian should at this moment open his eyes. He glared at the babe a fierce question. Thereupon the babe thrust the round bulb behind him and with a face expressive of the deepest guilt, began a wild but elaborate series of gestures declaring his innocence.

The Italian howled. He sprang to his feet, and with three steps overtook the babe. He whirled him fiercely and took from the little fingers a lemon.

A Dark-Brown Dog

A child was standing on a street-corner. He leaned with one shoulder against a high board-fence and swayed the other to and fro, the while kicking carelessly at the gravel.

Sunshine beat upon the cobbles, and a lazy summer wind raised yellow dust which trailed in clouds down the avenue. Clattering trucks moved with indistinctness through it. The child stood dreamily gazing.

After a time, a little dark-brown dog came trotting with an intent air down the sidewalk. A short rope was dragging from his neck. Occasionally he trod upon the end of it and stumbled.

He stopped opposite the child, and the two regarded each other. The dog hesitated for a moment, but presently he made some little advances with his tail. The child put out his hand and called him. In an apologetic manner the dog came close, and the two had an interchange of friendly pattings and waggles. The dog became more enthusiastic with each moment of the interview, until with his gleeful caperings he threatened to overturn the child. Whereupon the child lifted his hand and struck the dog a blow upon the head.

This thing seemed to overpower and astonish the little dark-brown dog, and wounded him to the heart. He sank down in despair at the child's feet. When the blow was repeated, together with an admonition in childish sentences, he turned over upon his back, and held his paws in a peculiar manner. At the same time with his ears and his eyes he offered a small prayer to the child.

He looked so comical on his back, and holding his paws peculiarly, that the child was greatly amused and gave him little taps repeatedly, to keep him so. But the little dark-brown dog took this chastisement in the most serious way, and no doubt considered that he had committed some grave crime, for he wriggled contritely and showed his repentance in every way that was in his power. He pleaded with the child and petitioned him, and offered more prayers.

At last the child grew weary of this amusement and turned toward home. The dog was praying at the time. He lay on his back and turned his eyes upon the retreating form.

Presently he struggled to his feet and started after the child. The latter wandered in a perfunctory way toward his home, stopping at times to investigate various matters. During one of these pauses he discovered the little dark-brown dog who was following him with the air of a footpad.

The child beat his pursuer with a small stick he had found. The dog lay down and prayed until the child had finished, and resumed his journey. Then he scrambled erect and took up the pursuit again.

On the way to his home the child turned many times and beat the dog, proclaiming with childish gestures that he held him in contempt as an unimportant dog, with no value save for a moment. For being this quality of animal the dog apologized and eloquently expressed regret, but he continued stealthily to follow the child. His manner grew so very guilty that he slunk like an assassin.

When the child reached his door-step, the dog was industriously ambling a few yards in the rear. He became so agitated with shame when he again confronted the child that he forgot the dragging rope. He tripped upon it and fell forward.

The child sat down on the step and the two had another interview. During it the dog greatly exerted himself to please the child. He performed a few gambols with such abandon that the child suddenly saw him to be a valuable thing. He made a swift, avaricious charge and seized the rope.

He dragged his captive into a hall and up many long stairways in a dark tenement. The dog made willing efforts, but he could not hobble very skilfully up the stairs because he was very small and soft, and at last the pace of the engrossed child grew so energetic that the dog became panic-stricken. In his mind he was being dragged toward a grim unknown. His eyes grew wild with the terror of it. He began to wiggle his head frantically and to brace his legs.

The child redoubled his exertions. They had a battle on the stairs. The child was victorious because he was completely absorbed in his purpose, and because the dog was very small. He dragged his acquirement to the door of his home, and finally with triumph across the threshold.

No one was in. The child sat down on the floor and made overtures to the dog. These the dog instantly accepted. He beamed with affection upon his new friend. In a short time they were firm and abiding comrades.

When the child's family appeared, they made a great row. The dog was examined and commented upon and called names. Scorn was leveled at him from all eyes, so that he became much embarrassed and drooped like a scorched plant. But the child went sturdily to the center of the floor, and, at the top of his voice, championed the dog. It happened that he was roaring protestations, with his arms clasped about the dog's neck, when the father of the family came in from work.

The parent demanded to know what the blazes they were making the kid howl for. It was explained in many words that the infernal kid wanted to introduce a disreputable dog into the family.

A family council was held. On this depended the dog's fate, but he in no way heeded, being busily engaged in chewing the end of the child's dress.

The affair was quickly ended. The father of the family, it appears, was in a particularly savage temper that evening, and when he perceived that it would amaze and anger everybody if such a dog were allowed to remain, he decided that it should be so. The child, crying softly, took his friend off to a retired part of the room to hobnob with him, while the father quelled a fierce rebellion of his wife. So it came to pass that the dog was a member of the household.

He and the child were associated together at all times save when the child slept. The child became a guardian and a friend. If the large folk kicked the dog and threw things at him, the child made loud and violent objections. Once when the child had run, protesting loudly, with tears raining down his face and his arms outstretched, to protect his friend, he had been struck in the head with a very large saucepan from the hand of his father, enraged at some seeming lack of courtesy in the dog. Ever after, the family were careful how they threw things at the dog. Moreover, the latter grew very skilful in avoiding missiles and feet. In a small room containing a stove, a table, a bureau and some chairs, he would display strategic ability of a high order, dodging, feinting and scuttling about among the furniture. He could force three or four people armed with brooms, sticks and handfuls of coal, to use all their ingenuity to get in a blow. And even when they did, it was seldom that they could do him a serious injury or leave any imprint.

But when the child was present, these scenes did not occur. It came to be recognized that if the dog was molested, the child would burst into sobs, and as the child, when started, was very riotous and practically unquenchable, the dog had therein a safeguard.

However, the child could not always be near. At night, when he was asleep, his dark-brown friend would raise from some black corner a wild, wailful cry, a song of infinite lowliness and despair, that would go shuddering and sobbing among the buildings of the block and cause people to swear. At these times the singer would often be chased all over the kitchen and hit with a great variety of articles.

Sometimes, too, the child himself used to beat the dog, although it is not known that he ever had what could be truly called a just cause. The dog always accepted these thrashings with an air of admitted guilt. He was too much of a dog to try to look to be a martyr or to plot revenge. He received the blows with deep humility, and furthermore he forgave his friend the moment the child had finished, and was ready to caress the child's hand with his little red tongue.

When misfortune came upon the child, and his troubles overwhelmed him, he would often crawl under the table and lay his small distressed head on the dog's back. The dog was ever sympathetic. It is not to be supposed that at such times he took occasion to refer to the unjust beatings his friend, when provoked, had administered to him.

He did not achieve any notable degree of intimacy with the other members of the family. He had no confidence in them, and the fear that he would express at their casual approach often exasperated them exceedingly. They used to gain a certain satisfaction in underfeeding him, but finally his friend the child grew to watch the matter with some care, and when he forgot it, the dog was often successful in secret for himself.

So the dog prospered. He developed a large bark, which came wondrously from such a small rug of a dog. He ceased to howl persistently at night. Sometimes, indeed, in his sleep, he would utter little yells, as from pain, but that occurred, no doubt, when in his dreams he encountered huge flaming dogs who threatened him direfully.

His devotion to the child grew until it was a sublime thing. He wagged at his approach; he sank down in despair at his departure. He could detect the sound of the child's step among all the noises of the neighborhood. It was like a calling voice to him.

The scene of their companionship was a kingdom governed by this terrible potentate, the child; but neither criticism nor rebellion ever lived for an instant in the heart of the one subject. Down in the mystic, hidden fields of his little dog-soul bloomed flowers of love and fidelity and perfect faith.

The child was in the habit of going on many expeditions to observe strange things in the vicinity. On these occasions his friend usually jogged aimfully along behind. Perhaps, though, he went ahead. This necessitated his turning around every quarter-minute to make sure the child was coming. He was filled with a large idea of the importance of these journeys. He would carry himself with such an air! He was proud to be the retainer of so great a monarch.

One day, however, the father of the family got quite exceptionally drunk. He came home and held carnival with the cooking utensils, the furniture and his wife. He was in the midst of this recreation when the child, followed by the dark-brown dog, entered the room. They were returning from their voyages.

The child's practised eye instantly noted his father's state. He dived under the table, where experience had taught him was a rather safe place. The dog, lacking skill in such matters, was, of course, unaware of the true condition of affairs. He looked with interested eyes at his friend's sudden dive. He interpreted it to mean: Joyous gambol. He started to patter across the floor to join him. He was the picture of a little dark-brown dog en route to a friend.

The head of the family saw him at this moment. He gave a huge howl of joy, and knocked the dog down with a heavy coffee-pot. The dog, yelling in supreme astonishment and fear, writhed to his feet and ran for cover. The man kicked out with a ponderous foot. It caused the dog to swerve as if caught in a tide. A second blow of the coffee-pot laid him upon the floor.

Here the child, uttering loud cries, came valiantly forth like a knight. The father of the family paid no attention to these calls of the child, but advanced with glee upon the dog. Upon being knocked down twice in swift succession, the latter apparently gave up all hope of escape. He rolled over on his back and held his paws in a peculiar manner. At the same time with his eyes and his ears he offered up a small prayer.

But the father was in a mood for having fun, and it occurred to him that it would be a fine thing to throw the dog out of the window. So he reached down and grabbing the animal by a leg, lifted him, squirming, up. He swung him two or three times hilariously about his head, and then flung him with great accuracy through the window.

The soaring dog created a surprise in the block. A woman watering plants in an opposite window gave an involuntary shout and dropped a flower-pot. A man in another window leaned perilously out to watch the flight of the dog. A woman, who had been hanging out clothes in a yard, began to caper wildly. Her mouth was filled with clothes-pins, but her arms gave vent to a sort of exclamation. In appearance she was like a gagged prisoner. Children ran whooping.

The dark-brown body crashed in a heap on the roof of a shed five stories below. From thence it rolled to the pavement of an alleyway.

The child in the room far above burst into a long, dirgelike cry, and toddled hastily out of the room. It took him a long time to reach the alley, because his size compelled him to go downstairs backward, one step at a time, and holding with both hands to the step above.

When they came for him later, they found him seated by the body of his dark-brown friend.

An Experiment in Misery

It was late at night, and a fine rain was swirling softly down, causing the pavements to glisten with hue of steel and blue and yellow in the rays of the innumerable lights. A youth was trudging slowly, without enthusiasm, with his hands buried deep in his trousers' pockets, toward the downtown places where beds can be hired for coppers. He was clothed in an aged and tattered suit, and his derby was a marvel of dust-covered crown and torn rim. He was going forth to eat as the wanderer may eat, and sleep as the homeless sleep. By the time he had reached City Hall Park he was so completely plastered with yells of "bum" and "hobo," and with various unholy epithets that small boys had applied to him at intervals, that he was in a state of the most profound dejection. The sifting rain saturated the old velvet collar of his overcoat, and as the wet cloth pressed against his neck, he felt that there no longer could be pleasure in life. He looked about him searching for an outcast of highest degree that the two might share miseries. But the lights threw a quivering glare over rows and circles of deserted benches that glistened damply, showing patches of wet sod behind them. It seemed that their usual freights had fled on this night to better things. There were only squads of well-dressed Brooklyn people who swarmed toward the Bridge.

The young man loitered about for a time and then went shuffling off down Park Row. In the sudden descent in style of the dress of the crowd he felt relief, and as if he were at last in his own country. He began to see tatters that matched his tatters. In Chatham Square there were aimless men strewn in front of saloons and lodging houses, standing sadly, patiently, reminding one vaguely of the attitudes of chickens in a storm. He aligned himself with these men, and turned slowly to occupy himself with the flowing life of the great street.

Through the mists of the cold and storming night, the cable cars went in silent procession, great affairs shining with red and brass, moving with formidable power, calm and irresistible, dangerful and gloomy, breaking silence only by the loud fierce cry of the gong. Two rivers of people swarmed along the sidewalks, spattered with black mud, which made each shoe leave a scar-like impression. Overhead elevated trains with a shrill grinding of the wheels stopped at the station, which upon its leg-like pillars seemed to resemble some monstrous kind of crab squatting over the street. The quick fat puffings of the engines could be heard. Down an alley there were sombre curtains of purple and black, on which street lamps dully glittered like embroidered flowers.

A saloon stood with a voracious air on a corner. A sign leaning against the front of the doorpost announced: "Free hot soup tonight." The swing doors snapping to and fro like ravenous lips, made gratified smacks as the saloon gorged itself with plump men, eating with astounding and endless appetite, smiling in some indescribable manner as the men came from all directions like sacrifices to a heathenish superstition.

Caught by the delectable sign, the young man allowed himself to be swallowed. A bartender placed a schooner of dark and portentous beer on the bar. Its monumental form upreared until the froth a-top was above the crown of the young man's brown derby.

"Soup over there, gents," said the bartender, affably. A little yellow man in rags and the youth grasped their schooners and went with speed toward a lunch counter, where a man with oily but imposing whiskers ladled genially from a kettle until he had furnished his two mendicants with a soup that was steaming hot and in which there were little floating suggestions of chicken. The young man, sipping his broth, felt the cordiality expressed by the warmth of the mixture, and he beamed at the man with oily but imposing whiskers, who was presiding like a priest behind an altar. "Have some more, gents?" he inquired of the two sorry figures before him. The little yellow man accepted with a swift gesture, but the youth shook his head and went out, following a man whose wondrous seediness promised that he would have a knowledge of cheap lodging houses.

On the side-walk he accosted the seedy man. "Say, do you know a cheap place t' sleep?"

The other hesitated for a time, gazing sideways. Finally he nodded in the direction of up the street. "I sleep up there," he said, "when I've got th' price."

"How much?"

"Ten cents."

The young man shook his head dolefully. "That's too rich for me."

At that moment there approached the two a reeling man in strange garments. His head was a fuddle of bushy hair and whiskers from which his eyes peered with a guilty slant. In a close scrutiny it was possible to distinguish the cruel lines of a mouth, which looked as if its lips had just closed with satisfaction over some tender and piteous morsel. He appeared like an assassin steeped in crimes performed awkwardly.

But at this time his voice was tuned to the coaxing key of an affectionate puppy. He looked at the men with wheedling eyes and began to sing a little melody for charity.

"Say, gents, can't yeh give a poor feller a couple of cents t' git a bed. I got five an I gits anudder two I gits me a bed. Now, on th' square, gents, can't yeh jest gimme two cents t' git a bed. Now, yeh know how a respecter'ble gentlem'n feels when he's down on his luck an' I——"

The seedy man, staring with imperturbable countenance at a train which clattered overhead, interrupted in an expressionless voice: "Ah, go t' h——!"

But the youth spoke to the prayerful assassin in tones of astonishment and inquiry. "Say, you must be crazy! Why don't yeh strike somebody that looks as if they had money?"

The assassin, tottering about on his uncertain legs, and at intervals brushing imaginary obstacles from before his nose, entered into a long explanation of the psychology of the situation. It was so profound that it was unintelligible.

When he had exhausted the subject the young man said to him: "Let's see th' five cents."

The assassin wore an expression of drunken woe at this sentence, filled with suspicion of him. With a deeply pained air he began to fumble in his clothing, his red hands trembling. Presently he announced in a voice of bitter grief, as if he had been betrayed: "There's on'y four."

"Four," said the young man thoughtfully. "Well, look-a-here, I'm a stranger here, an' if ye'll steer me to your cheap joint I'll find the other three."

The assassin's countenance became instantly radiant with joy. His whiskers quivered with the wealth of his alleged emotions. He seized the young man's hand in a transport of delight and friendliness.

"B'gawd," he cried, "if ye'll do that, b'gawd, I'd say yeh was a damned good feller, I would, an' I'd remember yeh all m' life, I would, b'gawd, an' if I ever got a chance I'd return th' compliment"—he spoke with drunken dignity—"b'gawd, I'd treat yeh white, I would, an' I'd allus remember yeh——"

The young man drew back, looking at the assassin coldly. "Oh, that's all right," he said. "You show me th' joint—that's all you've got t' do."

The assassin, gesticulating gratitude, led the young man along a dark street. Finally he stopped before a little dusty door. He raised his hand impressively. "Look-a-here," he said, and there was a thrill of deep and ancient wisdom upon his face, "I've brought yeh here, an' that's my part, ain't it? If th' place don't suit yeh yeh needn't git mad at me, need yeh? There won't be no bad feelin', will there?"

"No," said the young man.

The assassin waved his arm tragically and led the march up the steep stairway. On the way the young man furnished the assassin with three pennies. At the top a man with benevolent spectacles looked at them through a hole in the board. He collected their money, wrote some names on a register, and speedily was leading the two men along a gloom shrouded corridor.

Shortly after the beginning of this journey the young man felt his liver turn white, for from the dark and secret places of the building there suddenly came to his nostrils strange and unspeakable odors that assailed him like malignant diseases with wings. They seemed to be from human bodies closely packed in dens; the exhalations from a hundred pairs of reeking lips; the fumes from a thousand bygone debauches; the expression of a thousand present miseries.

A man, naked save for a little snuff colored undershirt, was parading sleepily along the corridor. He rubbed his eyes, and, giving vent to a prodigious yawn, demanded to be told the time.

"Half past one."

The man yawned again. He opened a door, and for a moment his form was outlined against a black, opaque interior. To this door came the three men, and as it was again opened the unholy odors rushed out like released fiends, so that the young man was obliged to struggle as against an overpowering wind.

It was some time before the youth's eyes were good in the intense gloom within, but the man with benevolent spectacles led him skillfully, pausing but a moment to deposit the limp assassin upon a cot. He took the youth to a cot that lay tranquilly by the window, and, showing him a tall locker for clothes that stood near the head with the ominous air of a tombstone, left him.

The youth sat on his cot and peered about him. There was a

gas jet in a distant part of the room that burned a small flickering orange hued flame. It caused vast masses of tumbled shadows in all parts of the place, save where, immediately about it, there was a little gray haze. As the young man's eyes became used to the darkness he could see upon the cots that thickly littered the floor the forms of men sprawled out, lying in death-like silence or heaving and snoring with tremendous effort, like stabbed fish.

The youth locked his derby and his shoes in the mummy case near him and then lay down with his old and familiar coat around his shoulders. A blanket he handled gingerly, drawing it over part of the coat. The cot was leather covered and cold as melting snow. The youth was obliged to shiver for some time on this affair, which was like a slab. Presently, however, his chill gave him peace, and during this period of leisure from it he turned his head to stare at his friend, the assassin, whom he could dimly discern where he lay sprawled on a cot in the abandon of a man filled with drink. He was snoring with incredible vigor. His wet hair and beard dimly glistened and his inflamed nose shone with subdued luster like a red light in a fog.

Within reach of the youth's hand was one who lay with yellow breast and shoulders bare to the cold drafts. One arm hung over the side of the cot and the fingers lay full length upon the wet cement floor of the room. Beneath the inky brows could be seen the eyes of the man exposed by the partly opened lids. To the youth it seemed that he and this corpse-like being were exchanging a prolonged stare and that the other threatened with his eyes. He drew back, watching his neighbor from the shadows of his blanket edge. The man did not move once through the night, but lay in this stillness as of death, like a body stretched out, expectant of the surgeon's knife.

And all through the room could be seen the tawny hues of naked flesh, limbs thrust into the darkness, projecting beyond the cots; up-reared knees; arms hanging, long and thin, over the cot edges. For the most part they were statuesque, carven, dead. With the curious lockers standing all about like tombstones there was a strange effect of a graveyard, where bodies were merely flung.

Yet occasionally could be seen limbs wildly tossing in fantastic, nightmare gestures, accompanied by guttural cries, grunts, oaths. And there was one fellow off in a gloomy corner, who in his dreams was oppressed by some frightful calamity, for of a sudden he began to utter long wails that went almost like yells from a hound, echoing wailfully and weird through this chill place of tombstones, where men lay like the dead.

The sound, in its high piercing beginnings that dwindled to final melancholy moans, expressed a red and grim tragedy of the unfathomable possibilities of the man's dreams. But to the youth these were not merely the shrieks of a vision pierced man. They were an utterance of the meaning of the room and its occupants. It was to him the protest of the wretch who feels the touch of the imperturbable granite wheels and who then cries with an impersonal eloquence, with a strength not from him, giving voice to the wail of a whole section, a class, a people. This, weaving into the young man's brain and mingling with his views of these vast and somber shadows that like mighty black fingers curled around the naked bodies, made the young man so that he did not sleep, but lay carving biographies for these men from his meager experience. At times the fellow in the corner howled in a writhing agony of his imaginations.

Finally a long lance point of gray light shot through the dusty panes of the window. Without, the young man could see roofs drearily white in the dawning. The point of light yellowed and grew brighter, until the golden rays of the morning sun came in bravely and strong. They touched with radiant color the form of a small, fat man, who snored in stuttering fashion. His round and shiny bald head glowed suddenly with the valor of a decoration. He sat up, blinked at the sun, swore fretfully and pulled his blanket over the ornamental splendors of his head.

The youth contentedly watched this rout of the shadows before the bright spears of the sun and presently he slumbered.

When he awoke he heard the voice of the assassin raised in valiant curses. Putting up his head he perceived his comrade seated on the side of the cot engaged in scratching his neck with long finger nails that rasped like files.

"Hully Jee dis is a new breed. They've got can openers on their feet," he continued in a violent tirade.

The young man hastily unlocked his closet and took out his shoes and hat. As he sat on the side of the cot, lacing his shoes, he glanced about and saw that daylight had made the room comparatively commonplace and uninteresting. The men, whose faces seemed stolid, serene or absent, were engaged in dressing, while a great crackle of bantering conversation arose.

A few were parading in unconcerned nakedness. Here and there were men of brawn, whose skins shone clear and ruddy. They took splendid poses, standing massively, like chiefs. When they had dressed in their ungainly garments there was an extraordinary change. They then showed bumps and deficiencies of all kinds.

There were others who exhibited many deformities. Shoulders were slanting, humped, pulled this way and pulled that way. And notable among these latter men was the little fat man who had refused to allow his head to be glorified. His pudgy form, builded like a pear, bustled to and fro, while he swore in fishwife fashion. It appeared that some article of his apparel had vanished.

The young man, attired speedily, went to his friend, the assassin. At first the latter looked dazed at the sight of the youth. This face seemed to be appealing to him through the cloud wastes of his memory. He scratched his neck and reflected. At last he grinned, a broad smile gradually spreading until his countenance was a round illumination. "Hello, Willie," he cried, cheerily.

"Hello," said the young man. "Are yeh ready t' fly?"

"Sure." The assassin tied his shoe carefully with some twine and came ambling.

When he reached the street the young man experienced no sudden relief from unholy atmospheres. He had forgotten all about them, and had been breathing naturally and with no sensation of discomfort or distress.

He was thinking of these things as he walked along the street, when he was suddenly startled by feeling the assassin's hand, trembling with excitement, clutching his arm, and when the assassin spoke, his voice went into quavers from a supreme agitation.

"I'll be hully, bloomin' blowed, if there wasn't a feller with a nightshirt on up there in that joint!"

The youth was bewildered for a moment, but presently he turned to smile indulgently at the assassin's humor.

"Oh, you're a d—— liar," he merely said.

Whereupon the assassin began to gesture extravagantly and take oath by strange gods. He frantically placed himself at the mercy of remarkable fates if his tale were not true. "Yes, he did! I cross m' heart thousan' times!" he protested, and at the time his eyes were large with amazement, his mouth wrinkled in unnatural glee. "Yessir! A nightshirt! A hully white nightshirt!"

"You lie!"

"Nosir! I hope ter die b'fore I kin git anudder ball if there wasn't a jay wid a hully, bloomin' white nightshirt!"

His face was filled with the infinite wonder of it. "A hully white nightshirt," he continually repeated.

The young man saw the dark entrance to a basement restaurant. There was a sign which read, "No mystery about our hash," and there were other age stained and world battered legends which told him that the place was within his means. He stopped before it and spoke to the assassin. "I guess I'll git somethin' t' eat."

At this the assassin, for some reason, appeared to be quite embarrassed. He gazed at the seductive front of the eating place for a moment. Then he started slowly up the street. "Well, goodby, Willie," he said, bravely.

For an instant the youth studied the departing figure. Then he called out, "Hol' on a minnet." As they came together he spoke

in a certain fierce way, as if he feared that the other would think
him to be weak. "Look-a-here, if yeh wanta git some breakfas'
I'll lend yeh three cents t' do it with. But say, look-a-here, you've
gota git out an' hustle. I ain't goin' t' support yeh, or I'll go broke
b'fore night. I ain't no millionaire."

"I take me oath, Willie," said the assassin, earnestly, "th' on'y
thing I really needs is a ball. Me t'roat feels like a fryin' pan. But
as I can't git a ball, why, th' next bes' thing is breakfast, an' if
yeh do that fer me, b'gawd, I'd say yeh was th' whitest lad I ever
see."

They spent a few moments in dexterous exchanges of phrases,
in which they each protested that the other was, as the assassin
had originally said, a "respecter'ble gentlem'n." And they concluded with mutual assurances that they were the souls of intelli-
gence and virtue. Then they went into the restaurant.

There was a long counter, dimly lighted from hidden sources.
Two or three men in soiled white aprons rushed here and there.

The youth bought a bowl of coffee for two cents and a roll for
one cent. The assassin purchased the same. The bowls were
webbed with brown seams, and the tin spoons wore an air of
having emerged from the first pyramid. Upon them were black,
moss-like encrustations of age, and they were bent and scarred
from the attacks of long forgotten teeth. But over their repast the
wanderers waxed warm and mellow. The assassin grew affable
as the hot mixture went soothingly down his parched throat, and
the young man felt courage flow in his veins.

Memories began to throng in on the assassin, and he brought
forth long tales, intricate, incoherent, delivered with a chattering
swiftness as from an old woman. "——great job out'n Orange.
Boss keep yeh hustlin', though, all time. I was there three days,
and then I went an' ask'im t' lend me a dollar. 'G-g-go ter the
devil,' he ses, an' I lose me job.

——"South no good. Damn niggers work for twenty-five an'
thirty cents a day. Run white man out. Good grub, though. Easy
livin'.

——"Yas; useter work little in Toledo, raftin' logs. Make two or three dollars er day in the spring. Lived high. Cold as ice, though, in the winter——

"I was raised in northern N'York. O-o-o-oh, yeh jest oughto live there. No beer ner whisky, though, way off in the woods. But all th' good hot grub yeh can eat. B'gawd, I hung around there long as I could till th' ol' man fired me. 'Git t'hell outa here, yeh wuthless skunk, git t'hell outa here an' go die,' he ses. 'You're a hell of a father,' I ses, 'you are,' an' I quit 'im."

As they were passing from the dim eating place they encountered an old man who was trying to steal forth with a tiny package of food, but a tall man with an indomitable mustache stood dragon fashion, barring the way of escape. They heard the old man raise a plaintive protest. "Ah, you always want to know what I take out, and you never see that I usually bring a package in here from my place of business."

As the wanderers trudged slowly along Park Row, the assassin began to expand and grow blithe. "B'gawd, we've been livin' like kings," he said, smacking appreciative lips.

"Look out or we'll have t' pay fer it t' night," said the youth, with gloomy warning.

But the assassin refused to turn his gaze toward the future. He went with a limping step, into which he injected a suggestion of lamb-like gambols. His mouth was wreathed in a red grin.

In the City Hall Park the two wanderers sat down in the little circle of benches sanctified by traditions of their class. They huddled in their old garments, slumbrously conscious of the march of the hours which for them had no meaning.

The people of the street hurrying hither and thither made a blend of black figures, changing, yet frieze-like. They walked in their good clothes as upon important missions, giving no gaze to the two wanderers seated upon the benches. They expressed to the young man his infinite distance from all that he valued. Social position, comfort, the pleasures of living, were unconquerable kingdoms. He felt a sudden awe.

And in the background a multitude of buildings, of pitiless hues and sternly high, were to him emblematic of a nation forcing its regal head into the clouds, throwing no downward glances; in the sublimity of its aspirations ignoring the wretches who may flounder at its feet. The roar of the city in his ear was to him the confusion of strange tongues, babbling heedlessly; it was the clink of coin, the voice of the city's hopes which were to him no hopes.

He confessed himself an outcast, and his eyes from under the lowered rim of his hat began to glance guiltily, wearing the criminal expression that comes with certain convictions.

An Experiment in Luxury

"If you accept this invitation you will have an opportunity to make another social study," said the old friend.

The youth laughed. "If they caught me making a study of them they'd attempt a murder. I would be pursued down Fifth avenue by the entire family."

"Well," persisted the old friend who could only see one thing at a time, "it would be very interesting. I have been told all my life that millionaires have no fun, and I know that the poor are always assured that the millionaire is a very unhappy person. They are informed that miseries swarm around all wealth, that all crowned heads are heavy with care, and——"

"But still——" began the youth.

"And, in the irritating, brutalizing, enslaving environment of their poverty, they are expected to solace themselves with these assurances," continued the old friend. He extended his gloved palm and began to tap it impressively with a finger of his other hand. His legs were spread apart in a fashion peculiar to his oratory. "I believe that it is mostly false. It is true that wealth does not release a man from many things from which he would gladly purchase release. Consequences cannot be bribed. I suppose that every man believes steadfastly that he has a private tragedy which makes him yearn for other existences. But it is impossible for me to believe that these things equalize themselves; that there are burrs under all rich cloaks and benefits in all ragged jackets, and the preaching of it seems wicked to me. There are those who have opportunities; there are those who are robbed of——"

"But look here," said the young man; "what has this got to do with my paying Jack a visit?"

"It has got a lot to do with it," said the old friend sharply. "As I said, there are those who have opportunities; there are those who are robbed——"

"Well, I won't have you say Jack ever robbed anybody of anything, because he's as honest a fellow as ever lived," interrupted the youth, with warmth. "I have known him for years, and he is a perfectly square fellow. He doesn't know about these infernal things. He isn't criminal because you say he is benefited by a condition which other men created."

"I didn't say he was," retorted the old friend. "Nobody is responsible for anything. I wish to Heaven somebody was, and then we could all jump on him. Look here, my boy, our modern civilization is——"

"Oh, the deuce!" said the young man.

The old friend then stood very erect and stern. "I can see by your frequent interruptions that you have not yet achieved sufficient pain in life. I hope one day to see you materially changed. You are yet——"

"There he is now," said the youth, suddenly. He indicated a young man who was passing. He went hurriedly toward him, pausing once to gesture adieu to his old friend.

The house was broad and brown and stolid like the face of a peasant. It had an inanity of expression, an absolute lack of artistic strength that was in itself powerful because it symbolized something. It stood, a homely pile of stone, rugged, grimly self reliant, asserting its quality as a fine thing when in reality the beholder usually wondered why so much money had been spent to obtain a complete negation. Then from another point of view it was important and mighty because it stood as a fetich, formidable because of traditions of worship.

When the great door was opened the youth imagined that the footman who held a hand on the knob looked at him with a quick, strange stare. There was nothing definite in it; it was all vague and elusive, but a suspicion was certainly denoted in some way. The youth felt that he, one of the outer barbarians, had been detected to be a barbarian by the guardian of the portal, he of the refined nose, he of the exquisite sense, he who must be more atrociously aristocratic than any that he serves. And the youth, detesting himself for it, found that he would rejoice to take a frightful revenge upon this lackey who, with a glance of his eyes, had called him a name. He would have liked to have been for a time a dreadful social perfection whose hand, waved lazily, would cause hordes of the idolatrous imperfect to be smitten in the eyes. And in the tumult of his imagination he did not think it strange that he should plan in his vision to come around to this house and with the power of his new social majesty, reduce this footman to ashes.

He had entered with an easy feeling of independence, but after this incident the splendor of the interior filled him with awe. He was a wanderer in a fairy land, and who felt that his presence marred certain effects. He was an invader with a shamed face, a man who had come to steal certain colors, forms, impressions that were not his. He had a dim thought that some one might come to tell him to begone.

His friend, unconscious of this swift drama of thought, was already upon the broad staircase. "Come on," he called. When the youth's foot struck from a thick rug and changed upon the tiled floor he was almost frightened.

There was cool abundance of gloom. High up stained glass caught the sunlight, and made it into marvelous hues that in places touched the dark walls. A broad bar of yellow gilded the leaves of lurking plants. A softened crimson glowed upon the head and shoulders of a bronze swordsman, who perpetually strained in a terrific lunge, his blade thrust at random into the shadow, piercing there an unknown something.

An immense fire place was at one end, and its furnishings gleamed until it resembled a curious door of a palace, and on the threshold, where one would have to pass a fire burned redly. From some remote place came the sound of a bird twittering busily. And from behind heavy portieres came a subdued noise of the chatter of three, twenty or a hundred women.

He could not relieve himself of this feeling of awe until he had reached his friend's room. There they lounged carelessly and smoked pipes. It was an amazingly comfortable room. It expressed to the visitor that he could do supremely as he chose, for it said plainly that in it the owner did supremely as he chose. The youth wondered if there had not been some domestic skirmishing to achieve so much beautiful disorder. There were various articles left about defiantly, as if the owner openly flaunted the feminine ideas of precision. The disarray of a table that stood prominently defined the entire room. A set of foils, a set of boxing gloves, a lot of illustrated papers, an inkstand and a hat lay entangled upon it. Here was surely a young man, who, when his menacing mother, sisters or servants knocked, would open a slit in the door like a Chinaman in an opium joint, and tell them to leave him to his beloved devices. And yet, withal, the effect was good, because the disorder was not necessary, and because there are some things that when flung down, look to have been flung by an artist. A baby can create an effect with a guitar. It would require genius to deal with the piled up dishes in a Cherry street sink.

The youth's friend lay back upon the broad seat that followed the curve of the window and smoked in blissful laziness. Without one could see the windowless wall of a house overgrown with a green, luxuriant vine. There was a glimpse of a side street. Below were the stables. At intervals a little fox terrier ran into the court and barked tremendously.

The youth, also blissfully indolent, kept up his part of the conversation on the recent college days, but continually he was beset by a stream of sub-conscious reflection. He was beginning to see a vast wonder in it that they two lay sleepily chatting with no more apparent responsibility than rabbits, when certainly there were men, equally fine perhaps, who were being blackened and mashed in the churning life of the lower places. And all this had merely happened; the great secret hand had guided them here and had guided others there. The eternal mystery of social condition exasperated him at this time. He wondered if incomprehensible justice were the sister of open wrong.

And, above all, why was he impressed, awed, overcome by a mass of materials, a collection of the trophies of wealth, when he knew that to him their dominant meaning was that they represented a lavish expenditure? For what reason did his nature so deeply respect all this? Perhaps his ancestors had been peasants bowing heads to the heel of appalling pomp of princes or rows of little men who stood to watch a king kill a flower with his cane. There was one side of him that said there were finer things in life, but the other side did homage.

Presently he began to feel that he was a better man than many—entitled to a great pride. He stretched his legs like a man in a garden, and he thought that he belonged to the garden. Hues and forms had smothered certain of his comprehensions. There had been times in his life when little voices called to him continually from the darkness; he heard them now as an idle, half-smothered babble on the horizon edge. It was necessary that it should be so, too. There was the horizon, he said, and, of course, there should be a babble of pain on it. Thus it was written; it was a law, he thought. And, anyway, perhaps it was not so bad as those who babbled tried to tell.

In this way and with this suddenness he arrived at a stage. He was become a philosopher, a type of the wise man who can eat but three meals a day, conduct a large business and understand the purposes of infinite power. He felt valuable. He was sage and important.

There were influences, knowledges that made him aware that he was idle and foolish in his new state, but he inwardly reveled like a barbarian in his environment. It was delicious to feel so high and mighty, to feel that the unattainable could be purchased like a penny bun. For a time, at any rate, there was no impossible. He indulged in monarchical reflections.

As they were dressing for dinner his friend spoke to him in this wise: "Be sure not to get off anything that resembles an original thought before my mother. I want her to like you, and I know that when any one says a thing cleverly before her he ruins himself with her forever. Confine your talk to orthodox expressions. Be dreary and unspeakably commonplace in the true sense of the word. Be damnable."

"It will be easy for me to do as you say," remarked the youth.

"As far as the old man goes," continued the other, "he's a blooming good fellow. He may appear like a sort of a crank if he happens to be in that mood, but he's all right when you come to know him. And besides he doesn't dare do that sort of thing with me, because I've got nerve enough to bully him. Oh, the old man is all right."

On their way down the youth lost the delightful mood that he had enjoyed in his friend's rooms. He dropped it like a hat on the stairs. The splendor of color and form swarmed upon him again. He bowed before the strength of this interior; it said a word to him which he believed he should despise, but instead he crouched. In the distance shone his enemy, the footman.

"There will be no people here to-night, so you may see the usual evening row between my sister Mary and me, but don't be alarmed or uncomfortable, because it is quite an ordinary matter," said his friend, as they were about to enter a little drawing room that was well apart from the grander rooms.

The head of the family, the famous millionaire, sat on a low stool before the fire. He was deeply absorbed in the gambols of a kitten who was plainly trying to stand on her head that she might use all four paws in grappling with an evening paper with which her playmate was poking her ribs. The old man chuckled in complete glee. There was never such a case of abstraction, of want of care. The man of millions was in a far land where mechanics and bricklayers go, a mystic land of little, universal emotions, and he had been guided to it by the quaint gestures of a kitten's furry paws.

His wife, who stood near, was apparently not at all a dweller in thought lands. She was existing very much in the present. Evidently she had been wishing to consult with her husband on some tremendous domestic question, and she was in a state of rampant irritation, because he refused to acknowledge at this moment that she or any such thing as a tremendous domestic question was in existence. At intervals she made savage attempts to gain his attention.

As the youth saw her she was in a pose of absolute despair. And her eyes expressed that she appreciated all the tragedy of it. Ah, they said, hers was a life of terrible burden, of appalling responsibility; her pathway was beset with unsolved problems, her horizon was lined with tangled difficulties, while her husband— the man of millions—continued to play with the kitten. Her expression was an admission of heroism.

The youth saw that here at any rate was one denial of his oratorical old friend's statement. In the face of this woman there was no sign that life was sometimes a joy. It was impossible that there could be any pleasure in living for her. Her features were as lined and creased with care and worriment as those of an apple woman. It was as if the passing of each social obligation, of each binding form of her life had left its footprints, scarring her face.

Somewhere in her expression there was terrible pride, that kind of pride which, mistaking the form for the real thing, worships itself because of its devotion to the form.

In the lines of the mouth and the set of the chin could be seen the might of a grim old fighter. They denoted all the power of machination of a general, veteran of a hundred battles. The little scars at the corners of her eyes made a wondrously fierce effect, baleful, determined, without regard somehow to ruck of pain. Here was a savage, a barbarian, a spear woman of the Philistines, who fought battles to excel in what are thought to be the refined and worthy things in life; here was a type of Zulu chieftainess who scuffled and scrambled for place before the white altars of social excellence. And woe to the socially weaker who should try to barricade themselves against that dragon.

It was certain that she never rested in the shade of the trees. One could imagine the endless churning of that mind. And plans and other plans coming forth continuously, defeating a rival here, reducing a family there, bludgeoning a man here, a maid there. Woe and wild eyes followed like obedient sheep upon her trail.

Too, the youth thought he could see that here was the true abode of conservatism—in the mothers, in those whose ears displayed their diamonds instead of their diamonds displaying their ears, in the ancient and honorable controllers who sat in remote corners and pulled wires and respected themselves with a magnitude of respect that heaven seldom allows on earth. There lived tradition and superstition. They were perhaps ignorant of that which they worshiped, and, not comprehending it at all, it naturally followed that the fervor of their devotion could set the sky ablaze.

As he watched, he saw that the mesmeric power of a kitten's waving paws was good. He rejoiced in the spectacle of the little fuzzy cat trying to stand on its head, and by this simple antic defeating some intention of a great domestic Napoleon.

The three girls of the family were having a musical altercation over by the window. Then and later the youth thought them adorable. They were wonderful to him in their charming gowns. They had time and opportunity to create effects, to be beautiful. And it would have been a wonder to him if he had not found them charming, since making themselves so could but be their principal occupation.

Beauty requires certain justices, certain fair conditions. When in a field no man can say: "Here should spring up a flower; here one should not." With incomprehensible machinery and system, nature sends them forth in places both strange and proper, so that, somehow, as we see them each one is a surprise to us. But at times, at places, one can say: "Here no flower can flourish." The youth wondered then why he had been sometimes surprised at seeing women fade, shrivel, their bosoms flatten, their shoulders crook forward, in the heavy swelter and wrench of their toil. It must be difficult, he thought, for a woman to remain serene and uncomplaining when she contemplated the wonder and the strangeness of it.

The lights shed marvelous hues of softened rose upon the table. In the encircling shadows the butler moved with a mournful, deeply solemn air. Upon the table there was color of pleasure, of festivity, but this servant in the background went to and fro like a slow religious procession.

The youth felt considerable alarm when he found himself involved in conversation with his hostess. In the course of this talk he discovered the great truth that when one submits himself to a thoroughly conventional conversation he runs risks of being most amazingly stupid. He was glad that no one cared to overhear it.

The millionaire, deprived of his kitten, sat back in his chair and laughed at the replies of his son to the attacks of one of the girls. In the rather good wit of his offspring he took an intense delight, but he laughed more particularly at the words of the son.

Indicated in this light chatter about the dinner table there was an existence that was not at all what the youth had been taught to see. Theologians had for a long time told the poor man that riches did not bring happiness, and they had solemnly repeated this phrase until it had come to mean that misery was commensurate with dollars, that each wealthy man was inwardly a miserable wretch. And when a wail of despair or rage had come from the night of the slums they had stuffed this epigram down the throat of he who cried out and told him that he was a lucky fellow. They did this because they feared.

The youth, studying this family group, could not see that they had great license to be pale and haggard. They were no doubt fairly good, being not strongly induced toward the bypaths. Various worlds turned open doors toward them. Wealth in a certain sense is liberty. If they were fairly virtuous he could not see why they should be so persistently pitied.

And no doubt they would dispense their dollars like little seeds upon the soil of the world if it were not for the fact that since the days of the ancient great political economist, the more exalted forms of virtue have grown to be utterly impracticable.

Mr. Binks' Day Off

When Binks was coming up town in a Broadway cable car one afternoon he caught some superficial glimpses of Madison square as he ducked his head to peek through between a young woman's bonnet and a young man's newspaper. The green of the little park vaguely astonished Binks. He had grown accustomed to a white and brown park; now, all at once, it was radiant green. The grass, the leaves, had come swiftly, silently, as if a great green light from the sky had shone suddenly upon the little desolate hued place.

The vision cheered the mind of Binks. It cried to him that nature was still supreme; he had begun to think the banking business to be the pivot on which the universe turned. Produced by this wealth of young green, faint faraway voices called to him. Certain subtle memories swept over him. The million leaves looked into his soul and said something sweet and pure in an unforgotten song, the melody of his past. Binks began to dream.

When he arrived at the little Harlem flat he sat down to dinner with an air of profound dejection, which Mrs. Binks promptly construed into an insult to her cooking, and to the time and thought she had expended in preparing the meal. She promptly resented it. "Well, what's the matter now?" she demanded. Apparently she had asked this question ten thousand times.

"Nothin'," said Binks, shortly, filled with gloom. He meant by this remark that his ailment was so subtle that her feminine mind would not be enlightened by any explanation.

The head of the family was in an ugly mood. The little Binkses suddenly paused in their uproar and became very wary children. They knew that it would be dangerous to do anything irrelevant to their father's bad temper. They studied his face with their large eyes, filled with childish seriousness and speculation. Meanwhile they ate with the most extraordinary caution. They handled their little forks with such care that there was barely a sound. At each slight movement of their father they looked apprehensively at him, expecting the explosion.

The meal continued amid a somber silence. At last, however, Binks spoke, clearing his throat of the indefinite rage that was in it and looking over at his wife. The little Binkses seemed to inwardly dodge, but he merely said: "I wish I could get away into the country for awhile!"

His wife bristled with that brave anger which agitates a woman when she sees fit to assume that her husband is weak spirited. "If I worked as hard as you do, if I slaved over those old books the way you do, I'd have a vacation once in awhile or I'd tear their old office down." Upon her face was a Roman determination. She was a personification of all manner of courages and rebellions and powers.

Binks felt the falsity of her emotion in a vague way, but at that time he only made a sullen gesture. Later, however, he cried out in a voice of sudden violence: "Look at Tommie's dress! Why the dickens don't you put a bib on that child?"

His wife glared over Tommie's head at her husband, as she leaned around in her chair to tie on the demanded bib. The two looked as hostile as warring redskins. In the wife's eyes there was an intense opposition and defiance, an assertion that she now considered the man she had married to be beneath her in intellect, industry, valor. There was in this glance a jeer at the failures of his life. And Binks, filled with an inexpressible rebellion at what was to him a lack of womanly perception and sympathy in her, replied with a look that called his wife a drag, an uncomprehending thing of vain ambitions, the weight of his existence.

The baby meanwhile began to weep because his mother, in her exasperation, had yanked him and hurt his neck. Her anger, groping for an outlet, had expressed itself in the nervous strength of her fingers. "Keep still, Tommie," she said to him. "I didn't hurt you. You needn't cry the minute anybody touches you!" He made a great struggle and repressed his loud sobs, but the tears continued to fall down his cheeks and his under lip quivered from a baby sense of injury, the anger of an impotent child who seems as he weeps to be planning revenges.

"I don't see why you don't keep that child from eternally crying," said Binks, as a final remark. He then arose and went away to smoke, leaving Mrs. Binks with the children and the disheveled table.

Later that night, when the children were in bed, Binks said to his wife: "We ought to get away from the city for awhile at least this spring. I can stand it in the summer, but in the spring——" He made a motion with his hand that represented the new things that are born in the heart when spring comes into the eyes.

"It will cost something, Phil," said Mrs. Binks.

"That's true," said Binks. They both began to reflect, contemplating the shackles of their poverty. "And besides, I don't believe I could get off," said Binks after a time.

Nothing more was said of it that night. In fact, it was two or three days afterward that Binks came home and said: "Margaret, you get the children ready on Saturday noon and we'll all go out and spend Sunday with your Aunt Sarah!"

When he came home on Saturday his hat was far back on the back of his head from the speed he was in. Mrs. Binks was putting on her bonnet before the glass, turning about occasionally to admonish the little Binkses, who, in their new clothes, were wandering around, stiffly, and getting into all sorts of small difficulties. They had been ready since 11 o'clock. Mrs. Binks had

been obliged to scold them continually, one after the other, and
sometimes three at once.

"Hurry up," said Binks, immediately, "ain't got much time.
Say, you ain't going to let Jim wear that hat, are you? Where's
his best one? Good heavens, look at Margaret's dress! It's soiled
already! Tommie, stop that, do you hear? Well, are you ready?"

Indeed, it was not until the Binkses had left the city far behind
and were careering into New Jersey that they recovered their bal-
ances. Then something of the fresh quality of the country stole
over them and cooled their nerves. Horse cars and ferryboats
were maddening to Binks when he was obliged to convoy a wife
and three children. He appreciated the vast expanses of green,
through which ran golden hued roads. The scene accented his
leisure and his lack of responsibility.

Near the track a little river jostled over the stones. At times the
cool thunder of its roar came faintly to the ear. The Ramapo
Hills were in the background, faintly purple, and surmounted
with little peaks that shone with the luster of the sun. Binks began to joke heavily with the children. The little Binkses, for their
part, asked the most superhuman questions about details of the
scenery. Mrs. Binks leaned contentedly back in her seat and
seemed to be at rest, which was a most extraordinary thing.

When they got off the train at the little rural station they created considerable interest. Two or three loungers began to view
them in a sort of concentrated excitement. They were apparently
fascinated by the Binkses and seemed to be indulging in all manner of wild and intense speculation. The agent, as he walked into
his station, kept his head turned. Across the dusty street, wide at
this place, a group of men upon the porch of a battered grocery
store shaded their eyes with their hands. The Binkses felt dimly
like a circus and were a trifle bewildered by it. Binks gazed up
and down, this way and that; he tried to be unaware of the stare
of the citizens. Finally, he approached the loungers, who straightened their forms suddenly and looked very expectant.

"Can you tell me where Miss Pattison lives?"

The loungers arose as one man. "It's th' third house up that road there."

"It's a white house with green shutters!"

"There, that's it—yeh can see it through th' trees!" Binks discerned that his wife's aunt was a well known personage, and also that the coming of the Binkses was an event of vast importance. When he marched off at the head of his flock, he felt like a drum-major. His course was followed by the unwavering, intent eyes of the loungers.

The street was lined with two rows of austere and solemn trees. In one way it was like parading between the plumes on an immense hearse. These trees, lowly sighing in a breath-like wind, oppressed one with a sense of melancholy and dreariness. Back from the road, behind flower beds, controlled by box-wood borders, the houses were asleep in the drowsy air. Between them one could get views of the fields lying in a splendor of gold and green. A monotonous humming song of insects came from the regions of sunshine, and from some hidden barnyard a hen suddenly burst forth in a sustained cackle of alarm. The tranquillity of the scene contained a meaning of peace and virtue that was incredibly monotonous to the warriors from the metropolis. The sense of a city is battle. The Binkses were vaguely irritated and astonished at the placidity of this little town. This life spoke to them of no absorbing nor even interesting thing. There was something unbearable about it. "I should go crazy if I had to live here," said Mrs. Binks. A warrior in the flood-tide of his blood, going from the hot business of war to a place of utter quiet, might have felt that there was an insipidity in peace. And thus felt the Binkses from New York. They had always named the clash of the swords of commerce as sin, crime, but now they began to imagine something admirable in it. It was high wisdom. They put aside their favorite expressions: "The curse of gold," "A mad passion to get rich," "The rush for the spoils." In the light of their contempt for this stillness, the conflicts of the city were exalted. They were at any rate wondrously clever.

But what they did feel was the fragrance of the air, the radiance of the sunshine, the glory of the fields and the hills. With their ears still clogged by the tempest and fury of city uproars, they heard the song of the universal religion, the mighty and mystic hymn of nature, whose melody is in each landscape. It appealed to their elemental selves. It was as if the earth had called recreant and heedless children and the mother word, of vast might and significance, brought them to sudden meekness. It was the universal thing whose power no one escapes. When a man hears it he usually remains silent. He understands then the sacrilege of speech.

When they came to the third house, the white one, with the green blinds, they perceived a woman, in a plaid sun bonnet, walking slowly down a path. Around her was a riot of shrubbery and flowers. From the long and tangled grass of the lawn grew a number of cherry trees. Their dark green foliage was thickly sprinkled with bright red fruit. Some sparrows were scuffling among the branches. The little Binkses began to whoop at sight of the woman in the plaid sun bonnet.

"Hay-oh, Aunt Sarah, hay-oh!" they shouted.

The woman shaded her eyes with her hand. "Well, good gracious, if it ain't Marg'ret Binks! An' Phil, too! Well, I am surprised!"

She came jovially to meet them. "Why, how are yeh all? I'm awful glad t' see yeh!"

The children, filled with great excitement, babbled questions and ejaculations while she greeted the others.

"Say, Aunt Sarah, gimme some cherries!"

"Look at th' man over there!"

"Look at th' flowers!"

"Gimme some flowers, Aunt Sarah!"

And little Tommie, red faced from the value of his information, bawled out: "Aunt Sah-wee, dey have horse tars where I live!" Later he shouted: "We come on a twain of steam tars!"

Aunt Sarah fairly bristled with the most enthusiastic hospital-

ity. She beamed upon them like a sun. She made desperate attempts to gain possession of everybody's bundles that she might
carry them to the house. There was a sort of a little fight over
the baggage. The children clamored questions at her; she tried
heroically to answer them. Tommie, at times, deluged her with
news.

The curtains of the dining room were pulled down to keep out
the flies. This made a deep, cool gloom in which corners of the
old furniture caught wandering rays of light and shone with a
mild luster. Everything was arranged with an unspeakable neatness that was the opposite of comfort. A branch of an apple tree
moved by the gentle wind, brushed softly against the closed
blinds.

"Take off yer things," said Aunt Sarah.

Binks and his wife remained talking to Aunt Sarah, but the
children speedily swarmed out over the farm, raiding in countless
directions. It was only a matter of seconds before Jimmie discovered the brook behind the barn. Little Margaret roamed among
the flowers, bursting into little cries at sight of new blossoms,
new glories. Tommie gazed at the cherry trees for a few moments
in profound silence. Then he went and procured a pole. It was
very heavy, relatively. He could hardly stagger under it, but with
infinite toil he dragged it to the proper place and somehow managed to push it erect. Then with a deep earnestness of demeanor
he began a little onslaught upon the trees. Very often his blow
missed the entire tree and the pole thumped on the ground. This
necessitated the most extraordinary labor. But then at other
times he would get two or three cherries at one wild swing of his
weapon.

Binks and his wife spent the larger part of the afternoon out
under the apple trees at the side of the house. Binks lay down on
his back, with his head in the long lush grass. Mrs. Binks moved
lazily to and fro in a rocking chair that had been brought from
the house. Aunt Sarah, sometimes appearing, was strenuous in an
account of relatives, and the Binkses had only to listen. They

were glad of it, for this warm, sleepy air, pulsating with the sounds of insects, had enchained them in a great indolence.

It was to this place that Jimmie ran after he had fallen into the brook and scrambled out again. Holding his arms out carefully from his dripping person, he was roaring tremendously. His new sailor suit was a sight. Little Margaret came often to describe the wonders of her journeys, and Tommie, after a frightful struggle with the cherry trees, toddled over and went to sleep in the midst of a long explanation of his operations. The breeze stirred the locks on his baby forehead. His breath came in long sighs of content. Presently he turned his head to cuddle deeper into the grass. One arm was thrown in childish abandon over his head. Mrs. Binks stopped rocking to gaze at him. Presently she bended and noiselessly brushed away a spear of grass that was troubling the baby's temple. When she straightened up she saw that Binks, too, was absorbed in a contemplation of Tommie. They looked at each other presently, exchanging a vague smile. Through the silence came the voice of a plowing farmer berating his horses in a distant field.

The peace of the hills and the fields came upon the Binkses. They allowed Jimmie to sit up in bed and eat cake while his clothes were drying. Uncle Daniel returned from a wagon journey and recited them a ponderous tale of a pig that he had sold to a man with a red beard. They had no difficulty in feeling much interest in the story.

Binks began to expand with enormous appreciations. He would not go into the house until they compelled him. And as soon as the evening meal was finished he dragged his wife forth on a trip to the top of the hill behind the house. There was a great view from there, Uncle Daniel said.

The path, gray with little stones in the dusk, extended above them like a pillar. The pines were beginning to croon in a mournful key, inspired by the evening winds. Mrs. Binks had great difficulty in climbing this upright road. Binks was obliged to assist her, which he did with a considerable care and tenderness. In it there was a sort of a reminiscence of their courtship. It was a repetition of old days. Both enjoyed it because of this fact, although they subtly gave each other to understand that they disdained this emotion as an altogether un-American thing, for she, as a woman, was proud, and he had great esteem for himself as a man.

At the summit they seated themselves upon a fallen tree, near the edge of a cliff. The evening silence was upon the earth below them. Far in the west the sun lay behind masses of corn colored clouds, tumbled and heaved into crags, peaks and canyons. On either hand stood the purple hills in motionless array. The valley lay wreathed in somber shadows. Slowly there went on the mystic process of the closing of the day. The corn colored clouds faded to yellow and finally to a faint luminous green, inexpressibly vague. The rim of the hills was then an edge of crimson. The mountains became a profound blue. From the night, approaching in the east, came a wind. The trees of the mountain raised plaintive voices, bending toward the faded splendors of the day.

This song of the trees arose in low, sighing melody into the still air. It was filled with an infinite sorrow—a sorrow for birth, slavery, death. It was a wail telling the griefs, the pains of all ages. It was the symbol of agonies. It celebrated all suffering. Each man finds in this sound the expression of his own grief. It is the universal voice raised in lamentations.

As the trees huddled and bended as if to hide from their eyes a certain sight the green tints became blue. A faint suggestion of yellow replaced the crimson. The sun was dead.

The Binkses had been silent. These songs of the trees awe. They had remained motionless during this ceremony, their eyes fixed upon the mighty and indefinable changes which spoke to them of the final thing—the inevitable end. Their eyes had an impersonal expression. They were purified, chastened by this sermon, this voice calling to them from the sky. The hills had spoken and the trees had crooned their song. Binks finally stretched forth his arm in a wondering gesture.

"I wonder why," he said; "I wonder why the dickens it—why it—why——"

Tangled in his tongue was the unformulated question of the centuries, but Mrs. Binks had stolen forth her arm and linked it with his. Her head leaned softly against his shoulder.

The Men in the Storm

At about three o'clock of the February afternoon, the blizzard began to swirl great clouds of snow along the streets, sweeping it down from the roofs and up from the pavements until the faces of pedestrians tingled and burned as from a thousand needle-prickings. Those on the walks huddled their necks closely in the collars of their coats and went along stooping like a race of aged people. The drivers of vehicles hurried their horses furiously on their way. They were made more cruel by the exposure of their positions, aloft on high seats. The street cars, bound up-town, went slowly, the horses slipping and straining in the spongy brown mass that lay between the rails. The drivers, muffled to the eyes, stood erect and facing the wind, models of grim philosophy. Overhead the trains rumbled and roared, and the dark structure of the elevated railroad, stretching over the avenue, dripped little streams and drops of water upon the mud and snow beneath it.

All the clatter of the street was softened by the masses that lay upon the cobbles until, even to one who looked from a window, it became important music, a melody of life made necessary to the ear by the dreariness of the pitiless beat and sweep of the storm. Occasionally one could see black figures of men busily shovelling the white drifts from the walks. The sounds from their labor created new recollections of rural experiences which every man manages to have in a measure. Later, the immense windows of the shops became aglow with light, throwing great beams of orange and yellow upon the pavement. They were infinitely cheerful, yet in a way they accented the force and discomfort of the storm, and gave a meaning to the pace of the people and the vehicles, scores of pedestrians and drivers, wretched with cold faces, necks and feet, speeding for scores of unknown doors and entrances, scattering to an infinite variety of shelters, to places which the imagination made warm with the familiar colors of home.

There was an absolute expression of hot dinners in the pace of the people. If one dared to speculate upon the destination of those who came trooping, he lost himself in a maze of social calculations; he might fling a handful of sand and attempt to follow the flight of each particular grain. But as to the suggestion of hot dinners, he was in firm lines of thought, for it was upon every hurrying face. It is a matter of tradition; it is from the tales of childhood. It comes forth with every storm.

However, in a certain part of a dark West-side street, there was a collection of men to whom these things were as if they were not. In this street was located a charitable house where for five cents the homeless of the city could get a bed at night and, in the morning, coffee and bread.

During the afternoon of the storm, the whirling snows acted as drivers, as men with whips, and at half-past three, the walk before the closed doors of the house was covered with wanderers of the street, waiting. For some distance on either side of the place they could be seen lurking in doorways and behind projecting parts of buildings, gathering in close bunches in an effort to get warm. A covered wagon drawn up near the curb sheltered a dozen of them. Under the stairs that led to the elevated railway station, there were six or eight, their hands stuffed deep in their pockets, their shoulders stooped, jiggling their feet. Others always could be seen coming, a strange procession, some slouching along with the characteristic hopeless gait of professional strays, some coming with hesitating steps wearing the air of men to whom this sort of thing was new.

It was an afternoon of incredible length. The snow, blowing in twisting clouds, sought out the men in their meagre hiding-places and skilfully beat in among them, drenching their persons with showers of fine, stinging flakes. They crowded together, muttering, and fumbling in their pockets to get their red, inflamed wrists covered by the cloth.

Newcomers usually halted at one of the groups and addressed a question, perhaps much as a matter of form, "Is it open yet?"

Those who had been waiting inclined to take the questioner seriously and become contemptuous. "No; do yeh think we'd be standin' here?"

The gathering swelled in numbers steadily and persistently. One could always see them coming, trudging slowly through the storm.

Finally, the little snow plains in the street began to assume a leaden hue from the shadows of evening. The buildings upreared gloomily save where various windows became brilliant figures of light that made shimmers and splashes of yellow on the snow. A street lamp on the curb struggled to illuminate, but it was reduced to impotent blindness by the swift gusts of sleet crusting its panes.

In this half-darkness, the men began to come from their shelter places and mass in front of the doors of charity. They were of all types, but the nationalities were mostly American, German and Irish. Many were strong, healthy, clear-skinned fellows with that stamp of countenance which is not frequently seen upon seekers after charity. There were men of undoubted patience, industry and temperance, who in time of ill-fortune, do not habitually turn to rail at the state of society, snarling at the arrogance of the rich and bemoaning the cowardice of the poor, but who at these times are apt to wear a sudden and singular meekness, as if they saw the world's progress marching from them and were trying to perceive where they had failed, what they had lacked, to be thus vanquished in the race. Then there were others of the shifting, Bowery lodging-house element who were used to paying ten cents for a place to sleep, but who now came here because it was cheaper.

But they were all mixed in one mass so thoroughly that one could not have discerned the different elements but for the fact that the laboring men, for the most part, remained silent and impassive in the blizzard, their eyes fixed on the windows of the house, statues of patience.

The sidewalk soon became completely blocked by the bodies of the men. They pressed close to one another like sheep in a winter's gale, keeping one another warm by the heat of their bodies. The snow came down upon this compressed group of men until, directly from above, it might have appeared like a heap of snow-covered merchandise, if it were not for the fact that the crowd swayed gently with a unanimous, rhythmical motion. It was wonderful to see how the snow lay upon the heads and shoulders of these men, in little ridges an inch thick perhaps in places, the flakes steadily adding drop and drop, precisely as they fall upon the unresisting grass of the fields. The feet of the men were all wet and cold and the wish to warm them accounted for the slow, gentle, rhythmical motion. Occasionally some man whose ears or nose tingled acutely from the cold winds would wriggle down until his head was protected by the shoulders of his companions.

There was a continuous murmuring discussion as to the probability of the doors being speedily opened. They persistently lifted their eyes toward the windows. One could hear little combats of opinion.

"There's a light in th' winder!"

"Naw; it's a reflection f'm across th' way."

"Well, didn't I see 'em lite it?"

"You did?"

"I did!"

"Well, then, that settles it!"

As the time approached when they expected to be allowed to enter, the men crowded to the doors in an unspeakable crush, jamming and wedging in a way that it seemed would crack bones. They surged heavily against the building in a powerful wave of pushing shoulders. Once a rumor flitted among all the tossing heads.

"They can't open th' doors! Th' fellers er smack up ag'in 'em."

Then a dull roar of rage came from the men on the outskirts; but all the time they strained and pushed until it appeared to be impossible for those that they cried out against to do anything but be crushed to pulp.

"Ah, git away f'm th' door!"

"Git outa that!"

"Throw 'em out!"

"Kill 'em!"

"Say, fellers, now, what th' 'ell? Give 'em a chanct t' open th' door!"

"Yeh damned pigs, give 'em a chanct t' open th' door!"

Men in the outskirts of the crowd occasionally yelled when a boot-heel of one of frantic trampling feet crushed on their freezing extremities.

"Git off me feet, yeh clumsy tarrier!"

"Say, don't stand on me feet! Walk on th' ground!"

A man near the doors suddenly shouted: "O-o-oh! Le' me out—le' me out!" And another, a man of infinite valor, once twisted his head so as to half face those who were pushing behind him. "Quit yer shovin', yeh ——" and he delivered a volley of the most powerful and singular invective straight into the faces of the men behind him. It was as if he was hammering the noses of them with curses of triple brass. His face, red with rage, could be seen; upon it, an expression of sublime disregard of consequences. But nobody cared to reply to his imprecations; it was too cold. Many of them snickered and all continued to push.

In occasional pauses of the crowd's movement the men had opportunity to make jokes; usually grim things, and no doubt very uncouth. Nevertheless, they are notable—one does not expect to find the quality of humor in a heap of old clothes under a snow-drift.

The winds seemed to grow fiercer as time wore on. Some of the gusts of snow that came down on the close collection of heads cut like knives and needles, and the men huddled, and swore, not like dark assassins, but in a sort of an American fashion, grimly and desperately, it is true, but yet with a wondrous under-effect, indefinable and mystic, as if there was some kind of humor in this catastrophe, in this situation in a night of snow-laden winds.

Once, the window of the huge dry-goods shop across the street furnished material for a few moments of forgetfulness. In the brilliantly-lighted space appeared the figure of a man. He was rather stout and very well clothed. His whiskers were fashioned charmingly after those of the Prince of Wales. He stood in an at-titude of magnificent reflection. He slowly stroked his moustache with a certain grandeur of manner, and looked down at the snow-encrusted mob. From below, there was denoted a supreme complacence in him. It seemed that the sight operated inversely, and enabled him to more clearly regard his own environment, de-lightful relatively.

One of the mob chanced to turn his head and perceive the fig-ure in the window. "Hello, lookit 'is whiskers," he said genially.

Many of the men turned then, and a shout went up. They called to him in all strange keys. They addressed him in every manner, from familiar and cordial greetings to carefully-worded advice concerning changes in his personal appearance. The man presently fled, and the mob chuckled ferociously like ogres who had just devoured something.

They turned then to serious business. Often they addressed the stolid front of the house.

"Oh, let us in fer Gawd's sake!"

"Let us in or we'll all drop dead!"

"Say, what's th' use o' keepin' all us poor Indians out in th' cold?"

And always some one was saying, "Keep off me feet."

The crushing of the crowd grew terrific toward the last. The men, in keen pain from the blasts, began almost to fight. With the pitiless whirl of snow upon them, the battle for shelter was going to the strong. It became known that the basement door at the foot of a little steep flight of stairs was the one to be opened, and they jostled and heaved in this direction like laboring fiends. One could hear them panting and groaning in their fierce exertion.

Usually some one in the front ranks was protesting to those in the rear: "O—o—ow! Oh, say, now, fellers, let up, will yeh? Do yeh wanta kill somebody?"

A policeman arrived and went into the midst of them, scolding and berating, occasionally threatening, but using no force but that of his hands and shoulders against these men who were only struggling to get in out of the storm. His decisive tones rang out sharply: "Stop that pushin' back there! Come, boys, don't push! Stop that! Here, you, quit yer shovin'! Cheese that!"

When the door below was opened, a thick stream of men forced a way down the stairs, which were of an extraordinary narrowness and seemed only wide enough for one at a time. Yet they somehow went down almost three abreast. It was a difficult and painful operation. The crowd was like a turbulent water forcing itself through one tiny outlet. The men in the rear, excited by the success of the others, made frantic exertions, for it seemed that this large band would more than fill the quarters and that many would be left upon the pavements. It would be disastrous to be of the last, and accordingly men with the snow biting their faces, writhed and twisted with their might. One expected that from the tremendous pressure, the narrow passage to the basement door would be so choked and clogged with human limbs and bodies that movement would be impossible. Once indeed the crowd was forced to stop, and a cry went along that a man had been injured at the foot of the stairs. But presently the slow movement began again, and the policeman fought at the top of the flight to ease the pressure on those who were going down.

A reddish light from a window fell upon the faces of the men when they, in turn, arrived at the last three steps and were about to enter. One could then note a change of expression that had come over their features. As they thus stood upon the threshold of their hopes, they looked suddenly content and complacent. The fire had passed from their eyes and the snarl had vanished from their lips. The very force of the crowd in the rear, which had previously vexed them, was regarded from another point of view, for it now made it inevitable that they should go through the little doors into the place that was cheery and warm with light.

The tossing crowd on the sidewalk grew smaller and smaller. The snow beat with merciless persistence upon the bowed heads of those who waited. The wind drove it up from the pavements in frantic forms of winding white, and it seethed in circles about the huddled forms, passing in, one by one, three by three, out of the storm.

When Man Falls, a Crowd Gathers

A man and a boy were trudging slowly along an East-Side street. It was nearly six o'clock in the evening and this street, which led to one of the East River ferries, was crowded with laborers, shop men and shop women, hurrying to their dinners. The store windows were a-glare.

The man and the boy conversed in Italian, mumbling the soft syllables and making little quick egotistical gestures. They walked with the lumbering peasant's gait, slowly, and blinking their black eyes at the passing show of the street.

Suddenly the man wavered on his limbs and glared bewildered and helpless as if some blinding light had flashed before his vision; then he swayed like a drunken man and fell. The boy grasped his companion's arm frantically and made an attempt to support him so that the limp form slid to the side-walk with an easy motion as a body sinks in the sea. The boy screamed.

Instantly, from all directions people turned their gaze upon the prone figure. In a moment there was a dodging, pushing, peering group about the man. A volley of questions, replies, speculations flew to and fro above all the bobbing heads.

"What's th' matter? What's th' matter?"

"Oh, a jag, I guess!"

"Nit; he's got a fit!"

"What's th' matter? What's th' matter?"

Two streams of people coming from different directions met at this point to form a crowd. Others came from across the street.

Down under their feet, almost lost under this throng, lay the man, hidden in the shadows caused by their forms which in fact barely allowed a particle of light to pass between them. Those in the foremost rank bended down, shouldering each other, eager, anxious to see everything. Others behind them crowded savagely for a place like starving men fighting for bread. Always, the question could be heard flying in the air. "What's the matter?" Some, near to the body and perhaps feeling the danger of being forced over upon it, twisted their heads and protested violently to those unheeding ones who were scuffling in the rear. "Say, quit yer shovin', can't yeh? What d' yeh want, anyhow? Quit!"

A man back in the crowd suddenly said: "Say, young feller, you're a peach wid dose feet o' yours. Keep off me!"

Another voice said: "Well, dat's all right——"

The boy who had been walking with the man who fell was standing helplessly, a terrified look in his eyes. He held the man's hand. Sometimes he gave it a little jerk that was at once an appeal, a reproach, a caution. And, withal, it was a timid calling to the limp and passive figure as if he half expected to arouse it from its coma with a pleading touch of his fingers. Occasionally, he looked about him with swift glances of indefinite hope, as if assistance might come from the clouds. The men near him questioned him, but he did not seem to understand. He answered them "Yes" or "No," blindly, with no apparent comprehension of their language. They frequently jostled him until he was obliged to put his hand upon the breast of the body to maintain his balance.

Those that were nearest to the man upon the side-walk at first saw his body go through a singular contortion. It was as if an invisible hand had reached up from the earth and had seized him by the hair. He seemed dragged slowly, relentlessly backward, while his body stiffened convulsively, his hands clenched, and his arms swung rigidly upward. A slight froth was upon his chin. Through his pallid half-closed lids could be seen the steel-colored

gleam of his eyes that were turned toward all the bending, swaying faces and in the inanimate thing upon the pave yet burned
threateningly, dangerously, shining with a mystic light, as a
corpse might glare at those live ones who seemed about to trample it under foot.

As for the men near, they hung back, appearing as if they expected it to spring erect and clutch at them. Their eyes however
were held in a spell of fascination. They seemed scarcely to
breathe. They were contemplating a depth into which a human
being had sunk and the marvel of this mystery of life or death
held them chained. Occasionally from the rear, a man came
thrusting his way impetuously, satisfied that there was a horror
to be seen and apparently insane to get a view of it. Less curious
persons swore at these men when they trod upon their toes.

The loaded street-cars jingled past this scene in endless parade.
Occasionally, from where the elevated railroad crossed the street
there came a rhythmical roar, suddenly begun and suddenly
ended. Over the heads of the crowd hung an immovable canvas
sign. "Regular dinner twenty cents."

After the first spasm of curiosity had passed away, there were
those in the crowd who began to consider ways to help. A voice
called: "Rub his wrists." The boy and some one on the other side
of the man began to rub his wrists and slap his palms, but still
the body lay inert, rigid. When a hand was dropped the arm fell
like a stick. A tall German suddenly appeared and resolutely began to push the crowd back. "Get back there—get back," he continually repeated as he pushed them. He had psychological
authority over this throng; they obeyed him. He and another
knelt by the man in the darkness and loosened his shirt at the
throat. Once they struck a match and held it close to the man's
face. This livid visage suddenly appearing under their feet in the
light of the match's yellow glare, made the throng shudder. Half
articulate exclamations could be heard. There were men who
nearly created a battle in the madness of their desire to see the
thing.

Meanwhile others with magnificent passions for abstract statis-

tical information were questioning the boy. "What's his name?"
"Where does he live?"

Then a policeman appeared. The first part of the little play had
gone on without his assistance but now he came swiftly, his hel-
met towering above the multitude of black derbys and shading
that confident, self-reliant police face. He charged the crowd as if
he were a squadron of Irish lancers. The people fairly withered
before this onslaught. He shouted: "Come, make way there!
Make way!" He was evidently a man whose life was half-
pestered out of him by the inhabitants of the city who were sufficiently unreasonable and stupid as to insist on being in the
streets. His was the rage of a placid cow, who wishes to lead a
life of tranquillity, but who is eternally besieged by flies that
hover in clouds.

When he arrived at the centre of the crowd he first demanded
threateningly: "Well, what's th' matter here?" And then when he
saw that human bit of wreckage at the bottom of the sea of men
he said to it: "Come, git up outa that! Git outa here!"

Whereupon hands were raised in the crowd and a volley of
decorated information was blazed at the officer.

"Ah, he's got a fit! Can't yeh see!"

"He's got a fit!"

"He's sick!"

"What th' 'ell yeh doin'? Leave 'm be!"

The policeman menaced with a glance the crowd from whose
safe interior the defiant voices had emerged.

A doctor had come. He and the policeman bended down at the
man's side. Occasionally the officer upreared to create room. The
crowd fell away before his threats, his admonitions, his sarcastic
questions and before the sweep of those two huge buckskin
gloves.

At last, the peering ones saw the man on the side-walk begin to
breathe heavily, with the strain of overtaxed machinery, as if he
had just come to the surface from some deep water. He uttered a
low cry in his foreign tongue. It was a babyish squeal or like the

sad wail of a little storm-tossed kitten. As this cry went forth to all those eager ears the jostling and crowding recommenced until the doctor was obliged to yell warningly a dozen times. The policeman had gone to send an ambulance call.

When a man struck another match and in its meagre light the doctor felt the skull of the prostrate one to discover if any wound or fracture had been caused by his fall to the stone side-walk, the crowd pressed and crushed again. It was as if they fully anticipated a sight of blood in the gleam of the match and they scrambled and dodged for positions. The policeman returned and fought with them. The doctor looked up frequently to scold at them and to sharply demand more space.

At last out of the golden haze made by the lamps far up the street, there came the sound of a gong beaten rapidly, impatiently. A monstrous truck loaded to the sky with barrels scurried to one side with marvelous agility. And then the black ambulance with its red light, its galloping horse, its dull gleam of lettering and bright shine of gong clattered into view. A young man, as imperturbable always as if he were going to a picnic, sat thoughtfully upon the rear seat.

When they picked up the limp body, from which came little moans and howls, the crowd almost turned into a mob, a silent mob, each member of which struggled for one thing. Afterward some resumed their ways with an air of relief, as if they themselves had been in pain and were at last recovered. Others still continued to stare at the ambulance on its banging, clanging return journey until it vanished into the golden haze. It was as if they had been cheated. Their eyes expressed discontent at this curtain which had been rung down in the midst of the drama. And this impenetrable fabric suddenly intervening between a suffering creature and their curiosity, seemed to appear to them as an injustice.

An Eloquence of Grief

The windows were high and saintly, of the shape that is found in churches. From time to time a policeman at the door spoke sharply to some incoming person. "Take your hat off!" He displayed in his voice the horror of a priest when the sanctity of a chapel is defied or forgotten. The court-room was crowded with people who sloped back comfortably in their chairs, regarding with undeviating glances the procession and its attendant and guardian policemen that moved slowly inside the spear-topped railing. All persons connected with a case went close to the magistrate's desk before a word was spoken in the matter, and then their voices were toned to the ordinary talking strength. The crowd in the court-room could not hear a sentence; they could merely see shifting figures, men that gestured quietly, women that sometimes raised an eager eloquent arm. They could not always see the judge, although they were able to estimate his location by the tall stands surmounted by white globes that were at either hand of him. And so those who had come for curiosity's sweet sake wore an air of being in wait for a cry of anguish, some loud painful protestation that would bring the proper thrill to their jaded, world-weary nerves—wires that refused to vibrate for ordinary affairs.

Inside the railing the court officers shuffled the various groups with speed and skill; and behind the desk the magistrate patiently toiled his way through mazes of wonderful testimony.

In a corner of this space, devoted to those who had business
before the judge, an officer in plain clothes stood with a girl that
wept constantly. None seemed to notice the girl and there was no
reason why she should be noticed if the curious in the body of
the court-room were not interested in the devastation which tears
bring upon some complexions. Her tears seemed to burn like acid
and they left fierce pink marks on her face. Occasionally the girl
looked across the room where two well-dressed young women
and a man stood waiting with the serenity of people who are not
concerned as to the interior fittings of a jail.

The business of the court progressed and presently the girl, the
officer and the well-dressed contingent stood before the judge.
Thereupon two lawyers engaged in some preliminary fire-wheels
which were endured, generally, in silence. The girl, it appeared,
was accused of stealing fifty dollars' worth of silk clothing from
the room of one of the well-dressed women. She had been a servant in the house.

In a clear way and with none of the ferocity that an accuser often exhibits in a police-court, calmly and moderately, the two
young women gave their testimony. Behind them stood their escort, always mute. His part, evidently, was to furnish the dignity,
and he furnished it heavily, almost massively.

When they had finished, the girl told her part. She had full, almost Afric, lips, and they had turned quite white. The lawyer for
the others asked some questions, which he did—be it said, in
passing—with the air of a man throwing flower-pots at a stone
house.

It was a short case and soon finished. At the end of it the judge
said that, considering the evidence, he would have to commit the
girl for trial. Instantly the quick-eyed court officer began to clear
the way for the next case. The well-dressed women and their escort turned one way and the girl turned another, toward a door
with an austere arch leading into a stone-paved passage. Then it
was that a great cry rang through the court-room, the cry of this
girl who believed that she was lost.

The loungers, many of them, underwent a spasmodic movement as if they had been knived. The court officers rallied quickly. The girl fell back opportunely for the arms of one of them, and her wild heels clicked twice on the floor. "I am innocent! Oh, I am innocent!"

People pity those who need none, and the guilty sob alone; but innocent or guilty, this girl's scream described such a profound depth of woe—it was so graphic of grief, that it slit with a dagger's sweep the curtain of common-place, and disclosed the gloom-shrouded spectre that sat in the young girl's heart so plainly, in so universal a tone of the mind, that a man heard expressed some far-off midnight terror of his own thought.

The cries died away down the stone-paved passage. A patrolman leaned one arm composedly on the railing, and down below him stood an aged, almost toothless wanderer, tottering and grinning.

"Plase, yer honer," said the old man as the time arrived for him to speak, "if ye'll lave me go this time, I've niver been dhrunk befoor, sir."

A court officer lifted his hand to hide a smile.

Adventures of a Novelist

[*The headline above Crane's report in the
September 20, 1896, edition of the New York* Journal *read:*
ADVENTURES OF A NOVELIST
BY STEPHEN CRANE
THE DISTINGUISHED AUTHOR'S NARRATIVE OF HOW HE SOUGHT
'MATERIAL' IN REAL LIFE IN THE 'TENDERLOIN' AND
FOUND MORE THAN HE BARGAINED FOR.]

This is a plain tale of two chorus girls, a woman of the streets and a reluctant laggard witness. The tale properly begins in a resort on Broadway, where the two chorus girls and the reluctant witness sat the entire evening. They were on the verge of departing their several ways when a young woman approached one of the chorus girls, with outstretched hand.

"Why, how do you do?" she said. "I haven't seen you for a long time."

The chorus girl recognized some acquaintance of the past, and the young woman then took a seat and joined the party. Finally they left the table in this resort, and the quartet walked down Broadway together. At the corner of Thirty-first street one of the chorus girls said that she wished to take a car immediately for home, and so the reluctant witness left one of the chorus girls and the young woman on the corner of Thirty-first street while he placed the other chorus girl aboard an uptown cable car. The two girls who waited on the corner were deep in conversation.

The reluctant witness was returning leisurely to them. In the semi-conscious manner in which people note details which do not appear at the time important, he saw two men passing along Broadway. They passed swiftly, like men who are going home. They paid attention to none, and none at the corner of Thirty-first street and Broadway paid attention to them.

The two girls were still deep in conversation. They were standing at the curb facing the street. The two men passed unseen—in
all human probability—by the two girls. The reluctant witness
continued his leisurely way. He was within four feet of these two
girls when suddenly and silently a man appeared from nowhere
in particular and grabbed them both.

The astonishment of the reluctant witness was so great for the
ensuing seconds that he was hardly aware of what transpired during that time, save that both girls screamed. Then he heard this
man, who was now evidently an officer, say to them: "Come to
the station house. You are under arrest for soliciting two men."

With one voice the unknown woman, the chorus girl and the
reluctant witness cried out: "What two men?"

The officer said: "Those two men who have just passed."

And here began the wildest and most hysterical sobbing of the
two girls, accompanied by spasmodic attempts to pull their arms
away from the grip of the policeman. The chorus girl seemed
nearly insane with fright and fury. Finally she screamed:

"Well, he's my husband." And with her finger she indicated
the reluctant witness. The witness at once replied to the swift,
questioning glance of the officer, "Yes; I am."

If it was necessary to avow a marriage to save a girl who is not
a prostitute from being arrested as a prostitute, it must be done,
though the man suffer eternally. And then the officer forgot immediately—without a second's hesitation, he forgot that a moment previously he had arrested this girl for soliciting, and so,
dropping her arm, released her.

"But," said he, "I have got this other one." He was as pic-
turesque as a wolf.

"Why arrest her, either?" said the reluctant witness.

"For soliciting those two men."

"But she didn't solicit those two men."

"Say," said the officer, turning, "do you know this woman?"

The chorus girl had it in mind to lie then for the purpose of
saving this woman easily and simply from the palpable wrong

she seemed to be about to experience. "Yes; I know her"—
"I have seen her two or three times"—"Yes; I have met her before——" But the reluctant witness said at once that he knew
nothing whatever of the girl.

"Well," said the officer, "she's a common prostitute."

There was a short silence then, but the reluctant witness
presently said: "Are you arresting her as a common prostitute?
She has been perfectly respectable since she has been with us. She
hasn't done anything wrong since she has been in our company."

"I am arresting her for soliciting those two men," answered the
officer, "and if you people don't want to get pinched, too, you
had better not be seen with her."

Then began a parade to the station house—the officer and his
prisoner ahead and two simpletons following.

At the station house the officer said to the sergeant behind the
desk that he had seen the woman come from the resort on Broadway alone, and on the way to the corner of Thirty-first street solicit two men, and that immediately afterward she had met a man
and a woman—meaning the chorus girl and the reluctant witness—on the said corner, and was in conversation with them
when he arrested her. He did not mention to the sergeant at this
time the arrest and release of the chorus girl.

At the conclusion of the officer's story the sergeant said,
shortly: "Take her back." This did not mean to take the woman
back to the corner of Thirty-first street and Broadway. It
meant to take her back to the cells, and she was accordingly led
away.

The chorus girl had undoubtedly intended to be an intrepid
champion; she had avowedly come to the station house for that
purpose, but her entire time had been devoted to sobbing in the
wildest form of hysteria. The reluctant witness was obliged to de-
vote his entire time to an attempt to keep her from making an uproar of some kind. This paroxysm of terror, of indignation,
and the extreme mental anguish caused by her unconventional
and strange situation, was so violent that the reluctant wit-

ness could not take time from her to give any testimony to the sergeant.

After the woman was sent to the cell the reluctant witness reflected a moment in silence; then he said:

"Well, we might as well go."

On the way out of Thirtieth street the chorus girl continued to sob. "If you don't go to court and speak for that girl you are no man!" she cried. The arrested woman had, by the way, screamed out a request to appear in her behalf before the Magistrate.

"By George! I cannot," said the reluctant witness. "I can't afford to do that sort of thing. I—I——"

After he had left this girl safely, he continued to reflect: "Now this arrest I firmly believe to be wrong. This girl may be a courtesan, for anything that I know at all to the contrary. The sergeant at the station house seemed to know her as well as he knew the Madison square tower. She is then, in all probability, a courtesan. She is arrested, however, for soliciting those two men. If I have ever had a conviction in my life, I am convinced that she did not solicit those two men. Now, if these affairs occur from time to time, they must be witnessed occasionally by men of character. Do these reputable citizens interfere? No, they go home and thank God that they can still attend piously to their own affairs. Suppose I were a clerk and I interfered in this sort of a case. When it became known to my employers they would say to me: 'We are sorry, but we cannot have men in our employ who stay out until 2:30 in the morning in the company of chorus girls.'

"Suppose, for instance, I had a wife and seven children in Harlem. As soon as my wife read the papers she would say: 'Ha! You told me you had a business engagement! Half-past two in the morning with questionable company!'

"Suppose, for instance, I were engaged to the beautiful Countess of Kalamazoo. If she were to hear it, she would write: 'All is over between us. My future husband cannot rescue prostitutes at 2:30 in the morning.'

"These, then, must be three small general illustrations of why men of character say nothing if they happen to witness some possible affair of this sort, and perhaps these illustrations could be multiplied to infinity. I possess nothing so tangible as a clerkship, as a wife and seven children in Harlem, as an engagement to the beautiful Countess of Kalamazoo; but all that I value may be chanced in this affair. Shall I take this risk for the benefit of a girl of the streets?

"But this girl, be she prostitute or whatever, was at this time manifestly in my escort, and—Heaven save the blasphemous philosophy—a wrong done to a prostitute must be as purely a wrong as a wrong done to a queen," said the reluctant witness— this blockhead.

"Moreover, I believe that this officer has dishonored his obligation as a public servant. Have I a duty as a citizen, or do citizens have duty, as a citizen, or do citizens have no duties? Is it a mere myth that there was at one time a man who possessed a consciousness of civic responsibility, or has it become a distinction of our municipal civilization that men of this character shall be licensed to deprecate in such a manner upon those who are completely at their mercy?"

He returned to the sergeant at the police station, and, after asking if he could send anything to the girl to make her more comfortable for the night, he told the sergeant the story of the arrest, as he knew it.

"Well," said the sergeant, "that may be all true. I don't defend the officer. I do not say that he was right, or that he was wrong, but it seems to me that I have seen you somewhere before and know you vaguely as a man of good repute; so why interfere in this thing? As for this girl, I know her to be a common prostitute. That's why I sent her back."

"But she was not arrested as a common prostitute. She was arrested for soliciting two men, and I know that she didn't solicit the two men."

"Well," said the sergeant, "that, too, may all be true, but I give you the plain advice of a man who has been behind this desk for years, and knows how these things go, and I advise you simply to stay home. If you monkey with this case, you are pretty sure to come out with mud all over you."

"I suppose so," said the reluctant witness. "I haven't a doubt of it. But I don't see how I can, in honesty, stay away from court in the morning."

"Well, do it anyhow," said the sergeant.

"But I don't see how I can do it."

The sergeant was bored. "Oh, I tell you, the girl is nothing but a common prostitute," he said, wearily.

The reluctant witness on reaching his room set the alarm clock for the proper hour.

In the court at 8:30 he met a reporter acquaintance. "Go home," said the reporter, when he had heard the story. "Go home; your own participation in the affair doesn't look very respectable. Go home."

"But it is a wrong," said the reluctant witness.

"Oh, it is only a temporary wrong," said the reporter. The definition of a temporary wrong did not appear at that time to the reluctant witness, but the reporter was too much in earnest to consider terms. "Go home," said he.

Thus—if the girl was wronged—it is to be seen that all circumstances, all forces, all opinions, all men were combined to militate against her. Apparently the united wisdom of the world declared that no man should do anything but throw his sense of justice to the winds in an affair of this description. "Let a man have a conscience for the daytime," said wisdom. "Let him have a conscience for the daytime, but it is idiocy for a man to have a conscience at 2:30 in the morning, in the case of an arrested prostitute."

The officer who had made the arrest told a story of the occurrence. The girl at the bar told a story of the occurrence. And the girl's story as to this affair was, to the reluctant witness, perfectly true. Nevertheless, her word could not be accounted of any value. It was impossible that any one in the courtroom could suppose that she was telling the truth, save the reluctant witness and the reporter to whom he had told the tale.

The reluctant witness recited what he believed to be a true accounting, and the Magistrate discharged the prisoner.

The reluctant witness has told this story merely because it is a story which the public of New York should know for once.

CLICK ON A CLASSIC
www.penguinclassics.com

The world's greatest literature at your fingertips

Constantly updated information on more than a thousand titles,
from Icelandic sagas to ancient Indian epics, Russian drama to
Italian romance, American greats to African masterpieces

•

The latest news on recent additions to the list, updated
editions, and specially commissioned translations

•

Original essays by leading writers

•

A wealth of background material, including biographies
of every classic author from Aristotle to Zamyatin, plot
synopses, readers' and teachers' guides, useful web links

•

Online desk and examination copy assistance for academics

•

Trivia quizzes, competitions, giveaways, news on
forthcoming screen adaptations

FOR THE BEST IN PAPERBACKS, LOOK FOR THE

In every corner of the world, on every subject under the sun, Penguin represents quality and variety—the very best in publishing today.

For complete information about books available from Penguin—including Penguin Classics, Penguin Compass, and Puffins—and how to order them, write to us at the appropriate address below. Please note that for copyright reasons the selection of books varies from country to country.

In the United States: Please write to *Penguin Group (USA), P.O. Box 12289 Dept. B, Newark, New Jersey 07101-5289* or call 1-800-788-6262.

In the United Kingdom: Please write to *Dept. EP, Penguin Books Ltd, Bath Road, Harmondsworth, West Drayton, Middlesex UB7 0DA.*

In Canada: Please write to *Penguin Books Canada Ltd, 10 Alcorn Avenue, Suite 300, Toronto, Ontario M4V 3B2.*

In Australia: Please write to *Penguin Books Australia Ltd, P.O. Box 257, Ringwood, Victoria 3134.*

In New Zealand: Please write to *Penguin Books (NZ) Ltd, Private Bag 102902, North Shore Mail Centre, Auckland 10.*

In India: Please write to *Penguin Books India Pvt Ltd, 11 Panchsheel Shopping Centre, Panchsheel Park, New Delhi 110 017.*

In the Netherlands: Please write to *Penguin Books Netherlands bv, Postbus 3507, NL-1001 AH Amsterdam.*

In Germany: Please write to *Penguin Books Deutschland GmbH, Metzlerstrasse 26, 60594 Frankfurt am Main.*

In Spain: Please write to *Penguin Books S. A., Bravo Murillo 19, 1° B, 28015 Madrid.*

In Italy: Please write to *Penguin Italia s.r.l., Via Benedetto Croce 2, 20094 Corsico, Milano.*

In France: Please write to *Penguin France, Le Carré Wilson, 62 rue Benjamin Baillaud, 31500 Toulouse.*

In Japan: Please write to *Penguin Books Japan Ltd, Kaneko Building, 2-3-25 Koraku, Bunkyo-Ku, Tokyo 112.*

In South Africa: Please write to *Penguin Books South Africa (Pty) Ltd, Private Bag X14, Parkview, 2122 Johannesburg.*